MARKED

ALSO BY P. C. CAST and KRISTIN CAST

Betrayed

Chosen

Untamed

Hunted

Tempted

MARKED

THE HOUSE OF NIGHT BOOK I

P. C. CAST and KRISTIN CAST

ST. MARTIN'S GRIFFIN
NEW YORK

MARKED. Copyright © 2007 by P. C. Cast and Kristin Cast. All rights reserved. Printed in the United States of America. For information, address St. Martin's Press, 175 Fifth Avenue, New York, N.Y. 10010.

www.stmartins.com

The Library of Congress has catalogued the paperback edition as follows:

Cast, P. C.
    Marked : a house of night novel / P. C. Cast and Kristin Cast.—1st ed.
        p. cm.
    ISBN 978-0-312-36026-9
    1. Vampires—Fiction. I. Title.
    PS3603.A869 M37 2007
    813'.6—dc22

                                                                2007006735

ISBN 978-0-312-36025-2 (hardcover)

First Hardcover St. Martin's Griffin Edition: October 2009

10 9 8 7 6 5 4 3 2 1

For our wonderful agent, Meredith Bernstein, who said the three magic words: vampyre finishing school. We heart you!

ACKNOWLEDGMENTS

I would like to thank a wonderful student of mine, John Maslin, for research help and for reading and giving feedback on many early versions of the book. His input was invaluable.

A big THANKS GUYS goes out to my Creative Writing classes in the school year 2005–2006. Your brainstorming was lots of help (and quite amusing).

I also want to thank my fabulous daughter, Kristin, for making sure we sound like teenagers. I couldn't have done it without you. (She made me write that.)   —PC

I want to thank my lovely "mam," better known as PC, for being such an unbelievably talented author and so easy to work with. (Okay, she made me write that.)   —Kristin

PC and Kristin would both like to thank their dad/grandpa, Dick Cast, for the biological hypothesis he helped create as the basis for the House of Night's vampyres. We love you Dad/G-pa!

From Hesiod's poem to Nyx, the Greek personification of night:

"There also stands the gloomy house of Night;
ghastly clouds shroud it in darkness.
Before it Atlas stands erect and on his head
and unwearying arms firmly supports the broad sky,
where Night and Day cross a bronze threshold
and then come close and greet each other."
(Hesiod, *Theogony*, 744 ff.)

MARKED

CHAPTER ONE

—

Just when I thought my day couldn't get any worse I saw the dead guy standing next to my locker. Kayla was talking nonstop in her usual K-babble, and she didn't even notice him. At first. Actually, now that I think about it, no one else noticed him until he spoke, which is, tragically, more evidence of my freakish inability to fit in.

"No, but Zoey, I *swear to God* Heath didn't get *that* drunk after the game. You really shouldn't be so hard on him."

"Yeah," I said absently. "Sure." Then I coughed. Again. I felt like crap. I must be coming down with what Mr. Wise, my more-than-slightly-insane AP biology teacher, called the Teenage Plague.

If I died, would it get me out of my geometry test tomorrow? One could only hope.

"Zoey, please. Are you even listening? I think he only had like four—I dunno—maybe six beers, and maybe like three shots. But that's totally beside the point. He probably wouldn't even have had hardly any if your stupid parents hadn't made you go home right after the game."

We shared a long-suffering look, in total agreement about the latest injustice committed against me by my mom and the Step-Loser she'd married three really long years ago. Then, after barely half a breath break, K was back with the babbling.

"Plus, he was celebrating. I mean we beat Union!" K shook my shoulder and put her face close to mine. "Hello! Your boyfriend—"

"My almost-boyfriend," I corrected her, trying my best not to cough on her.

"Whatever. Heath is our quarterback so of course he's going to celebrate. It's been like a million years since Broken Arrow beat Union."

"Sixteen." I'm crappy at math, but K's math impairment makes me look like a genius.

"Again, *whatever*. The point is, he was happy. You should give the boy a break."

"The point is that he was wasted for like the fifth time this week. I'm sorry, but I don't want to go out with a guy whose main focus in life has changed from trying to play college football to trying to chug a six-pack without puking. Not to mention the fact that he's going to get fat from all that beer." I had to pause to cough. I was feeling a little dizzy and forced myself to take slow, deep breaths when the coughing fit was over. Not that K-babble noticed.

"Eww! Heath, *fat!* Not a visual I want."

I managed to ignore another urge to cough. "And kissing him is like sucking on alcohol-soaked feet."

K scrunched up her face. "Okay, sick. Too bad he's so hot."

I rolled my eyes, not bothering to try to hide my annoyance at her typical shallowness.

"You're so grumpy when you're sick. Anyway, you have no idea how lost-puppy-like Heath looked after you ignored him at lunch. He couldn't even . . ."

Then I saw him. The dead guy. Okay, I realized pretty quick that he wasn't technically "dead." He was undead. Or un-human. Whatever. Scientists said one thing, people said another, but the end result was the same. There was no mistaking what he was and even if I hadn't felt the power and darkness that radiated from him, there was no frickin' way I could miss his Mark, the sapphire-blue crescent moon on his forehead and the additional tattooing of entwining knot work that framed his equally blue eyes. He was a vampyre, and worse. He was a Tracker.

Well, crap! He was standing by my locker.

"Zoey, you're *so* not listening to me!"

Then the vampyre spoke and his ceremonial words slicked across the space between us, dangerous and seductive, like blood mixed with melted chocolate.

"Zoey Montgomery! Night has chosen thee; thy death will be thy birth. Night calls to thee; hearken to Her sweet voice. Your destiny awaits you at the House of Night!"

He lifted one long, white finger and pointed at me. As my forehead exploded in pain Kayla opened her mouth and screamed.

When the bright splotches finally cleared from my eyes I looked up to see K's colorless face staring down at me.

As usual, I said the first ridiculous thing that came to mind. "K, your eyes are popping out of your head like a fish."

"He Marked you. Oh, Zoey! You have the outline of that thing on your forehead!" Then she pressed a shaking hand against her white lips, unsuccessfully trying to hold back a sob.

I sat up and coughed. I had a killer headache, and I rubbed at the spot right between my eyebrows. It stung as if a wasp had bit me and radiated pain down around my eyes, all the way across my cheekbones. I felt like I might puke.

"Zoey!" K was really crying now and had to speak between wet little hiccups. "Oh. My. God. That guy was a Tracker—a vampyre Tracker!"

"K." I blinked hard, trying to clear the pain from my head.

"Stop crying. You know I hate it when you cry." I reached out to attempt a comforting pat on her shoulders.

And she automatically cringed, and moved away from me.

I couldn't believe it. She actually cringed, like she was afraid of me. She must have seen the hurt in my eyes because she instantly started a string of breathless K-babble.

"Oh, *God,* Zoey! What are you going to do? You can't go to that place. You can't be one of those things. This can't be happening! Who am I supposed to go to all of our football games with?"

I noticed that all during her tirade she didn't once move any closer to me. I clamped down on the sick, hurt feeling inside that threatened to make me burst into tears. My eyes dried instantly. I was good at hiding tears. I should be; I'd had three years to get good at it.

"It's okay. I'll figure this out. It's probably some . . . some bizarre mistake," I lied.

I wasn't really talking; I was just making words come out of my mouth. Still grimacing at the pain in my head, I stood up. Looking around I felt a small measure of relief that K and I were the only ones in the math hall, and then I had to choke back what I knew was hysterical laughter. Had I not been totally psycho about the geometry test from hell scheduled for tomorrow, and had run back to my locker to get my book so I could attempt to obsessively (and pointlessly) study tonight, the Tracker would have found me standing outside in front of the school with the majority of the 1,300 kids who went to Broken Arrow's South Intermediate High School waiting for what my stupid Barbie-clone sister liked to smugly call "the big yellow limos." I have a car, but standing around with the less fortunate who have to ride the buses is a time-honored tradition, not to mention an excellent way to check out who's hitting on who. As it was, there was only one other kid in the math hall—a tall thin dork with messed-up teeth, which I could, unfortunately, see too much of because he was standing there with his mouth flapping open staring at me like I'd just given birth to a litter of flying pigs.

I coughed again, this time a really wet, disgusting cough. The dork made a squeaky little sound and scuttled down the hall to Mrs. Day's room clutching a flat board to his bony chest. Guess the chess club had changed its meeting time to Mondays after school.

Do vampyres play chess? Were there vampyre dorks? How about Barbie-like vampyre cheerleaders? Did any vampyres play in the band? Were there vampyre Emos with their guy-wearing-girl's-pants weirdness and those awful bangs that cover half their faces? Or were they all those freaky Goth kids who didn't like to bathe much? Was I going to turn into a Goth kid? Or worse, an Emo? I didn't particularly like wearing black, at least not exclusively, and I wasn't feeling a sudden and unfortunate aversion to soap and water, nor did I have an obsessive desire to change my hairstyle and wear too much eyeliner.

All this whirled through my mind while I felt another little hysterical bubble of laughter try to escape from my throat, and was almost thankful when it came out as a cough instead.

"Zoey? Are you okay?" Kayla's voice sounded too high, like someone was pinching her, and she'd taken another step away from me.

I sighed and felt my first sliver of anger. It wasn't like I'd asked for this. K and I had been best friends since third grade, and now she was looking at me like I had turned into a monster.

"Kayla, it's just me. The same me I was two seconds ago and two hours ago and two days ago." I made a frustrated gesture toward my throbbing head. "This doesn't change who I am!"

K's eyes teared up again, but, thankfully, her cell phone started singing Madonna's "Material Girl." Automatically, she glanced at the caller ID. I could tell by her rabbit-in-the-headlights expression that it was her boyfriend, Jared.

"Go on," I said in a flat, tired voice. "Ride home with him."

Her look of relief was like a slap in my face.

"Call me later?" she threw over her shoulder as she beat a hasty retreat out the side door.

I watched her rush across the east lawn to the parking lot. I could see that she had her cell phone smashed to her ear and was talking in animated little bursts to Jared. I'm sure she was already telling him I was turning into a monster.

The problem, of course, was that turning into a monster was the brighter of my two choices. Choice Number 1: I turn into a vampyre, which equals a monster in just about any human's mind. Choice Number 2: My body rejects the Change and I die. Forever.

So the good news is that I wouldn't have to take the geometry test tomorrow.

The bad news was that I'd have to move into the House of Night, a private boarding school in Tulsa's Midtown, known by all my friends as the Vampyre Finishing School, where I would spend the next four years going through bizarre and unnameable physical changes, as well as a total and permanent life shake-up. And that's only if the whole process didn't kill me.

Great. I didn't want to do either. I just wanted to attempt to be normal, despite the burden of my mega-conservative parents, my troll-like younger brother, and my oh-so-perfect older sister. I wanted to pass geometry. I wanted to keep my grades up so that I could get accepted into the veterinary college at OSU and get out of Broken Arrow, Oklahoma. But most of all, I wanted to fit in—at least at school. Home had become hopeless, so all I was left with were my friends and my life away from my family.

Now that was being taken away from me, too.

I rubbed my forehead and then messed with my hair until it

semi-covered my eyes, and, with any luck, the mark that had appeared above them. Keeping my head ducked down, like I was fascinated with the goo that had somehow formed in my purse, I hurried toward the door that led to the student parking lot.

But I stopped short of going outside. Through the side-by-side windows in the institutional-looking doors I could see Heath. Girls flocked around him, posing and flipping their hair, while guys revved ridiculously big pickup trucks and tried (but mostly failed) to look cool. Doesn't it figure that I would choose *that* to be attracted to? No, to be fair to myself I should remember that Heath used to be incredibly sweet, and even now he had his moments. Mostly when he bothered to be sober.

High-pitched girl giggles flitted to me from the parking lot. Great. Kathy Richter, the biggest ho in school, was pretending to smack Heath. Even from where I was standing it was obvious she thought hitting him was some kind of mating ritual. As usual, clueless Heath was just standing there grinning. Well, hell, my day just wasn't going to get any better. And there sat my robin's egg–blue 1966 VW Bug right in the middle of them. No. I couldn't go out there. I couldn't walk into the middle of all of them with this thing on my forehead. I'd never be able to be part of them again. I already knew too well what they'd do. I remembered the last kid a Tracker had Chosen at SIHS.

It happened at the beginning of the school year last year. The Tracker had come before school started and had targeted the kid as he was walking to his first hour. I didn't see the Tracker, but I did see the kid afterward, for just a second, after he dropped his books and ran out of the building, his new Mark glowing on his pale forehead and tears washing down his too white cheeks. I never forgot how crowded the halls had been that morning, and how everyone had backed away from him like he had the plague as he rushed to escape out the front doors of the school. I had been one of those kids who had backed out of his way and stared, even though I'd felt really sorry for him. I just hadn't wanted to be labeled as that-one-girl-who's-friends-with-those-freaks. Sort of ironic now, isn't it?

Instead of going to my car I headed for the nearest restroom, which was, thankfully, empty. There were three stalls—yes, I double-checked each for feet. On one wall were two sinks, over which hung two medium-sized mirrors. Across from the sinks the opposite wall was covered with a huge mirror that had a ledge below it for holding brushes and makeup and whatnot. I put my purse and my geometry book on the ledge, took a deep breath, and in one motion lifted my head and brushed back my hair.

It was like staring into the face of a familiar stranger. You know, that person you see in a crowd and swear you know, but you really don't? Now she was me—the familiar stranger.

She had my eyes. They were the same hazel color that could never decide whether it wanted to be green or brown, but my eyes had never been that big and round. Or had they? She had my hair—long and straight and almost as dark as my grandma's had been before hers had begun to turn silver. The stranger had my high cheekbones, long, strong nose, and wide mouth—more features from my grandma and her Cherokee ancestors. But my face had never been that pale. I'd always been olive-ish, much darker skinned than anyone else in my family. But maybe it wasn't that my skin was suddenly so white . . . maybe it just looked pale in comparison to the dark blue outline of the crescent moon that was perfectly positioned in the middle of my forehead. Or maybe it was the horrid fluorescent lighting. I hoped it was the lighting.

I stared at the exotic-looking tattoo. Mixed with my strong Cherokee features it seemed to brand me with a mark of wildness . . . as if I belonged to ancient times when the world was bigger . . . more barbaric.

From this day on my life would never be the same. And for a moment—just an instant—I forgot about the horror of not belonging and felt a shocking burst of pleasure, while deep inside of me the blood of my grandmother's people rejoiced.

CHAPTER TWO

When I figured that enough time had passed for everyone to have left school, I flopped my hair back over my forehead and left the bathroom, hurrying to the doors that led to the student parking lot. Everything seemed all clear—there was just some random kid wearing those seriously unattractive gang wanna-be baggy pants cutting across the far end of the lot. Keeping his pants from falling down as he walked was taking all his concentration; he wouldn't even notice me. I gritted my teeth against the throbbing pain in my head and bolted out the door, heading straight for my little Bug.

The moment I stepped outside the sun began to batter me. I mean, it wasn't a particularly sunny day; there were plenty of those big, puffy clouds that looked so pretty in pictures floating around the sky, semi-blocking the sun. But that didn't matter. I had to squint my eyes painfully and hold my hand up as a make-believe sun block against even that intermittent light. I guess it was because I was focusing so hard on the pain the ordinary sunlight was causing me that I didn't notice the truck until it squealed to a stop in front of me.

"Hey Zo! Didn't you get my message?"

Oh crap crap crap! It was Heath. I glanced up, looking at him from between my fingers like I was watching one of those stupid slasher movies. He was sitting on the open tailgate of his friend Dustin's pickup truck. Over his shoulder I could see into the cab of the truck where Dustin and his brother, Drew, were doing what they were usually doing—wrestling around and arguing over God only knows what stupid boy thing. Thankfully, they were ignoring me. I glanced back at Heath and sighed. He had a beer in his hand and a goofy grin on his face. Momentarily forgetting that I'd just been Marked and was destined to become an outcast blood-sucking monster, I scowled at Heath.

"You're drinking at school! Are you crazy?"

His little boy grin got bigger. "Yes I am crazy, 'bout you, baby!"

I shook my head while I turned my back to him, opening the creaky door to my Bug and shoving my books and backpack into the passenger's seat.

"Why aren't you guys at football practice?" I said, still keeping my face angled away from him.

"Didn't you hear? We got the day off 'cause of the ass-kicking we gave Union on Friday!"

Dustin and Drew, who must have been kinda paying attention to Heath and me after all, did a couple of very Okie "Whoo-hoo!" and "Yeah!" yells from inside the truck.

"Oh. Uh. No. I musta missed the announcement. I've been busy today. You know, big geometry test tomorrow." I tried to sound normal and nonchalant. Then I coughed and added, "Plus, I'm getting a crappy cold."

"Zo, really. Are you pissed or somethin'? Like, did Kayla say some shit about the party? You know I didn't really cheat on you."

Huh? Kayla had not said one solitary word about Heath *cheating* on me. Like a moron, I forgot (okay, temporarily) about my new Mark. My head snapped around so I could glare at him.

"What did you do, Heath?"

"Zo, me? You know I wouldn't . . ." but his innocent act and his excuses faded into an unattractive open-mouthed look of shock when he caught sight of my Mark. "What the—" he started to say, but I cut him off.

"Shh!" I jerked my head in the direction of the still clueless Dustin and Drew, who were now singing at the top of their totally tonedeaf lungs to the latest Toby Keith CD.

Heath's eyes were still wide and shocked, but he lowered his voice. "Is that some kinda makeup thing you're doing for drama class?"

"No," I whispered. "It's not."

"But you can't be Marked. We're going out."

"We are not going out!" And just like that my semi-reprieve from coughing ended. I practically doubled over, hacking a seriously nasty, phlegmy cough.

"Hey, Zo!" Dustin called from the cab. "You gotta lay off those cigarettes."

"Yeah, you sound like you're gonna cough up a lung or somethin'," Drew said.

"Dude! Leave her alone. You know she don't smoke. She's a vampyre."

Great. Wonderful. Heath, with his usual total and complete lack of anything resembling good sense, thought he was actually standing up for me as he yelled at his friends, who instantly stuck their heads out of the open windows and gawked at me like I was a science experiment.

"Well, shit. Zoey's a fucking freak!" Drew said.

Drew's insensitive words made the anger that had been simmering somewhere inside my chest ever since Kayla had cringed from me bubble up and boil over. Ignoring the pain the sun caused me, I stared straight at Drew, meeting his eyes.

"Shut the hell up! I've had a really bad day and I do not need this crap from you." I paused to look from the now wide-eyed and silent Drew to Dustin and added, "Or you." And as I kept eye contact with Dustin I realized something—something that shocked and weirdly excited me: Dustin looked scared. Really scared. I glared back at Drew. He looked scared, too. Then I felt it. A tingling sensation that crawled over my skin and made my new Mark burn.

Power. I felt power.

"Zo? What the fuck?" Heath's voice broke my attention and pulled my gaze from the brothers.

"We're outta here!" Dustin said, throwing the truck into gear and stepping on the gas. The pickup lurched forward, causing Heath to lose his balance and slide, with a windmill of arms and flying beer, onto the blacktop of the parking lot.

Automatically, I rushed forward. "Are you okay?" Heath was on his hands and knees, and I bent down to help pull him to his feet.

Then I smelled it. Something smelled amazing—hot and sweet and delicious.

Was Heath wearing new cologne? One of those weird pheromone things that are supposed to attract women like a big genetically engineered bug zapper? I didn't realize how close I was to him until he stood up straight and our bodies were almost pressed together. He looked down at me, a question in his eyes.

I didn't back away from him. I should have. I would have before . . . but not now. Not today.

"Zo?" he said softly, his voice deep and husky.

"You smell really good," I couldn't stop myself from saying. My heart was pounding so loud that I could hear its echo in my throbbing temples.

"Zoey, I've really missed you. We need to get back together. You know I really love you." He reached up to touch my face and both of us noticed the blood that smeared the palm of his hand. "Ah, shit. I guess I—" his voice closed off when he glanced at my face. I could only imagine what I must look like, with my face all white, my new Mark blazingly outlined in sapphire blue, and my eyes staring at the blood on his hand. I couldn't move; I couldn't look away.

"I want . . ." I whispered. "I want . . ." What did I want? I couldn't put it into words. No, that wasn't it. I *wouldn't* put it into words. Wouldn't say aloud the overwhelming surge of white-hot desire that was trying to drown me. And it wasn't because Heath was standing so near. He'd been close to me before. Hell, we'd been making out for a year, but he'd never made me feel like this—nothing ever like this. I bit my lip and moaned.

The pickup truck squealed to a halt, fishtailing beside us. Drew jumped out and grabbed Heath around the waist, and jerked him backward into the cab of the truck.

"Knock it off! I'm talking to Zoey!"

Heath tried to struggle against Drew, but the kid was Broken Arrow's senior linebacker, and truly ginormous. Dustin reached around them and slammed the door to the truck.

"Leave him alone, you freak!" Drew yelled at me as Dustin floored the truck and this time they really did speed off.

I got into my Bug. My hands were shaking so hard I had to try three times before I got the engine started.

"Just get home. Just get home." I said the words over and over between wrenching coughs as I drove. I wouldn't think about what had just happened. I couldn't think about what had just happened.

The drive home took fifteen minutes, but it seemed to pass in the blink of an eye. Too soon I was sitting in the driveway, trying to get ready for the scene I knew, sure as lightning follows thunder, was waiting inside for me.

Why had I been so eager to get here? I suppose I hadn't technically been all that eager. I suppose I'd just been escaping from what had happened in the parking lot with Heath.

No! I wasn't going to think about that now. And, anyway, there was probably some kind of rational explanation for everything, a rational and simple explanation. Dustin and Drew were retards—totally immature beer-brains. I hadn't used a creepy new power to intimidate them. They'd just been freaked that I'd been Marked. That was it. I mean, people were scared of vampyres.

"But I'm *not* a vampyre!" I said. Then I coughed while I remember how hypnotically beautiful Heath's blood had been, and the rush of desire I'd felt for *it*. Not Heath, but Heath's blood.

No! No! No! Blood was not beautiful or desirable. I must be in shock. That's it. That had to be it. I was in shock and not thinking clearly. Okay . . . okay . . . absently, I touched my forehead. It had stopped burning, but it still felt different. I coughed for the zillionth time. Fine. I wouldn't think about Heath, but I couldn't deny it any more. *I* felt different. My skin was ultrasensitive. My chest hurt, and even though I had my cool Maui Jim sunglasses on, my eyes kept tearing up painfully.

"I'm dying . . ." I moaned, and then promptly clamped my lips shut. I might actually be dying. I glanced up at the big brick house that, after three years, still didn't seem like home. "Get it over with. Just get it over with." At least my sister wouldn't be home yet—cheerleading practice. Hopefully, the troll would be totally hypnotized by his new Delta Force: Black Hawk Down video game (um . . . ew). I might have Mom to myself. Maybe she would understand . . . maybe she would know what to do. . . .

Ah, hell! I was sixteen years old, but I suddenly realized that I wanted nothing as much as I wanted my mom.

"Please let her understand," I whispered a simple prayer to whatever god or goddess might be listening to me.

As usual, I went in through the garage. I walked down the hall to my room and dumped my geometry book, purse, and backpack on my bed. Then I took a deep breath and headed, a little shakily, to find my mom.

She was in the family room, curled up on the edge of the couch, sipping a cup of coffee and reading *Chicken Soup for a Woman's Soul.* She looked so normal, so much like she used to look. Except that she used to read exotic romances and actually wear makeup. Both were things her new husband didn't allow (what a turd).

"Mom?"

"Hum?" She didn't look up at me.

I swallowed hard. "Mama." I used the name I used to call her, back in the days before she married John. "I need your help."

I don't know whether it was the unexpected use of "Mama" or if something in my voice touched an old piece of mom-intuition she still had somewhere inside her, but the eyes she lifted immediately from the book were soft and filled with concern.

"What is it, baby—" she began, and then her words seemed to freeze on her lips as her eyes found the Mark on my forehead.

"Oh, God! What have you done now?"

My heart started to hurt again. "Mom, I didn't *do* anything. This is something that happened *to* me, not because of me. It's not my fault."

"Oh, please, no!" she wailed as if I hadn't said a word. "What is your father going to say?"

I wanted to scream *how the hell would any of us know what my father was going to say, we haven't seen or heard from him for fourteen years!* But I knew it wouldn't do any good, and it always just made her mad when I reminded her that John was not my "real" father. So I tried a different tactic—one I'd given up on three years ago.

"Mama, please. Can't you just not tell him? At least for a day or two? Just keep it between the two of us until we . . . I don't know . . . get used to it or something." I held my breath.

"But what would I say? You can't even cover that thing up with makeup." Her lips curled weirdly as she gave the crescent moon a nervous glance.

"Mom, I didn't mean that I'd stay here while we got used to it. I have to go; you know that." I had to pause while a huge cough made my shoulders shake. "The Tracker Marked me. I have to move to the House of Night or I'm just going to get sicker and sicker." *And then die,* I tried to tell her with my eyes. I couldn't actually say the words. "I just want a couple of days before I have to deal with . . ." I broke off so I didn't have to say his name, this time purposefully making myself cough, which wasn't hard.

"What would I tell your father?"

I felt a rush of fear at the panic in her voice. Wasn't she the mom? Wasn't she supposed to have the answers instead of the questions?

"Just . . . just tell him that I'm spending the next couple days at Kayla's house because we have a big biology project due."

I watched my mom's eyes change. The concern faded from them and was replaced by a hardness that I recognized all too well.

"So what you're saying is that you want me to lie to him."

"No, Mom. What I'm saying is that I want you, for once, to put what I need before what he wants. I want you to be my mama. To help me pack and to drive with me to this new school because I'm scared and sick and I don't know if I can do it all by myself!" I finished in a rush, breathing hard and coughing into my hand.

"I wasn't aware that I had stopped being your mom," she said coldly.

She made me feel even more tired than Kayla had. I sighed. "I think that's the problem, Mom. You don't care enough to be aware of it. You haven't cared about anything but John since you married him."

Her eyes narrowed at me. "I don't know how you can be so selfish. Don't you realize all that he's done for us? Because of him I quit that awful job at Dillards. Because of him we don't have to worry about money and we have this big, beautiful house. Because of him we have security and a bright future."

I'd heard these words so often I could have recited them with her. It was at this point in our non-conversations that I usually apologized and went back to my room. But today I couldn't apologize. Today I was different. Everything was different.

"No, Mother. The truth is that because of him you haven't paid any attention to your kids for three years. Did you know that your oldest daughter has turned into a sneaky, spoiled slut who's screwed half of the football team? Do you know what nasty, bloody video games Kevin keeps hidden from you? No, of course you don't! The two of them *act* happy and *pretend* to like John and the whole damn make-believe family thing, so you smile at them and pray for them and let them do whatever. And me? You think I'm the bad one because I don't pretend—because I'm honest. You know what? I'm so sick of my life that I'm glad the Tracker Marked me! They call that vampyre school the House of Night, but it can't be any darker than this *perfect* home!" Before I could cry or scream I whirled around and stalked back to my bedroom, slamming the door behind me.

I hope they all drown.

Through the too thin walls I could hear her making a hysterical call to John. There was no doubt that he'd rush home to deal with me. The Problem. Instead of sitting on the bed and crying like I was tempted to, I emptied the school crap out of my backpack. Like I'd need it where I was going? They probably don't even have normal classes. They probably have classes like Ripping Peoples

Throats Out 101 and . . . and . . . Intro to How to See in the Dark. Whatever.

No matter what my mom did or didn't do, I couldn't stay here. I had to leave.

So what did I need to take with me?

My two favorite pairs of jeans, besides what I had on. A couple of black T-shirts. I mean, what else do vampyres wear? Plus, they are slimming. I almost passed on my cute aqua-colored sparkly cami, but all that black was bound to make me more depressed . . . so I included it. Then I stuffed tons of bras and thongs and hair and makeup things into the side pouch. I almost left my stuffed animal, Otis the Shish (couldn't say fish when I was two), on my pillow, but . . . well . . . vampyre or not I didn't think I could sleep very well without him. So I tucked him gently into the damn backpack.

Then I heard the knock on my door, and *its* voice called me out of my room.

"What?" I yelled, and then I convulsed in a bout of nasty coughing.

"Zoey. Your mother and I need to speak with you."

Great. Clearly they didn't drown.

I patted Otis the Shish. "Otis, this sucks." I squared my shoulders, coughed again, and went out to face the enemy.

CHAPTER THREE

—

At first glance my step-loser, John Heffer, appears to be an okay guy, even normal. (Yes, that's really his last name—and, sadly, it is also now my mom's last name. She's Mrs. Heffer. Can you believe it?) When he and my mom started dating I actually overheard some of my mom's friends calling him "handsome" and "charming." At first. Of course now Mom has a whole new group of friends, ones Mr. Handsome and Charming thinks are more appropriate than the group of fun single women she used to hang with.

I never liked him. Really. I'm not just saying that because I can't stand him now. From the first day I met him I saw only one thing—a fake. He fakes being a nice guy. He fakes being a good husband. He even fakes being a good father.

He looks like every other dad-age guy. He has dark hair, skinny chicken legs, and is getting a gut. His eyes are like his soul, a washed-out, cold, brownish color.

I walked into the family room to find him standing by the couch. My mother was crumpled near the end of it, clutching his hand. Her eyes were already red and watery. Great. She was going to play Hurt Hysterical Mother. It's an act she does well.

John had begun to attempt to skewer me with his eyes, but my Mark distracted him. His face twisted in disgust.

"Get thee behind me, Satan!" he quoted in what I like to think of as his sermon voice.

I sighed. "It's not Satan. It's just me."

"Now is not the time for sarcasm, Zoey," Mom said.

"I'll handle this, hon," the step-loser said, patting her shoulder absently before he turned his attention back to me. "I told you that your bad behavior and your attitude problem would catch up with you. I'm not even surprised it happened this soon."

I shook my head. I expected this. I really expected this, and still it was a shock. The entire world knew that there was nothing anyone could do to bring on the Change. The whole "if you get bit by a vampyre you'll die and become one" thing is strictly fiction. Scientists have been trying to figure out what causes the sequence of physical events that lead to vampyrism for years, hoping that if they figure it out they could cure it, or at the very least invent a vaccine to fight against it. So far, no such luck. But now John Heffer, my step-loser, had suddenly discovered that bad teenage behavior—specifically my bad behavior, which mostly consisted of an occasional lie, some pissed off thoughts and smart-ass comments directed primarily against my parents, and maybe some semi-harmless lust for Ashton Kutcher (sad to say he likes older women)—actually brought about this physical reaction in my body. Well, hell! Who knew?

"This wasn't something I caused," I finally managed to say. "This wasn't done *because* of me. It was done *to* me. Every scientist on the planet agrees with that."

"Scientists are not all-knowing. They are not men of God."

I just stared at him. He was an Elder of the People of Faith, a position he was oh, so proud of. It was one of the reasons Mom had been attracted to him, and on a strictly logical level I could understand why. Being an Elder meant that a man was successful. He had the right job. A nice house. The perfect family. He was supposed to do the right things and believe the right way. On paper he should have been a great choice for her new husband and our father. Too bad the paper wouldn't have shown the full story. And now, predictably, he was going to play the Elder card and throw God in my face. I would bet my cool new Steve Madden flats that it irritated God as much as it annoyed me.

I tried again. "We studied this in AP biology. It's a physiological reaction that takes place in some teenagers' bodies as their hormone levels rise." I paused, thinking really hard and totally proud of myself for remembering something I learned last semester. "In certain people the hormones trigger something-or-other in a . . . a . . ." I thought harder and remembered: "a Junk DNA strand, which starts the whole Change." I smiled, not really at John, but because I was thrilled by my ability to recall stuff from a unit we'd been done with for months. I knew the smile was a mistake when I saw the familiar clenching of his jaw.

"God's knowledge surpasses science, and it's blasphemous for you to say otherwise, young lady."

"I never said scientists are smarter than God!" I threw my hands up and tried to stifle a cough. "I'm just trying to explain this thing to you."

"I don't need to have anything explained to me by a sixteen-year-old."

Well, he was wearing those really bad pants and that awful shirt. Clearly he did need some things explained to him by a teenager, but I didn't think it was the right time to mention his unfortunate and obvious fashion impairment.

"But John, honey, what are we going to do about her? What will the neighbors say?" Her face paled even more and she stifled a little sob. "What will people say at Meeting on Sunday?"

He narrowed his eyes when I opened my mouth to answer, and interrupted before I could speak.

"We are going to do what any good family should do. We are going to give this to God."

They were sending me to a convent? Unfortunately, I had to deal with another round of coughing, so he kept right on talking.

"We are also going to call Dr. Asher. He'll know what to do to calm this situation."

Wonderful. Fabulous. He's calling in our family shrink, the Incredibly Expressionless Man. Perfect.

"Linda, call Dr. Asher's emergency number, and then I think it would be wise to activate the prayer phone tree. Make sure the other Elders know that they are to gather here."

My mom nodded and started to get up, but the words that burst from my mouth made her flop back down on the couch.

"What! Your answer is to call a shrink who is totally clueless about teenagers and get all those uptight Elders over here? Like they would even begin to try and understand? No! Don't you get it? I have to leave. Tonight." I coughed, a really gut-wrenching sound that hurt my chest. "See! This will just get worse if I don't get around the . . ." I hesitated. Why was it so hard to say "vampyres"? Because it sounded so foreign—so final—and, part of me admitted, so fantastic. "I have to get to the House of Night."

Mom jumped up, and for a second I thought she was actually going to save me. Then John put his arm around her shoulder possessively. She looked up at him and when she looked back at me her eyes seemed almost sorry, but her words, typically, reflected only what John would want her to say.

"Zoey, surely it wouldn't hurt anything if you spent just tonight at home?"

"Of course it wouldn't," John said to her. "I'm sure Dr. Asher will see the need for a house visit. With him here she'll be perfectly fine." He patted her shoulder, pretended to be caring, but instead of sweet he sounded slimy.

I looked from him to my mom. They weren't going to let me leave. Not tonight, and maybe not ever, or at least not until I had to be hauled out by the paramedics. I suddenly understood that it wasn't just about this Mark and the fact that my life had been totally changed. It was about control. If they let me go, somehow they lose. In Mom's case, I liked to think that she was afraid of losing me. I knew what John didn't want to lose. He didn't want to lose his precious authority and the illusion that we were the perfect little family. As Mom had already said, *What would the neighbors think—what will people think at Meeting on Sunday?* John had to preserve the illusion, and if that meant allowing me to get really, really sick, well then, that was a price he was willing to pay.

I wasn't willing to pay it, though.

I guess it was time I took things into my own hands (after all, they are well manicured).

"Fine," I said. "Call Dr. Asher. Start the prayer phone tree. But do you mind if I go lay down until everyone gets here?" I coughed again for good measure.

"Of course not, honey," Mom said, looking obviously relieved. "A little rest will probably make you feel better." Then she moved away from John's possessive arm. She smiled and then hugged me. "Would you like me to get you some NyQuil?"

"No, I'll be fine," I said, clinging to her for just a second, wishing so damn hard that it was three years ago and she was still mine—still on my side. Then I took a deep breath and stepped back. "I'll be fine," I repeated.

She looked at me and nodded, telling me she was sorry the only way she could, with her eyes.

I turned away from her and started to retreat to my bedroom. To my back the step-loser said, "And why don't you do us all a favor and see if you can find some powder or something to cover up that thing on your forehead?"

I didn't even pause. I just kept walking. And I wouldn't cry.

I'm going to remember this, I told myself sternly. *I'm going to remember how awful they made me feel today. So when I'm scared and alone and whatever else is going to happen to me starts to happen, I'm going to remember that nothing could be as bad as being stuck here. Nothing.*

CHAPTER FOUR

—

So I sat on my bed and coughed while I listened to my mom making a frantic call to our shrink's emergency line, followed quickly by another equally hysterical call that would activate the dreaded People of Faith prayer tree. Within thirty minutes our house would begin to fill up with fat women and their beady-eyed pedophile husbands. They'd call me out to the family room. My Mark would be considered a Really Big and Embarrassing Problem, so they'd probably anoint me with some crap that was sure to clog my pores and give me a Cyclops-sized zit before laying their hands on me and praying. They'd ask God to help me stop being such an awful teenager and a problem to my parents. Oh, and the little matter of my Mark needed to be cleared up, too.

If only it were that simple. I'd gladly make a deal with God to be a good kid versus changing school and species. I'd even take the geometry test. Well, okay. Maybe not the geometry test—but, still, it's not like I'd asked to become a freak. This whole thing meant that I was going to have to leave. To start my life over somewhere I'd be the new kid. Somewhere I didn't have any friends. I blinked hard, forcing myself not to cry. School was the only place I really felt at home anymore; my friends were my only family. I balled up my fists and squidged my face up to keep from crying. One step at a time—I'd just take this one step at a time.

No way was I going deal with clones of the step-loser on top of everything else. And, as if the People of Faith weren't bad enough, the horrid prayer session would be followed by an equally annoying session with Dr. Asher. He'd ask me a lot of questions about how this and that made me feel. Then he'd babble on and on about teenage anger and angst being normal but that only I could choose how it would have an impact on my life . . . blah . . . blah . . . and since this was an "emergency" he'd probably want me to draw something that represented my inner child or whatever.

I definitely had to get out of there.

Good thing I've always been "the bad kid" and was well prepared for a situation like this. Okay, I wasn't exactly thinking about escaping from my house so I could run off and join the vampyres when I put a spare key to my car under the flowerpot outside my window. I was just considering that I might want to sneak out and go to Kayla's house. Or, if I *really* wanted to be bad I might meet Heath at the park and make out. But then Heath started drinking and I started to change into a vampyre. Sometimes life doesn't make any sense.

I grabbed my backpack, opened my window, and with an ease that said more about my sinful nature than the step-loser's boring lectures, I popped out my window screen. I put on my sunglasses and peeked out. It was only four thirty or so, and not dark yet, so I was really glad that our privacy fence hid me from our totally nosy neighbors. On this side of the house the only other windows were to my sister's room, and she should still be at cheerleading practice. (Hell must truly be freezing over because for once I was sincerely glad my sister's world revolved around what she called "the sport of cheer.") I dropped my backpack out first and then slowly followed it out the window, being careful not to make even a small *oof* noise when I landed on the grass. I paused there for way too many minutes, burying my face in my arms to muffle my horrible cough. Then I bent over and lifted up the edge of the pot that held the lavender plant Grandma Redbird had given me, and let my fingers find the hard metal of the key where it nestled against the smushed grass.

The gate didn't even squeak when I cracked it open and inched out like one of Charlie's Angels. My cute Bug was sitting there where she always sat—right in front of the third door to our three car garage. The step-loser wouldn't let me park her inside because he said the lawnmower was more important. (More important than a vintage VW? How? That didn't even make sense. Jeesh, I just sounded like a guy. Since when did I care about the vintageness of my Bug? I must really be Changing.) I looked both ways. Nothing. I sprinted for my Bug, jumped in, put it in neutral, and was truly thankful that our driveway was ridiculously steep when my wonderful car rolled smoothly and silently into the street. From there it was east to start it and zip out of the neighborhood of Big Expensive Houses.

I didn't even glance in the rearview mirror.

I did reach over and turn off my cell phone. I didn't want to talk to anyone.

No, that wasn't exactly true. There was one person I really wanted to talk to. She was the one person in the world who I was positive wouldn't look at my Mark and think I was a monster or a freak or a really awful person.

Like my Bug could read my mind it seemed to turn all by itself onto the highway that led to the Muskogee Turnpike and, eventually, to the most wonderful place in this world—my Grandma Redbird's lavender farm.

Unlike the drive from school to home, the hour-and-a-half trip to Grandma Redbird's farm seemed to take forever. By the time

I pulled off the two-lane highway onto the hard-packed dirt road that led to Grandma's place, my body ached even worse than it did that time they hired that crazy new gym teacher who thought we should do insane weight circuits while she cracked her whip at us and cackled. Okay, so maybe she didn't have a whip, but still. My muscles hurt like hell. It was almost six o'clock and the sun was finally starting to set, but my eyes still stung. Actually, even the fading sunlight made my skin feel tingly and weird. It made me glad that it was the end of October and it had finally turned cool enough for me to wear my Borg Invasion 4D hoodie (sure, it is a *Star Trek: The Next Generation* ride in Vegas and, sadly, I am on occasion a total *Star Trek* nerd) which, thankfully, covered most of my skin. Before I got out of my Bug I dug around in the backseat until I found my old OSU trucker's hat and pulled it down on my head so that my face was out of the sun.

My grandma's house sat between two lavender fields and was shaded by huge old oaks. It was built in 1942 of raw Oklahoma stone, with a comfortable porch and unusually big windows. I loved this house. Just climbing the little wooden stairs that led to the porch made me feel better . . . safe. Then I saw the note taped on the outside of the door. It was easy to recognize Grandma Redbird's pretty handwriting: *I'm on the bluffs collecting wildflowers.*

I touched the soft lavender-scented paper. She always knew when I was coming for a visit. When I was a kid I used to think it was weird, but as I got older I appreciated the extra sense she had. All my life I've known that, no matter what, I could count on Grandma Redbird. During those awful first months after Mom married John I think I would have shriveled up and died if I hadn't been able to escape every weekend to Grandma's house.

For a second I considered going inside (Grandma never locked her doors) and waiting for her, but I needed to see her, to have her hug me and tell me what I had wanted Mom to say.

Don't be scared . . . it'll be okay . . . we'll make it be okay. So instead of going inside I found the little deer path at the edge of the northern-most lavender field that would lead to the bluffs and I followed it, letting my fingertips trail over the top of the closest plants so that as I walked they released their sweet, silvery scent into the air around me like they were welcoming me home.

It felt like years since I'd been here, even though I knew it had been only four weeks. John didn't like Grandma. He thought she was weird. I'd even overheard him tell Mom that Grandma was "a witch and going to hell." He's such an ass.

Then an amazing thought hit me and I came to a complete stop. My parents no longer controlled what I did. I wasn't going to live with them ever again. John couldn't tell me what to do anymore.

Whoa! How awesome!

So awesome that it sent me into a spasm of coughing that made me wrap my arms around myself, like I was trying to hold my chest together. I needed to find Grandma Redbird, and I needed to find her now.

CHAPTER FIVE

—

The path up the side of the bluffs had always been steep, but I'd climbed it about a gazillion times, with and without my grandma, and I'd never felt like this. It wasn't just the coughing anymore. And it wasn't just the sore muscles. I was dizzy and my stomach had started to gurgle so badly that I was reminding myself of Meg Ryan in the movie *French Kiss* after she ate all that cheese and had a lactose-intolerance fit. (Kevin Kline is really cute in that movie—well, for an old guy.)

And I was snotting. I don't mean just sniffling a little. I mean I was wiping my nose on the sleeve of my hoodie (gross). I couldn't breathe without opening my mouth, which made me cough more, and I couldn't believe how badly my chest hurt! I tried to remember what it was that officially killed the kids who didn't complete the Change into vampyres. Did they have heart attacks? Or was it possible that they coughed and snotted themselves to death?

Stop thinking about it!

I needed to find Grandma Redbird. If Grandma didn't have the answers, she'd figure them out. Grandma Redbird understood people. She said it was because she hadn't lost touch with her Cherokee heritage and the tribal knowledge of the ancestral Wise Women she carried in her blood. Even now it made me smile to think about the frown that came over Grandma's face whenever the subject of the step-loser came up (she's the only adult who knows I call him that). Grandma Redbird said that it was obvious that the Redbird Wise Woman blood had skipped over her daughter, but that was only because it had been saving up to give an extra dose of ancient Cherokee magic to me.

As a little girl I'd climbed this path holding Grandma's hand more times than I could count. In the meadow of tall grasses and wildflowers we'd lay out a brightly colored blanket and eat a picnic lunch while Grandma told me stories of the Cherokee people and taught me the mysterious-sounding words of their language. As I struggled up the winding path those ancient stories seemed to swirl around and around inside my head, like smoke from a ceremonial fire . . . including the sad story of how the stars were formed when a dog was discovered stealing cornmeal and the tribe whipped him. As the dog ran howling to his home in the north, the meal scattered across the sky and the magic in it made the Milky Way. Or how the Great Buzzard made the mountains and valleys with his wings. And my favorite, the story about young woman sun who lived in the east, and her brother, the moon, who lived in the west, and the Redbird who was the daughter of the sun.

"Isn't that weird? I'm a Redbird and the daughter of the sun, but I'm turning into a monster of the night." I heard myself talking out loud and was surprised that my voice sounded so weak, especially when my words seemed to echo around me, as if I were talking into a vibrating drum.

Drum . . .

Thinking the word reminded me of powwows Grandma had taken me to when I was a little girl, and then, my thoughts somehow breathing life into the memory, I actually heard the rhythmic beating of ceremonial drums. I looked around, squinting against even the weak light of the dying day. My eyes stung and my vision was all screwed up. There was no wind, but the shadows of the rocks and trees seemed to be moving . . . stretching . . . reaching out toward me.

"Grandma I'm scared . . ." I cried between wracking coughs.

The spirits of the land are nothing to be frightened of, Zoeybird.

"Grandma?" Did I hear her voice calling me by my nickname, or was it only more weirdness and echoes, this time coming from my memory? "Grandma!" I called again, and then stood still listening for an answer.

Nothing. Nothing except the wind.

U-no-le . . . the Cherokee word for wind drifted through my mind like a half-forgotten dream.

Wind? No, wait! There hadn't been any wind just a second ago, but now I had to hold my hat down with one hand and brush away the hair that was whipping wildly across my face with the other. Then in the wind I heard them—the sounds of many Cherokee voices chanting in time with the beating of the ceremonial drums. Through a veil of hair and tears I saw smoke. The nutty sweet scent of piñon wood filled my open mouth and I tasted the campfires of my ancestors. I gasped, fighting to catch my breath.

That's when I felt them. They were all around me, almost-visible shapes shimmering like heat waves lifting from a blacktop road in summer. I could feel them press against me as they twirled and moved with graceful, intricate steps around and around the shadowy image of a Cherokee campfire.

Join us, u-we-tsi-a-ge-ya . . . Join us, daughter . . .

Cherokee ghosts . . . drowning in my own lungs . . . the fight with my parents . . . my old life gone . . .

It was all just too much. I ran.

I guess what they teach us in biology about adrenaline taking over during the whole fight-or-flight thing is true because even though my chest felt like it was going to explode and it seemed as if I was trying to breathe underwater, I ran up the last and steepest part of the trail like they'd opened up all the stores at the mall and they were giving away free shoes.

Gasping for breath I stumbled up the path—higher and higher—fighting to get away from the frightening spirits that hovered around me like fog, but instead of leaving them behind it seemed I was running farther into their world of smoke and shadows. Was I dying? Was this what happens? Was that why I could see ghosts? Where's the white light? Completely panicked, I rushed forward, throwing my arms out wildly as if I could hold off the terror that was chasing me.

I didn't see the root that broke through the hard ground of the path. Completely disoriented I tried to catch myself, but all of my reflexes were off. I fell hard. The pain in my head was sharp, but it lasted only an instant before blackness swallowed me.

Waking up was weird. I expected my body to hurt, especially my head and my chest, but instead of pain I felt . . . well . . . I felt fine. Actually, I felt better than fine. I wasn't coughing. My arms and legs were amazingly light, tingly, and warm, like I had just slipped into a bubbly hot tub on a cold night.

Huh?

Surprise made me open my eyes. I was staring up at a light, which miraculously didn't hurt my eyes. Instead of the glaring light of the sun, this was more like a soft rain of candlelight filtering down from above. I sat up, and realized I was wrong. The light wasn't coming down. I was moving up toward it!

I'm going to heaven. Well, that'll shock some people.

I glanced down to see *my body!* I or it or . . . or . . . whatever was lying scarily close to the edge of the bluff. My body was very still. My forehead had been cut and it was bleeding badly. The blood dripped steadily into a gash in the rocky ground, making a trail of red tears that fell into the heart of the bluff.

It was incredibly weird to look down on myself. I wasn't scared. But I should be, shouldn't I? Didn't this mean I was dead? Maybe I'd be able to see the Cherokee ghosts better now. Even that thought didn't scare me. Actually, instead of being afraid it was more like I was an observer, as if none of this could really touch me. (Kinda like those girls who have sex with everyone and think that they're not going to get pregnant or a really nasty STD that eats your brains and stuff. Well, we'll see in ten years, won't we?)

I enjoyed the way the world looked, sparkling and new, but it was my body that kept drawing my attention. I floated closer to it. I was breathing in short, shallow pants. Well, my *body* was breathing like that, not the I that was me. (Talk about confusing pronoun usage.) And I/she didn't look good. I/she was all pale and her lips were blue. Hey! White face, blue lips, and red blood! Am I patriotic or what?

I laughed, and it was amazing! I swear I could see my laughter floating around me like the puffy things you blow off a dandelion, only instead of being white it was birthday-cake-frosting-blue. Wow! Who knew hitting my head and passing out would be so much fun? I wondered if this was what it was like to be high.

The dandelion icing laughter faded and I could hear the shining crystal sound of running water. I moved closer to my body, able to see that what I had at first thought was a gash in the ground was really a narrow crevasse. The living water sound was coming from deep inside it. Curious, I peered down, and the sparkling silver outline of words drifted up from within the rock. I strained to hear, and was rewarded by a faint, whispering of silver sound.

Zoey Redbird . . . come to me . . .

"Grandma!" I yelled into the slash in the rock. My words were bright purple and they filled the air around me. "Is that you, Grandma?"

Come to me . . .

The silver mixed with the purple of my visible voice, turning the words the glistening color of lavender blossoms. It was an omen! A sign! Somehow, like the spirit guides the Cherokee people have believed in for centuries, Grandma Redbird was telling me I had to go down into the rock.

Without any more hesitation, I flung my spirit forward and down into the crevasse, following the trail of my blood and the silver memory of my grandma's whisper until I came to the smooth floor of a cave-like room. In the middle of the room a small stream of water bubbled, giving off tinkling shards of visible sound, bright and glass-colored. Mixed with the scarlet drops of my blood it lit up the cave with a flickering light that was the color of dried leaves. I wanted to sit next to the bubbling water and let my fingers touch the air around it and play in the texture of its music, but the voice called to me again.

Zoey Redbird . . . follow me to your destiny . . .

So I followed the stream and the woman's call. The cave narrowed until it was a rounded tunnel. It curved and curled around and around, in a gentle spiral, ending abruptly at a wall that was covered with carved symbols that looked familiar and alien at the same time. Confused, I watched the stream pour down into a crack in the wall and disappear. What now? Was I supposed to follow it?

I looked back down the tunnel. Nothing there except dancing light. I turned to the wall and felt a jolt of electric shock. Whoa! There was a woman sitting cross-legged in front of the wall! She was wearing a white fringed dress that was beaded with the same symbols that were on the wall behind her. She was fantastically beautiful, with long straight hair so black it looked as if it had blue and purple highlights, like a raven's wing. Her full lips curved up as she spoke, filling the air between us with the silver power of her voice.

Tsi-lu-gi U-we-tsi a-ge-hu-tsa. Welcome, Daughter. You have done well.

She spoke in Cherokee, but even though I hadn't practiced the language much in the last couple years I understood the words.

"You're not my grandma!" I blurted, feeling awkward and out of place as my purple words joined with hers, making incredible patterns of sparkling lavender in the air around us.

Her smile was like the rising sun.

No, Daughter, I am not, but I know Sylvia Redbird very well.

I took a deep breath. "Am I dead?"

I was afraid she would laugh at me, but she didn't. Instead her dark eyes were soft and concerned.

No, u-we-tsi-a-ge-ya. You are far from dead, though your spirit has been temporarily freed to wander the realm of the Nunne 'hi.

"The spirit people!" I glanced around the tunnel, trying to see faces and forms within the shadows.

Your grandmother has taught you well, u-s-ti Do-tsu-wa . . . little Redbird. You are a unique mixture of the Old Ways and the New World—of ancient tribal blood and the heartbeat of outsiders.

Her words made me feel hot and cold at the same time. "Who are you?" I asked.

I am known by many names . . . Changing Woman, Gaea, A'akuluujjusi, Kuan Yin, Grandmother Spider, and even Dawn . . .

As she spoke each name her face was transformed so that I was dizzied by her power. She must have understood, because she paused and flashed her beautiful smile at me again, and her face settled back into the woman I had first seen.

But you, Zoeybird, my Daughter, may call me by the name by which your world knows me today, Nyx.

"Nyx," my voice was barely above a whisper. "The vampyre Goddess?"

In truth, it was the ancient Greeks touched by the Change who first worshiped me as the mother they searched for within their endless Night. I have been pleased to call their descendents my children for many ages. And, yes, in your world those children are called vampyre. Accept the name, u-we-tsi-a-ge-ya; in it you will find your destiny.

I could feel my Mark burning on my forehead, and all of a sudden I wanted to cry. "I—I don't understand. Find my destiny? I just want to find a way to deal with my new life—to make this all okay. Goddess, I just want to fit in someplace. I don't think I'm up to finding my destiny."

The Goddess's face softened again, and when she spoke her voice was like my mother's, only more—as though she had somehow sprinkled the love of every mother in the world into her words.

Believe in yourself, Zoey Redbird. I have Marked you as my own. You will be my first true u-we-tsi-a-ge-ya v-hna-i Sv-no-yi . . . Daughter of Night . . . in this age. You are special. Accept that about yourself, and you will begin to understand there is true power in your uniqueness. Within you is combined the magic blood of ancient Wise Women and Elders, as well as insight into and understanding of the modern world.

The Goddess stood up and walked gracefully toward me, her voice painting silver symbols of power in the air around us. When she reached me she wiped the tears from my cheeks before taking my face in her hands.

Zoey Redbird, Daughter of Night, I name you my eyes and ears in the world today, a world where good and evil are struggling to find balance.

"But I'm sixteen! I can't even parallel-park! How am I supposed to know how to be your eyes and ears?"

She just smiled serenely. *You are old beyond your years, Zoey-bird. Believe in yourself and you will find a way. But remember, darkness does not always equate to evil, just as light does not always bring good.*

Then the Goddess Nyx, the ancient personification of Night, leaned forward and kissed me on my forehead. And for the third time that day I passed out.

CHAPTER SIX

—

Beautiful, see the cloud, the cloud appear.
Beautiful, see the rain, the rain draw near . . .

The words of the ancient song floated through my mind. I must be dreaming about Grandma Redbird again. It made me feel warm and safe and happy, which was especially nice, since I'd felt so crappy lately . . . except I couldn't remember exactly why. Huh. Odd.

Who spoke?
The little corn ear,
High on top of the stalk . . .

My grandma's song continued and I curled up on my side, sighing as I rubbed my cheek against the soft pillow. Unfortunately, moving my head caused an ugly pain to shoot through my temples, and like a bullet through a pane of glass, it shattered my happy feeling as the memory of the last day overwhelmed me.

I was turning into a vampyre.

I had run away from home.

I'd had an accident and then some kind of weird near-death experience.

I was turning into a vampyre. Oh my God.

Man, my head hurt.

"Zoeybird! Are you awake, baby?"

I blinked my blurry eyes clear to see Grandma Redbird sitting on a little chair close beside my bed.

"Grandma!" I croaked and reached for her hand. My voice sounded as terrible as my head felt. "What happened? Where am I?"

"You're safe, Little Bird. You're safe."

"My head hurts." I reached up and felt the place on my head that was tight and sore, and my fingers found the prick of stitches.

"It should. You scared ten years of my life from me." Grandma rubbed the back of my hand gently. "All that blood . . ." She shuddered, and then shook her head and smiled at me. "How about you promise not to do that again?"

"Promise," I said. "So, you found me . . ."

"Bloody and unconscious, Little Bird." Grandma brushed the hair back from my forehead, her fingers lingering lightly on my Mark. "And so pale that your dark crescent seemed to glow against your skin. I knew you needed to be taken back to the House of Night, which is exactly what I did." She chuckled and the mischievous sparkle in her eyes made her look like a little girl. "I called your mother to tell her that I was returning you to the House of Night, and I had to pretend that my cell phone cut out so I could hang up on her. I'm afraid she's not happy with either of us."

I grinned back at Grandma Redbird. Hee hee, Mom was mad at her, too.

"But, Zoey, whatever were you doing out during the daylight? And why didn't you tell me earlier that you had been Marked?"

I struggled to sit up, grunting at the pain in my head. But, thankfully, it seemed I'd stopped coughing. *Must be because I'm finally really here—at the House of Night . . .* But the thought disappeared as my mind processed all of what Grandma had said.

"Wait, I couldn't have told you any earlier. The Tracker came to school today and Marked me. I went home first. I really hoped Mom would understand and take my side." I paused, remembering again the awful scene with my parents. In total understanding, Grandma squeezed my hand. "She and John basically locked me in my room while they called our shrink and started the prayer tree."

Grandma grimaced.

"So I crawled out my window and came straight to you," I concluded.

"I'm glad you did, Zoeybird, but it just doesn't make any sense."

"I know," I sighed. "I can't believe I got Marked, either. Why me?"

"That's not what I mean, baby. I'm not surprised you were Tracked and Marked. The Redbird blood has always held strong magic; it was only a matter of time before one of us was Chosen. What I mean is that it makes no sense that you were *just* Marked. The crescent isn't an outline. It's completely filled in."

"That's impossible!"

"Look for yourself, u-we-tsi-a-ge-ya." She used the Cherokee word for daughter, suddenly reminding me very much of a mysterious, ancient goddess.

Grandma searched through her purse for the antique silver compact she always carried. Without saying anything else, she handed it to me. I pushed the little clasp. It popped open to show me my reflection . . . the familiar stranger . . . the me who wasn't quite *me*. Her eyes were huge and her skin was too white, but I barely noticed that. It was the Mark that I couldn't quit staring at, the Mark that was now a completed crescent moon, filled in perfectly with the distinctive sapphire blue of the vampyre tattoo. Feeling like I was still moving through a dream, I reached up and let my fingers trace the exotic-looking Mark and I seemed to feel the Goddess's lips against my skin again.

"What does it mean?" I said, unable to look away from the Mark.

"We were hoping you would have an answer to that question, Zoey Redbird."

Her voice was amazing. Even before I looked up from my reflection I knew she would be unique and incredible. I was right. She was movie-star beautiful, Barbie beautiful. I'd never seen anyone up close who was so perfect. She had huge, almond-shaped eyes that were a deep, mossy green. Her face was an almost perfect heart and her skin was that kind of flawless creaminess that you see on TV. Her hair was deep red—not that horrid carrot-top orange-red or the washed-out blond-red, but a dark, glossy auburn that fell in heavy waves well past her shoulders. Her body was, well, perfect. She wasn't thin like the freak girls who puked and starved themselves into what they thought was Paris Hilton chic. ("That's Hott." Yeah, okay, whatever, Paris.) This woman's body was perfect because she was strong, but curvy. And she had great boobs. (I wish I had great boobs.)

"Huh?" I said. Speaking of boobs—I was totally sounding like one. (Boob . . . hee hee).

The woman smiled at me and showed amazingly straight, white teeth—without fangs. Oh, I guess I forgot to mention that in addition to her perfection she had a sapphire crescent moon neatly tattooed in the middle of her forehead, and from it, swirls of lines that reminded me of ocean waves framed her brows, extending down around her high cheekbones.

She was a vampyre.

"I said, we were hoping you would have some explanation about why a fledgling vampyre that hasn't Changed has the Mark of a mature being on her forehead."

Without her smile and the gentle concern in her voice her words would have seemed harsh. Instead, what she said came off as worried and a little confused.

"So I'm not a vampyre?" I blurted.

Her laughter was like music. "Not yet, Zoey, but I would say that already having your Mark complete is an excellent omen."

"Oh . . . I . . . well, good. That's good," I babbled.

Thankfully, Grandma saved me from total humiliation.

"Zoey, this is the High Priestess of the House of Night, Neferet. She's been taking good care of you while you've been"—Grandma paused, obviously not wanting to say the word unconscious—"while you've been asleep."

"Welcome to the House of Night, Zoey Redbird," Neferet said warmly.

I glanced at Grandma and then back at Neferet. Feeling more than a little lost I stuttered, "That's—that's not really my name. My last name is Montgomery."

"Is it?" Neferet said, raising her amber-tinted brows. "One benefit of beginning a new life is that you have the opportunity to start over—to make choices you weren't given before. If you could choose, what would your true name be?"

I didn't hesitate. "Zoey Redbird."

"Then from this moment on, you shall be Zoey Redbird. Welcome to your new life." She reached out like she wanted to shake my hand, and I automatically offered mine. But instead of taking my hand, she grasped my forearm, which was weird but somehow felt right.

Her touch was warm and firm. Her smile blazed with welcome. She was amazing and awe-inspiring. Actually, she was what all vampyres are, *more* than human—stronger, smarter, more talented. She looked like someone had turned on a blazing inner light within her, which I realize is definitely an ironic description considering the vampyre stereotypes (some of which I already knew were totally true): They avoid sunlight, they're most powerful at night, they need to drink blood to survive (eesh!), and they worship a goddess who is known as Night personified.

"Th-thank you. It's nice to meet you," I said, trying really hard to sound at least semi-intelligent and normal.

"As I was telling your grandmother earlier, we have never had a fledgling come to us in such an unusual manner before— unconscious and with a completed Mark. Can you remember what happened to you, Zoey?"

I opened my mouth to tell her that I totally remembered it— falling and hitting my head . . . seeing myself like I was a floating spirit . . . following the weirdly visible words into the cave . . . and finally meeting the Goddess Nyx. But right before I said the words I got a weird feeling, like someone had just hit me in my stomach. It was clear and it was specific, and it was telling me to shut up.

"I—I really don't remember much—" I broke off and my hand found the sore spot where my stitches poked out. "At least not after I hit my head. I mean, up until then I remember everything. The Tracker Marked me; I told my parents and got into a ginormic fight with them; then I ran away to my grandma's place. I was feeling really sick, so when I climbed the path up to the bluffs . . ." I remembered the rest of it—*all* of the rest of it—the spirits of the Cherokee people, the dancing and the campfire. *Shut up!* the feeling screamed at me. "I—I guess I slipped because I was coughing so much, and hit my head. The next thing I remember is Grandma Redbird singing and then I woke up here." I finished in a rush. I wanted to look away from the sharpness of her green-eyed gaze, but the same feeling that was ordering me to be quiet was also clearly telling me that I had to keep eye contact with her, that I had to try really hard to look like I wasn't hiding anything, even though I didn't really have a clue why I was hiding anything.

"It's normal to experience memory loss with a head wound." Grandma said matter-of-factly, breaking the silence.

I could have kissed her.

"Yes, of course it is," Neferet said quickly, her face losing its sharpness. "Do not fear for your granddaughter's health, Sylvia Redbird. All will be well with her."

She spoke to Grandma respectfully, and some of the tension that had been building inside me loosened. If she liked Grandma Redbird, she had to be an okay person, or vampyre or whatever. Right?

"As I'm sure you already know, vampyres"—Neferet paused and smiled at me—"even fledgling vampyres, have unusual powers of recovery. Her healing is proceeding so well that it is perfectly safe for her to leave the infirmary." She looked from Grandma to me. "Zoey, would you like to meet your new roommate?"

No. I swallowed hard and nodded. "Yes."

"Excellent!" Neferet said. Thankfully she ignored the fact that I was standing there like a smiling stupid garden gnome.

"Are you sure you shouldn't keep her here another day for observation?" Grandma asked.

"I understand your concern, but I assure you Zoey's physical wounds are already healing at a pace you would find extraordinary."

She smiled at me again and even though I was scared and nervous and just plain freaked out I smiled back at her. It seemed like she was genuinely happy that I was there. And, truthfully, she made me think turning into a vampyre might not be such a bad thing.

"Grandma, I'm fine. Really. My head just hurts a little, and the rest of me feels way better." I realized as I said it that it was true. I'd completely stopped coughing. My muscles didn't ache anymore. I felt perfectly normal except for a little headache.

Then Neferet did something that not only surprised me, but made me instantly like her—and begin to trust her. She walked over to Grandma and spoke slowly and carefully.

"Sylvia Redbird, I give you my solemn oath that your granddaughter is safe here. Each fledgling is paired with an adult mentor.

To ensure my oath to you I will be Zoey's mentor. And now you must entrust her to my care."

Neferet placed her fist over her heart and bowed formally to Grandma. My grandma hesitated for only a moment before answering her.

"I will hold you to your oath, Neferet, High Priestess of Nyx." Then she mimicked Neferet's actions by putting her own fist over her heart and bowing to her before turning to me and hugging me hard. "Call me if you need me, Zoeybird. I love you."

"I will, Grandma. I love you, too. And thank you for bringing me here," I whispered, breathing in her familiar lavender scent and trying not to cry.

She kissed me gently on my cheek and then with her quick, confident steps she walked out of the room, leaving me alone for the first time in my life with a vampyre.

"Well, Zoey, are you ready to begin your new life?"

I looked up at her and thought again how amazing she was. If I actually Changed into a vampyre, would I have her confidence and power, or was that something only a High Priestess got? For an instant it flashed though my mind how awesome it would be to be a High Priestess—and then my sanity returned. I was just a kid. A confused kid at that, and definitely not High Priestess material. I just want to figure out how to fit in here, but Neferet had certainly made what was happening to me seem easier to bear.

"Yes, I am." I was glad I sounded more confident than I felt.

CHAPTER SEVEN

—

"What time is it?"

We were walking down a narrow hall that curved gently. The walls were made of an odd mixture of dark stone and jutting brick. Every so often flickering gaslights that hung from old-fashioned-looking black iron sconces stuck out of the wall, giving off a soft yellow glow that was, thankfully, really easy on my eyes. There were no windows in the hall, and we didn't meet anyone else (even though I kept peeking nervously around, imagining my first glimpse of vampyre kids).

"It is nearly four A.M., which means classes have been out for almost an hour." Neferet said, and then she smiled slightly at what I'm sure was my totally shocked expression.

"Classes begin at eight P.M., and end at three A.M.," she explained. "Teachers are available until three thirty A.M. to give students extra help. The gym is open until dawn, the exact time of which you will always know as soon as you have completed the Change. Until then dawn time is clearly posted in all the classrooms, common rooms, and gathering areas, including the dining hall, library, and gym. Nyx's Temple is, of course, open at all hours, but formal rituals are held twice a week right after school. The next ritual will be tomorrow." Neferet glanced at me and her slight smile warmed. "It seems overwhelming now, but you'll catch on quickly. And your roommate will help you, as will I."

I was just getting ready to open my mouth to ask her another question when an orange ball of fur ran into the hall and without a sound, hurled itself into Neferet's arms. I jumped and made a stupid little *squee* sound—then I felt like a total retard when I saw that the orange ball of fur was not a flying boogieman or whatever, but a massively big cat.

Neferet laughed and scratched the fur ball's ears. "Zoey, meet Skylar. He's usually prowling around here waiting to launch himself at me."

"That's the biggest cat I've ever seen," I said, reaching my hand out to let him sniff me.

"Careful, he's a known biter."

Before I could jerk my hand out of the way, Skylar started rubbing his face on my fingers. I held my breath.

Neferet tilted her head to the side, as if she was listening to words in the wind. "He likes you, which is definitely unusual. He doesn't like anyone except me. He even keeps the other cats away from this end of campus. He's really a terrible bully," she said fondly.

I carefully scratched Skylar's ears like Neferet had been doing. "I like cats," I said softly. "I used to have one, but when my mom got remarried I had to give it to Street Cats to be adopted. John, her new husband, doesn't like cats."

"I've found that the way a person feels about cats—and the way they feel about him or her in return—is usually an excellent gauge by which to measure a person's character."

I looked up from the cat to meet her green eyes and saw that she understood a lot more about freaky family issues than she was saying. It made me feel connected to her, and automatically my stress level relaxed a little. "Are there a lot of cats here?"

"Yes, there are. Cats have always been closely allied with vampyres."

Okay, actually I already knew that. In World History with Mr. Shaddox (better known as Puff Shaddy, but don't tell him) we learned that in the past cats had been slaughtered because it was thought that they somehow turned people into vampyres. *Yeah, okay, talk about ridiculous. More evidence of the stupidity of humans* . . . the thought popped into my mind, shocking me by how easily I'd already started thinking of "normal" people as "humans," and therefore something different than me.

"Do you think I could have a cat?" I asked.

"If one chooses you, you will belong to him or her."

"Chooses me?"

Neferet smiled and stroked Skylar, who closed his eyes and purred loudly. "Cats choose us; we don't own them." As if to demonstrate what she said was true, Skylar jumped out of her arms and, with a stuck-up flick of his tail, disappeared down the hall.

Neferet laughed. "He's really awful, but I do adore him. I think I would, even were it not part of my gift from Nyx."

"Gift? Skylar is a gift from the Goddess?"

"Yes, in a way. Every High Priestess is given an affinity—what you would probably think of as special powers—by the Goddess. It's part of the way we identify our High Priestesses. The affinities can be unusual cognitive skills, like reading minds or having visions and being able to predict the future. Or the affinity can be for something in the physical realm, like a special connection to one of the four elements, or to animals. I have two Goddess gifts. My main affinity is for cats; I have a connection with them that is unusual, even for a vampyre. Nyx has also given me unusual powers of healing." She smiled. "Which is why I know you're healing well—my gift told me."

"Wow, that's amazing," was all I could think to say. My head was already reeling from the events of the past day.

"Come on. Let's get you to your room. I'm sure you're hungry and tired. Dinner will start in"—Neferet cocked her head to the side as if someone was weirdly whispering the time to her—"an hour." She gave me a knowing smile. "Vampyres always know what time it is."

"That's cool, too."

"That, my dear fledgling, is just the tip of the 'cool' iceberg."

I hoped her analogy didn't have anything to do with Titanic-sized disasters. As we continued walking down the hall I thought about time and stuff, and remembered the question I had started to ask when Skylar had interrupted my easily derailed train of thought.

"So, wait. You said that classes start at eight? At night?" Okay, I'm usually not this slow, but some of this was like she was speaking a foreign language to me. I was having a hard time getting it.

"Once you take a moment to think about it you'll understand that having classes at night is only logical. Of course you must know that vampyres, adult or fledgling, don't explode, or any other such fictional nonsense, if subjected to direct sunlight, but it is uncomfortable for us. Wasn't the sunlight already difficult for you to bear today?"

I nodded. "My Maui Jims didn't even help much." Then I added quickly, feeling moronic again, "Uh, Maui Jims are sunglasses."

"Yes, Zoey," Neferet said patiently. "I know sunglasses. Very well, actually."

"Oh, God, I'm sorry I—" I broke off, wondering whether it was okay for me to say "God." Would it offend Neferet, a High Priestess who wore her Goddess Mark so proudly? Hell, would it offend Nyx? Oh, God. What about saying "hell"? It was my favorite cuss word ever. (Okay, it was really the only cuss word I used regularly.) Could I still say it? The People of Faith preached that vampyres worshiped a false goddess and that they were mostly selfish, dark creatures who cared about nothing except money and luxury and drinking blood and they were all certainly going straight to hell, so wouldn't that mean that I should watch how and where I used . . .

"Zoey."

I looked up to find Neferet studying me with a concerned expression and realized that she had probably been trying to get my attention while I had been babbling inside my head.

"I'm sorry," I repeated.

Neferet stopped. She put her hands on my shoulders and turned me so that I had to face her.

"Zoey, quit apologizing. And remember, everyone here has been where you are. This was new to all of us once. We know what it feels like—the fear of the Change—the shock at your life being turned into something foreign."

"And not being able to control any of it," I added quietly.

"That, too. It won't always be this bad. When you're a mature vampyre your life will seem your own again. You'll make your own choices; go your own way; follow the path down which your heart and soul and talents lead you."

"*If* I become a mature vampyre."

"You will, Zoey."

"How can you be so sure?"

Neferet's eyes found the darkened Mark on my forehead. "Nyx has chosen you. For what, we do not know. But her Mark has been clearly placed upon you. She would not have touched you only to see you fail."

I remembered the Goddess's words, *Zoey Redbird, Daughter of Night, I name you my eyes and ears in the world today, a world where good and evil are struggling to find balance,* and looked quickly away from Neferet's sharp gaze, wishing desperately that I knew why my gut was still telling me to keep my mouth shut about my meeting with the Goddess.

"It's—it's just a lot to happen all in one day."

"It certainly is, especially on an empty stomach."

We had started walking again when the sound of a ringing cell phone made me jump. Neferet sighed and smiled apologetically at me, then she fished a small phone out of her pocket.

"Neferet," she said. She listened for a little while and I saw her forehead wrinkle, and her eyes narrow. "No, you were right to call me. I'll come back and check on her." And she flipped the phone shut. "I'm sorry, Zoey. One of the fledglings broke her leg earlier today. It seems she's having trouble resting, and I should go back and be sure all is well with her. Why don't you follow this hallway around to the left until you come to the main door? You can't miss it—it's large and made of very old wood. Right outside is a stone bench. You can wait there for me. I won't be long."

"Okay, no problem." But before I'd finished speaking Neferet had already disappeared back down the winding hallway. I sighed. I didn't like the idea of being by myself in a place that was full of vampyres and vampyre kids. And now that Neferet was gone the little flickering lights didn't seem so welcoming. They seemed weird, throwing ghostly shadows against the old stone hall.

Determined not to freak myself out, I started slowly down the hall in the direction we had been heading. Pretty soon I almost wished I'd run into some other people (even if they were vampyres). It was too quiet. And creepy. A couple of times the hall branched off to the right, but like Neferet had told me, I kept to the left. Actually, I also kept my eyes to the left because those other halls had hardly any lights in them.

Unfortunately at the next right-hand turn off the hall I *didn't* avert my eyes. Okay, so the reason made sense. I heard something.

To be more specific, I heard a laugh. It was a soft, girly laugh that for some reason made the hair on the back of my neck stand up. It also made me stop walking. I peeked down the hall and thought I saw movement in the shadows.

Zoey . . . My name was whispered from the shadows.

I blinked in surprise. Had I really heard my name or was I imagining things? The voice was almost familiar. Could it be Nyx again? Was the Goddess calling my name? Almost as afraid as I was intrigued, I held my breath and took a few steps into the side hallway.

As I walked around the gentle bend I saw something ahead of me that made me stop and automatically move closer to the wall. In a little alcove not far from me were two people. At first I couldn't make my mind process what I was seeing; then in a rush I understood.

I should have gotten out of there then. I should have backed silently away and tried not to think about what I'd seen. But I didn't do any of those things. It was like my feet were suddenly so heavy I couldn't pick them up. All I could do was watch.

The man—and then with a little jolt of additional shock I realized that he wasn't a man, he was a teenager—not more than a year or so older than me. He was standing with his back pressed against the stone of the alcove. His head was tilted back and he was breathing hard. His face was in the shadows, but even though he was only partially visible I could see that he was handsome. Then another breathy little laugh drew my eyes downward.

She was on her knees in front of him. All I could see of her was her blond hair. There was so much of it that it looked like she was wearing it as some kind of ancient veil. Then her hands moved up, running along the guy's thighs.

Go! my mind screamed at me. *Get out of there!* I started to take a step back, and then his voice made me freeze.

"Stop!"

My eyes got huge because for a second I thought he was talking to me.

"You don't really want me to."

I felt almost dizzy with relief when she spoke. He was talking to her, not me. They didn't even know I was there.

"Yes, I do." It sounded as if he was grinding his words from between his teeth. "Get off your knees."

"You like it—you know you like it. Just like you know you still want me."

Her voice was all husky and trying to be sexy, but I could also hear the whine in it. She sounded almost desperate. I watched her fingers move, and my eyes widened in amazement when she drew the nail of her index finger down his thigh. Unbelievably, her fingernail slashed through his jeans, just like it was a knife, and a line of fresh blood appeared, startling in its liquid redness.

I didn't want it to, and it grossed me out, but at the sight of the blood my mouth started watering.

"No!" He snapped, putting his hands on her shoulders and trying to push her away from him.

"Oh, quit pretending," she laughed again, a mean, sarcastic sound. "You know we'll always be together." She reached up with her tongue and licked along the line of blood.

I shuddered; against my will I was completely mesmerized.

"Cut it out!" He was still pushing at her shoulders. "I don't want to hurt you, but you're really starting to piss me off. Why can't you understand? We're not doing this anymore. I don't want you."

"You want me! You'll always want me!" She unzipped his pants.

I shouldn't be there. I shouldn't be seeing this. I tore my eyes from his bloody thigh and took one step back.

The guy's eyes lifted. He saw me.

And then something truly bizarre happened. I could feel his

touch through our eyes. I couldn't look away from him. The girl in front of him seemed to disappear, and all there was in the hallway was him and me and the sweet, beautiful smell of his blood.

"You don't want me? That's not how it looks now," she said with a nasty purr in her voice.

I felt my head begin to shake back and forth, back and forth. At the same moment he cried "No!" and tried to push her out of the way so that he could move toward me.

I ripped my eyes away from his and stumbled back.

"No!" he said again. This time I knew he was speaking to me and not her. She must have realized it, too, because with a cry that sounded uncomfortably like the snarl of a wild animal, she started to whirl around. My body unfroze. At the same instant I turned and ran back down the hall.

I expected them to come after me, so I kept running until I reached the huge old doors Neferet had described. Then I stood there, leaning against their cold wood, trying to get my breathing under control so I could listen for the sounds of running feet.

What would I do if they did chase me down? My head was pounding painfully again, and I felt weak and totally scared. And completely, utterly grossed out.

Yes, I was aware of the whole oral sex thing. I doubt if there's a teenager alive in America today who isn't aware that most of the adult public think we're giving guys blow jobs like they used to give guys gum (or maybe more appropriately suckers). Okay, that's just bullshit, and it's always made me mad. Of course there are girls who think it's "cool" to give guys head. Uh, they're wrong. Those of us with functioning brains know that it is not cool to be used like that.

Okay, so I *knew* about the whole blow job issue. I' d definitely never seen one. So, what I had just seen had definitely freaked me out. But what had freaked me out more than the fact that the blonde was doing the nasty to him was the way I'd responded to seeing the guy's blood.

I'd wanted to lick it, too.

And that's just not normal.

Then there's the whole issue about me sharing that weird look with him. What had that been all about?

"Zoey, are you all right?"

"Hell!" I gasped and jumped. Neferet was standing behind me looking at me with total confusion.

"Are you feeling ill?"

"I—I . . ." My mind flailed about. No way could I tell her what I'd just seen. "My head just really hurts," I finally managed to say. And it was true. I had a killer headache.

Her frown was full of concern. "Let me help you." Neferet placed her hand lightly over the line of stitches on my forehead. She closed her eyes and I could hear her whispering something in a language I could not understand. Then her hand started to feel warm and it was as if the warmth became liquid and my skin absorbed it. I closed my eyes and sighed in relief as the pain in my head began to fade.

"Better?"

"Yes," I barely whispered.

She took her hand away and I opened my eyes. "That should keep the pain away. I don't know why it suddenly came back with such force."

"Me, neither, but it's gone now," I said quickly.

She studied me silently for a little while more while I held my breath. Then she said, "Anything upset you?"

I swallowed. "I'm a little scared about meeting my new roommate." Which technically wasn't a lie. It wasn't what had upset me, but I was scared about it.

Neferet's smile was kind. "All will be well, Zoey. Now let me introduce you to your new life."

Neferet opened the thick wooden door and we walked out into a large courtyard that fronted the school. She stepped aside and let me gawk. Teenagers wearing uniforms that somehow looked cool and unique while still being similar walked in small groups across the courtyard and along the sidewalk. I could hear the deceptively normal sound of their voices as they laughed and talked. I kept staring from them to the school, not sure which to gawk at first. I chose the school. It was the less intimidating of the two (and I was scared I'd see *him*). The place was like something out of a creepy dream. It was the middle of the night, and it should have been deeply dark, but there was a brilliant moon shining above the huge old oaks that shaded everything. Freestanding gaslights housed in tarnished copper fixtures followed the sidewalk that ran parallel to the huge red brick and black rock building. It was three stories tall and had a weirdly high roof that pointed up and then flattened off at the top. I could see that heavy drapes had been opened and soft yellow lights made shadows dance up and down the rooms, giving the entire structure an alive and welcoming look. A round tower was attached to the front of the main building, furthering the illusion that the place was much more castle-like than school-like. I swear, a moat would have looked more like it belonged there than a sidewalk ringed by thick azalea bushes and a neat lawn.

Across from the main building was a smaller one that looked older and church-like. Behind it and the old oaks that shaded the schoolyard I could see the shadow of the enormous stone wall that surrounded the entire school. In front of the church building was a marble statue of a woman who was wearing long, flowing robes.

"Nyx!" I blurted.

Neferet lifted one eyebrow in surprise. "Yes, Zoey. That is a statue of the Goddess, and the building behind it is her temple." She motioned for me to walk with her down the sidewalk and gestured expansively at the impressive campus that stretched before us. "What is known today as the House of Night was built in the neo-French-Norman style, with stones imported from Europe. It originated in the mid-1920s as an Augustine monastery for the People of Faith. Eventually it was converted into Cascia Hall, a private preparatory school for affluent human teenagers. When we decided that we must open a school of our own in this part of the country, we bought it from Cascia Hall five years ago."

I only vaguely recalled the days when it had been a stuck-up private school—actually the only reason I'd ever thought about it at all was that I remembered hearing the news that a whole herd of kids who went to Cascia Hall had been busted for drugs, and how shocked the adults had been. Whatever. No one else had been shocked that those rich kids were majorly into drugs.

"I'm surprised they sold it to you guys," I said absently.

Her laugh was low and a little dangerous. "They didn't want to, but we made their arrogant headmaster an offer even he couldn't refuse."

I wanted to ask her what she meant, but her laugh gave me a skin-crawly feeling. And, plus, I was busy. I couldn't stop staring. Okay the first thing I noticed was that everyone who had a solid vampyre tattoo was incredibly good-looking. I mean, it was totally insane. Yes, I knew that vampyres were attractive. Everyone knew that. The most successful actors and actresses in the world were vampyres. They were also dancers and musicians, authors and singers. Vampyres dominated the arts, which is one reason they had so much money—and also one reason (of many) that the People of Faith considered them selfish and immoral. *But really, they're just jealous that they're not as good-looking.* The People of Faith would go see their movies, plays, concerts, buy their books and their art, but at the same time they'd talk about them and look down at them, and God knows they'd never, ever mix with them. Hello—can you say hypocrites?

Anyway, being surrounded by so many totally gorgeous people made me want to crawl under a bench, even though many of them greeted Neferet and then smiled and said hello to me, too. Between hesitantly returning their hellos I snuck looks at the kids who walked by us. Each of them nodded respectfully to Neferet. Several of them bowed formally to her and crossed their fists over their hearts, which made Neferet smile and bow slightly in response. Okay, the kids weren't as gorgeous as the adults. Sure, they were nice-looking—interesting actually, with their crescent moon outlines, and their uniforms that looked more like runway designs than school clothes—but they didn't have the glossy, inhumanly attractive light that radiated from inside each of the adult vampyres. Uh, I did notice that, as I had suspected, their uniforms had a lot of basic black in them (you'd think that a group of people so up on the arts would recognize a cliché when one goes walking by in boring Goth black. I'm just saying . . .). But I suppose if I was going to be honest I'd have to admit it looked good on them—the black mixed with tiny plaid lines of deep purple, dark blue, and emerald green. Each uniform had an ornate design embroidered in gold or silver on either its jacket breast pocket or blouse pocket. I could tell that some of the designs were the same, but I couldn't see exactly what they were. Also, there was a weirdly large amount of kids with long hair. Seriously, the girls had long hair, the guys had long hair, the teachers had long hair, even the cats that wandered across the sidewalk from time to time were long-haired balls of fur. Odd. Good thing I'd talked myself out of getting my hair cut in that short duck butt style Kayla had cut hers off in last week.

I also noticed that the adults and the kids had one other thing in common—their eyes all lingered with obvious curiosity on my Mark. Great. So I was beginning my new life as an anomaly, which figured about as much as it sucked.

CHAPTER EIGHT

—

The part of the House of Night that held the dorms was way across campus, so we had a fairly long walk, and Neferet seemed to be walking slowly on purpose, giving me plenty of time to ask questions and gawk. Not that I minded. Walking the length of the sprawling castle-like cluster of buildings, with Neferet pointing out little details about what was what, gave me a sense of the place. It was weird, but in a good way. Plus, walking felt normal. Actually, as odd as it sounds, I felt like myself again. I wasn't coughing. My body didn't ache. My head even had stopped hurting. I was absolutely, totally not thinking about the disturbing scene I'd accidentally witnessed. I was forgetting it—on purpose. The last thing I needed was to have more to deal with than a new life and a weird Mark. So, blow job—forgotten.

Deeply in denial I told myself that if I hadn't been walking through a school campus at an ungodly hour of the night beside a vampyre I almost could pretend that I was the same today as I had been yesterday. Almost.

Well, okay. Maybe not even *almost*, but my head did feel better, and I was just about ready to face my roommate when Neferet finally opened the door to the girl's dorm.

Inside was a surprise. I'm not sure what I expected—maybe everything to be all black and creepy. But it was nice, decorated in soft blue and antique yellow, with comfy couches and clumps of puffy pillows big enough to sit on dotting the room like giant pastel M&Ms. The soft gaslight coming from several antique crystal chandeliers made the place look like a princess's castle. On the cream-colored walls there were large oil paintings, all of them of ancient women who looked exotic and powerful. Fresh-cut flowers, mostly roses, sat in crystal vases on end tables that were cluttered with books and purses and fairly normal-looking teenage girl stuff. I saw several flat screen TVs, and recognized the sounds of MTV's *Real World* coming from one of them. I took in all of this fast, while I tried to smile and appear friendly to the girls who had shut up the instant I walked in the room and were now staring at me. Well, scratch that. They weren't exactly staring at *me.* They were staring at the Mark on my forehead.

"Ladies, this is Zoey Redbird. Greet her and welcome her to the House of Night."

For a second I didn't think anyone was going to say anything, and I wanted to die of new-kid mortification. Then a girl stood up from among the middle of a group that was clustered around one of the TVs. She was a tiny blonde and darn near perfect. Actually, she reminded me of a young version of Sarah Jessica Parker (who I don't like, by the by—she's just so . . . so . . . annoying and unnaturally perky).

"Hi Zoey. Welcome to your new home." The SJP look-alike's smile was warm and genuine, and she was clearly making an effort to make eye contact instead of gawk at my darkened-in Mark. Instantly I felt bad for making a negative comparison about her. "I'm Aphrodite," she said.

Aphrodite? Okay, maybe I *hadn't* been too hasty in my comparison. How could anyone normal choose Aphrodite as her name? Please. Talk about delusions of grandeur. I plastered a smile on my face, though, and said a bright, "Hi Aphrodite!"

"Neferet, would you like me to show Zoey to her room?"

Neferet hesitated, which felt really odd. Instead of answering right away she just stood there and locked eyes with Aphrodite. Then, just as quickly as the silent stare-down had started, Neferet's face broke into a wide smile.

"Thank you, Aphrodite, that would be lovely. I am Zoey's mentor, but I'm sure she would feel much more welcomed if someone her own age showed her the way to her room."

Was that anger I saw flash through Aphrodite's eyes? No, I must have imagined it—or at least I would have believed I'd imagined it if that weird new gut feeling of mine hadn't told me otherwise. And I didn't need my new intuition to clue me in that something was wrong, because Aphrodite laughed—*and I recognized the sound of it.*

Feeling like someone had punched me in the gut I realized that this girl—Aphrodite—had been the one I'd just watched with the guy in the hall!

Aphrodite's laugh, followed by her perky, "Of course I'd be happy to show her around! You know I'm always glad to help you, Neferet," was as fake and cold as Pamela Anderson's humongously huge boobs, but Neferet just nodded in response and then turned to face me.

"I'll leave you now, Zoey," Neferet said, squeezing my shoulder. "Aphrodite will take you to your room, and your new roommate can help you get ready for dinner. I'll see you in the dining room." She smiled her warm, mom-smile at me, and I had the ridiculously childish urge to hug her and beg her not to leave me alone with Aphrodite. "You'll be fine," she said, as if she could read my mind. "You'll see, Zoeybird. All will be well," she whispered, sounding so much like my grandma that I had to blink hard not to cry. Then she nodded a quick good-bye to Aphrodite and the other girls, and left the dorm.

The door closed with a muffled, dead sound. Oh, hell . . . I just wanted to go home!

"Come on, Zoey. The rooms are this way," Aphrodite said. She motioned for me to come with her up the wide stairs that curved to our right. As we walked upstairs I tried to ignore the buzz of voices that instantly erupted behind us.

Neither of us spoke, and I felt so uncomfortable that I wanted to scream. Had she seen me back there in the hall? Well, I sure as hell wasn't going to mention it. Ever. As far as I was concerned it never happened.

I cleared my throat and said, "The dorm seems nice. I mean, it's really pretty."

She cut her eyes sideways at me. "It's better than nice or really pretty here; it's amazing."

"Oh. Well. That's good to hear."

She laughed. The sound was totally unpleasant—almost a sneer—and it crawled up the back of my neck like it had when I'd first heard it.

"It's amazing here mostly because of me."

I glanced at her, thinking that she must be kidding, and met her cold blue eyes.

"Yeah, you heard me right. This place is cool because I'm cool."

Oh. My. God. What a bizarre thing for her to say. I didn't have a clue how to respond to that very stuck-up piece of info. I mean, like I needed the stress of a fight with slutty Ms. Thinking-She's-All-That added on top of a life/species/school change? And I still couldn't tell whether she knew it had been me watching her in the hall.

Okay, I just wanted to find a way to fit in. I wanted to be able to call this new school home. So I decided to take the safest road and keep my mouth shut.

Neither of us said anything more. The stairs led to a large

hallway lined with doors. I held my breath when Aphrodite stopped before one that was painted a pretty light purple, but instead of knocking, she turned to face me. Her perfect face suddenly looked hateful and cold and definitely not so pretty.

"Okay, here's the deal, Zoey. You have this weird Mark, so everyone's talking about you and wondering what the fuck is up with you." She rolled her eyes and clutched her pearls dramatically, changing her voice so that she sounded really silly and gushing. "Oooh! The new girl has a colored-in Mark! Whatever could that mean? Is she special? Does she have fabulous powers? Oh my—oh my!" She dropped her hand from her throat and narrowed her eyes at me. Her voice went as flat and mean as her gaze. "Here's what's what. I'm *it* here. Things go my way. You want to get along here, then you'd best remember that. If you don't, you'll be in for a world of shit."

Okay, she was starting to piss me off. "Look," I said, "I just got here. I'm not looking for trouble, and I have no control over what people are saying about my Mark."

Her eyes narrowed. Ah, crap. Was I going to have to actually fight this girl? I'd never been in a fight in my life! My stomach knotted up and I got ready to duck or run or whatever would not get me beat up.

Then, just as quickly as she'd gone all scary and hateful, her face relaxed into a smile and she turned back into sweet little blonde again. (Not that I was fooled.)

"Good. Just so we understand each other."

Huh? I understood she'd forgotten to take her meds, but that was all I understood.

Aphrodite didn't give me time to say anything. With one last, weirdly warm smile, she knocked on the door.

"Come on in!" called a perky voice with an Okie accent.

Aphrodite opened the door.

"Hi y'all! Ohmygosh, come on in." With a huge grin, my new roomie, also a blonde, rushed up like a little countrified tornado. But the instant she saw Aphrodite, her grin slid from her face and she stopped hurrying toward us.

"I brought your new roommate to you." There was nothing technically wrong with Aphrodite's words, but her tone was hateful and she was putting on a terrible, fake Oklahoma accent. "Stevie Rae Johnson, this is Zoey Redbird. Zoey Redbird, this is Stevie Rae Johnson. There, now ain't we all nice and cozy like three little corns on a cob?"

I glanced at Stevie Rae. She looked like a terrified little rabbit.

"Thanks for showing me up here, Aphrodite." I talked quickly, moving toward Aphrodite, who automatically stepped back, which put her out in the hall again. "See you around." I closed the door on her as her look of surprise was just beginning to change to anger. Then I turned to Stevie Rae, who was still pale.

"What's with her?" I asked.

"She's . . . she's . . . ,"

Even though I didn't know her at all, I could tell that Stevie Rae was struggling with how much she should or shouldn't say. So I decided to help her. I mean, we were going to be roommates. "She's a bitch!" I said.

Stevie Rae's eyes went round, and then she giggled. "She's not very nice, that's for sure."

"She needs pharmaceutical help, *that's* for sure," I added, making her laugh some more.

"I think we're gonna get along just fine, Zoey Redbird," she said, still smiling. "Welcome to your new home!" She stepped aside and made a sweeping arm gesture at the little room, like she was ushering me into a palace.

I looked around and blinked. Several times. The first thing I saw was the life-sized Kenny Chesney poster that hung over one of the two beds and the cowboy (cowgirl?) hat that rested on one of the bedside tables—the one that also had the old-fashioned-looking gas lamp with the base shaped like a cowboy boot. Oh, nu uh. Stevie Rae was a total Okie!

Then she shocked me with a big hello hug, reminding me of a cute puppy with her short, curly hair and her smiling round face. "Zoey, I'm so glad you're feelin' better! I was so worried when I heard you'd hurt yourself. I'm really glad you're finally here."

"Thanks," I said, still staring around what was now my room, too, feeling totally overwhelmed and weirdly on the edge of tears again.

"It's kinda scary, isn't it?" Stevie Rae was watching me with big, serious blue eyes that were filled with sympathetic tears. I nodded, not trusting my voice.

"I know. I cried the whole first night."

I swallowed back my own tears and asked, "How long have you been here?"

"Three months. And, man, I was glad when they told me I was getting a roommate!"

"You knew I was coming?"

She nodded vigorously. "Oh, yeah! Neferet told me day before yesterday that the Tracker had sensed you and was going to Mark you. I thought you'd be here yesterday, but then I heard that you'd had an accident and been brought to the clinic. What happened?"

I shrugged and said, "I was looking for my grandma and I fell and hit my head." I wasn't getting the weird feeling that told me to keep my mouth shut, but I wasn't sure how much I should say to Stevie Rae yet, and I was relieved when she nodded as though she understood and didn't ask any more questions about the accident—or mention my weird colored-in Mark.

"Your parents freaked when you got Marked?"

"Totally. Didn't yours?"

"Actually, my mama was okay with it. She said anything that got me out of Henrietta was a good thing."

"Henrietta, Oklahoma?" I asked, glad to move to a subject that was not all about me.

"Sadly, yes."

Stevie Rae flopped down on the bed in front of the Kenny Chesney poster and motioned for me to sit on the one across the room from her. I did, and then felt a little jolt of surprise when I realized that I was sitting on my cool hot-pink and green Ralph Lauren comforter from home. I looked at the little oak end table and blinked. There was my annoying, ugly alarm clock, nerdy glasses for when I'm sick of wearing my contacts, and the picture of Grandma and me from last summer. And in the bookshelves behind the computer on my side of the room I saw my Gossip Girls and Bubbles series books (along with some of my other favorites, including Bram Stoker's *Dracula*—which was more than a little ironic), some CDs, my laptop, and—*oh my dear sweet lord*—my *Monsters Inc.* figurines. *How incredibly embarrassing.* My backpack was sitting on the floor next to my bed.

"Your grandma brought your stuff up here. She's really nice," Stevie Rae said.

"She's more than nice. She's brave as hell to have faced my mom and her stupid husband to get this stuff for me. I can only imagine the overly dramatic scene my mom caused." I sighed and then shook my head.

"Yeah, I guess I'm lucky. At least my mama was cool about all of this," Stevie Rae pointed to the outline of the crescent moon on her forehead. "Even if my daddy lost every bit of his mind, me being his only 'baby girl' and all." She shrugged and then giggled. "My three brothers thought it was awesome and wanted to know if I could help them get vampyre chicks." She rolled her eyes. "Stupid boys."

"Stupid boys," I echoed and smiled at her. If she thought boys were stupid she and I would get along fine.

"Mostly now I'm okay with all of this. I mean, the classes are weird but I like them—especially the Tae Kwan Do class. I kinda like to kick butt." She grinned mischievously, like a little blonde elf. "I like the uniforms, which totally shocked me at first. I mean, would anyone expect to *like* school uniforms? But we can add stuff to them and make them unique, so they don't look like typical stuck-up, boring school uniforms. And there are some seriously hot guys here—even if boys are stupid." Her eyes sparkled. "Mostly I'm just so darn glad to be out of Henrietta that I don't mind all the other stuff, even if Tulsa is kinda scary because it's so big."

"Tulsa isn't scary," I said automatically. Unlike too many kids from our suburb of Broken Arrow, I actually knew my way around Tulsa, thanks to what Grandma liked to call "field-tripping" with her. "You just have to know where to go. There's a great bead gallery where you can make your own jewelry downtown on Brady Street, and next door to that is Lola's at the Bowery—she has the best desserts in town. Cherry Street is cool, too. We're not far from there now. Actually, we're right by the awesome Philbrook Museum and Utica Square. There's some excellent shopping there and—"

I suddenly realized what I was saying. Did vampyre kids get to mingle with regular kids? I searched my memory. No. I'd never seen kids with crescent moon outlines hanging around the Philbrook or Utica's Gap or Banana Republic or Starbucks. I'd never seen them at the movies. Hell! I'd never even *seen* a vampyre kid before today. So would they keep us locked up here for four years? Feeling a little short of breath and claustrophobic I asked, "Do we ever get out of here?"

"Yeah, but there are all sorts of rules you have to follow."

"Rules? Like what?"

"Well, you can't wear any part of the school uniform—" She broke off suddenly. "Shoot! That reminds me. We have to hurry. Dinner is in a few minutes and you need to change." She jumped up and started to rummage through the closet that was on my side of the room, chattering at me from over her shoulder the whole time. "Neferet had some clothes delivered here last night. Don't worry about the sizes not being right. Somehow they always know what size we'll be before they actually see us—it's kinda freaky how the adult vamps know way more than they should. Anyway, don't be scared. I was serious before when I said the uniforms aren't as awful as you'd think they'd be. You really can add your own stuff to them—like me."

I looked at her. I mean, really looked at her. She was wearing a pair of honest-to-God Roper jeans. You know, the kind those ag-kids wear that are way too tight and have no back pockets. How anyone could think no back pockets and tightness was cute, I'd honestly never understand. Stevie Rae was totally skinny, and the jeans even made her butt look wide. I knew before I looked at the girl's feet what she'd be wearing—cowboy boots. I glanced down and sighed. Yep. Brown leather, flat-heeled, pointy-tipped cowboy boots. Tucked into her countrified jeans was a black, long-sleeved cotton blouse that had the expensive look of something you'd find at Saks or Neiman Marcus, versus the cheaper see-through shirts that overpriced Abercrombie tries to make us believe aren't slutty. When she glanced over at me I saw that she had double-pierced ears with little silver hoops in them. She turned and held out in one hand a black blouse like the one she had on, and a pullover sweater in another, and I decided that even though the country look wasn't for me she was kinda cute with her mixture of hayseed and chic.

"Here ya go! Just throw these on over your jeans and we'll be ready."

The flickering light from the cowboy-boot lamp caught on a streak of silver embroidery that was on the breast of the sweater she was holding out. I got up and took the two shirts, holding the sweater up so I could see the front of it better. The silver embroidery was in the shape of a spiral that glittered around and around in a delicate circle that would rest over my heart.

"It's our sign," Stevie Rae said.

"Our sign?"

"Yeah, each class—here they call them third formers, fourth formers, fifth formers, and sixth formers—has their own sign. We're third formers, so our sign is the silver labyrinth of the Goddess Nyx."

"What does it mean?" I asked, more to myself than to her as I traced my finger around the sliver circles.

"It stands for our new beginning as we start walking the Path of Night and learn the ways of the Goddess and the possibilities of our new life."

I looked up at her, surprised that she suddenly sounded so serious. She grinned a little shyly at me and shrugged her shoulders. "It one of the first things you learn in Vampyre Sociology 101. That's the class Neferet teaches, and it sure beats the heck outta the boring classes I was taking at Henrietta High, home of the fighting hens. Ugh. Fighting hens! What kind of a mascot is that?" She shook her head and rolled her eyes while I laughed. "Anyway, I heard Neferet is your mentor, which is really lucky. She hardly takes on any new kids, and besides being High Priestess, she's way the coolest teacher here."

What she didn't say was that I'm not just lucky, I'm "special" with my weird colored-in Mark. Which reminded me . . .

"Stevie Rae, why haven't you asked me about my Mark? I

mean, I appreciate you not bombarding me with a hundred questions, but all the way up here everyone who saw me stared at my Mark. Aphrodite mentioned it almost the second we were alone. You haven't even really looked at it. Why?"

Then she did finally look at my forehead before she shrugged and met my eyes again. "You're my roommate. I figured you'd tell me what was up with it when you were ready. One thing growing up in a small town like Henrietta taught me is that it's best to mind your own business if you want someone to stay your friend. Well, we're gonna be rooming together for four years . . ." She paused and in the gap between words sat the big, ugly unsaid truth that we'd be roommates for four years only if both of us survived the Change. Stevie Rae swallowed hard and finished in a rush, "I guess what I'm trying to say is that I want us to be friends."

I smiled at her. She looked so young and hopeful—so nice and normal and not at all what I imagined a vampyre kid would be. I felt a little stirring of hope. Maybe I could find a way to fit in here. "I want to be friends, too."

"Yea for that!" I swear she looked like a wriggly puppy again. "But come on! Hurry—we don't want to be late."

She gave me a shove toward a door that sat between the two closets before she hurried over to a makeup mirror on her computer desk and started brushing at her short hair. I ducked inside to find a tiny bathroom, and quickly pulled off my BA Tigers T-shirt and put on the cotton blouse and over it the silk knit sweater that was a deep, pretty shade of purple with little black plaid lines going through it. I was just getting ready to go back into the room to grab my backpack so I could try to fix my face and hair with the makeup and stuff I'd brought, when I glanced in the mirror over the sink. My face was still white, but it had lost the scary, unhealthy paleness it had earlier. My hair looked insane, all wild and uncombed, and I could faintly see the slim line of dark stitches just above my left temple. But it was the sapphire-colored Mark that caught my eyes. While I stared at it, entranced by its exotic beauty, the bathroom light caught the silver labyrinth embroidered over my heart. I decided that the two symbols somehow matched, even though they were different shapes . . . different colors . . .

But did I match them? And did I match this strange new world?

I squeezed my eyes shut tightly and hoped desperately that whatever we were eating for dinner (oh, please let there not be any blood-drinking involved) wouldn't disagree with my already screwed-up, nervous stomach.

"Oh, no . . ." I whispered to myself, "it would be just my luck to get a raging case of diarrhea."

CHAPTER NINE

—

Okay, the cafeteria was cool—oops, I mean "dining hall," as the silver plaque outside the entrance proclaimed. It was nothing at all like SIHS's freezing cold monstrous cafeteria where the acoustics were so bad that even though I sat right next to Kayla I couldn't hear what she was babbling at me half the time. This room was warm and friendly. The walls were made of the same weird mixture of jutting bricks and black rock as the exterior of the building and the room was filled with heavy wooden picnic tables that had matching benches with padded seats and backs. Each table sat about six kids and radiated out from a large, unoccupied table situated at the center of the room that was practically overflowing with fruit and cheese and meat, and a crystal goblet that was filled with something that looked suspiciously like red wine. (Huh? Wine at school? What?) The ceiling was low and the rear wall was made up of windows with a glass door in the center. Heavy burgundy velvet drapes were pulled open so that I could see outside to a beautiful little courtyard with stone benches, winding paths, and ornamental bushes and flowers. In the middle of the courtyard was a marble fountain with water spouting from the top of something that looked an awful lot like a pineapple. It was very pretty, especially lit up by the moonlight and the occasional antique gaslight.

Most of the tables were already filled with eating, talking kids who glanced up with obvious curiosity when Stevie Rae and I entered the room. I took a deep breath and held my head high. Might as well give them a clear view of the Mark they all seemed so obsessed with. Stevie Rae led me to the side of the room that had the typical cafeteria servers handing out food from behind buffet-style glass thingies.

"What's the table in the middle of the room for?" I asked as we walked.

"It's the symbolic offering to the Goddess Nyx. There's always a place set at that table for her. It seems kinda weird at first, but pretty soon it won't seem so weird and it'll feel right to you."

Actually, it didn't seem that weird to me. In a way, it made sense. The Goddess was so alive here. Her Mark was everywhere. Her statue stood proudly in front of her Temple. I was also starting to notice all over the school little pictures and figurines that represented her. Her High Priestess was my mentor and, I had to admit to myself, I already felt connected to Nyx. With an effort, I stopped myself from touching the Mark on my forehead. Instead I grabbed a tray and moved behind Stevie Rae in line.

"Don't worry," she whispered to me. "The food's real good. They don't make you drink blood or eat raw meat or anything like that."

Relieved, I unclenched my jaws. Most of the kids were already eating, so the line was short, and as Stevie Rae and I got up to the food I felt my mouth start to water. Spaghetti! I sniffed deeply: *with garlic!*

"That whole vampyres can't stand garlic thing is total bullshit—pardon my French," Stevie Rae was saying under her breath to me as we loaded up our plates.

"Okay, what about that whole vampyres have to drink blood thing?" I whispered back.

"Not," she said softly.

"Not?"

"Not bullshit."

Great. Wonderful. Fantastic. Just exactly what I wanted to hear—*not*.

Trying not to think about blood and whatnot I got a glass of tea with Stevie Rae, and then followed her to a table where two other kids were already talking animatedly while they ate. Of course the conversation totally stopped when I joined them, which didn't seem to faze Stevie Rae at all. As I slid into the booth opposite her she made introductions in her Okie twang.

"Hey, y'all. Meet my new roommate, Zoey Redbird. Zoey, this is Erin Bates," she pointed to the ridiculously pretty blonde sitting on my side of the table. (Well, hell—how many pretty blondes could one school have? Isn't there some kind of limit?) Still in her matter-of-fact Okie voice, she went on, making little air quotes for emphasis. "Erin is 'the pretty one.' She's also funny and smart and has more shoes than anyone I've ever known."

Erin pulled her blue eyes away from staring at my Mark long enough to say a quick "Hi."

"And this is the token guy in our group, Damien Maslin. But he's gay, so I don't really think he counts as a guy."

Instead of getting pissed at Stevie Rae, Damien looked serene and unruffled. "Actually, since I'm gay I think I should count for two guys instead of just one. I mean, in me you get the male point of view *and* you don't have to worry about me wanting to touch your boobies."

He had a smooth face that was totally zit free, and dark brown hair and eyes that reminded me of a baby deer. Actually, he was cute. Not in the overly girly way so many teenage guys are when they decide to come out and tell everyone what everyone already knew (well, everyone except their typically clueless and/or in-denial parents). Damien wasn't a swishy girly-guy; he was just a cute kid with a likable smile. He was also noticeably trying not to stare at my Mark, which I appreciated.

"Well, maybe you're right. I hadn't really thought about it like that," Stevie Rae said through a big bite of garlic bread.

"Just ignore her, Zoey. The rest of us are almost normal," Damien said. "And we're desperately glad you finally got here. Stevie Ray's been driving everyone crazy wondering what you'd be like, when you'd get here—"

"If you'd be one of those freaky kids who smell bad and think being a vampyre means seeing who can be the biggest loser," Erin interrupted.

"Or wondering if you'd be one of *them*," Damien said, cutting his eyes at a table to our left.

I followed his gaze and felt a zap of nerves when I recognized who he was talking about. "You mean Aphrodite?"

"Yeah," Damien said. "And her stuck-up flock of sycophants."

Huh? I blinked at him.

Stevie Rae sighed. "You'll get used to Damien's vocabulary obsession. Thankfully, this isn't a new word so some of us actually know what he's talking about without having to beg him for a translation. Again. Sycophant—a servile flatterer," she twanged proudly like she was giving an answer in English class.

"Whatever. They make me want to retch," Erin said without looking up from her spaghetti.

"They?" I asked.

"The Dark Daughters," Stevie Rae said, and I noticed she automatically lowered her voice.

"Think of them like a sorority," Damien said.

"Of hags from hell," Erin said.

"Hey, y'all, I don't think we should prejudice Zoey against them. She might get along okay with them."

"Fuck that. They're hags from hell," Erin said.

"Watch that mouth, Er Bear. You have to eat out of it," Damien said a little primly.

Incredibly relieved that none of them liked Aphrodite, I was just getting ready to ask for more of an explanation when a girl rushed up and, with a big huff, slid herself and her tray into the booth beside Stevie Rae. She was the color of cappuccino (the kind you get from real coffee shops and not the nasty, too-sweet stuff you get from Quick Trip) and all curvy with pouty lips and high cheekbones that made her look like an African princess. She also had some seriously good hair. It was thick and fell in dark, glossy waves around her shoulders. Her eyes were so black they looked like they didn't have any pupils.

"Okay, please! Just please. Did *nobody*," she stared pointedly at Erin, "think to bother to wake me the hell up and tell me that we were going to dinner?"

"I do believe I'm your roommate, not your mamma," Erin said lazily.

"Do *not* make me cut that Jessica Simpson look-alike blond hair of yours off in the middle of the night," the African princess said.

"Actually, the consuetudinary way to phrase that would be 'Do not make me cut that Jessica Simpson look-alike blond hair of yours off in the middle of the day.' Technically day is night for us and so night would be day. Time is reversed here."

The black girl narrowed her eyes at him. "Damien, you are getting on my damn last nerve what that vocab shit."

"Shaunee," Stevie Rae broke in hastily. "My roommate finally got here. This is Zoey Redbird. Zoey, this is Erin's roommate, Shaunee Cole."

"Hi," I said through a mouthful of spaghetti when Shaunee turned from glaring at Erin to me.

"So, Zoey, what's up with your Mark being colored in? You're still a fledgling, aren't you?" Everyone at the table was shocked silent by Shaunee's question. She looked around. "What? Do not pretend that every last one of you isn't wondering the same thing."

"We might be, but we also might be polite enough not to ask," Stevie Rae said firmly.

"Oh, please. Whatever." She shrugged off Stevie Rae's protest. "This is too important for that. Everyone wants to know about her Mark. There's no time to play games when good gossip is involved." Shaunee turned back to me. "So, what's up with the weird Mark?"

Might as well face this now. I took a quick drink of tea to clear my throat. All four of them were staring at me, waiting impatiently for my answer.

"Well, I'm still a fledgling. I don't think I'm any different than the rest of you." Then I blurted something that I'd been considering while everyone else had been talking. I mean, I knew that I was going to have to answer this question eventually. I'm not stupid— confused, maybe, but not stupid—and my gut told me I needed to say something besides the real story about my out-of-body experience with Nyx. "I don't actually know for sure why my Mark is filled in. It wasn't that way when the Tracker first Marked me. But later that day I had an accident. I fell and hit my head. When I woke up the Mark was like it is now. I've been thinking about it, and all I can come up with is that it must have happened as some kind of reaction to my accident. I was unconscious and I lost a lot of blood. Maybe that did something to speed up the darkening-in process. That's my guess, anyway."

"Huh," Shaunee huffed. "I was hoping it'd be somethin' more interesting. Something good and gossipy."

"Sorry . . . ," I muttered.

"Careful, Twin," Erin said to Shaunee, jerking her head at the

Dark Daughters. "You're starting to sound like you should sit over at that table."

Shaunee's face twisted. "I wouldn't be caught undead with those bitches."

"You're confusing the crap outta Zoey," Stevie Rae said.

Damien gave a long-suffering sigh. "I'll explain, proving once again how valuable I am to this group, penis or no penis."

"I really wish you wouldn't use the P-word," Stevie Rae said. "Especially when I'm trying to eat."

"I like it," Erin chimed in. "If everyone called things what they are we'd all be a lot less confused. For instance, you know when I have to go to the bathroom I state the obvious—I have urine that needs to come out of my urethra. Simple. Easy. Clear."

"Disgusting. Gross. Crude," Stevie Rae said.

"I'm with you, Twin," Shaunee said. "I mean, if we talked plainly about things like urination and menstruation and such, life would be much simpler."

"Okay. Enough with the menstruation talk while we're eating spaghetti." Damien held up a hand like he could physically stop the conversation. "I may be gay, but there's only so much even I can handle." He leaned toward me and launched into his explanation. "First, Shaunee and Erin call each other Twin because even though they are *clearly* not related—Erin being an extremely white girl from Tulsa, and Shaunee being of Jamaican descent and a lovely mocha color from Connecticut—"

"Thank you for appreciating my blackness," Shaunee said.

"Don't mention it," Damien said, and then continued smoothly with his explanation. "Even though they aren't related by blood they are freakishly alike."

"It's like they were separated at birth or something," Stevie Rae said.

At the same moment Erin and Shaunee grinned at each other and shrugged. It was then that I noticed they were wearing the same outfit—dark jeans jackets with beautiful golden wings embroidered on the breast pockets, black T-shirts, and low-riding black slacks. They even had on the same earrings—huge gold hoops.

"We have the same shoe size," Erin said, sticking out her foot so we could see that she was wearing pointy-toed black leather stiletto boots.

"And what's a little melanin difference when a truly soul-deep love of shoes is involved?" Lifting up her foot Shaunee showed off another great pair of boots—only these were smooth black leather with sharp silver buckles across the ankles.

"Next!" Damien cut in, rolling his eyes. "The Dark Daughters. The short version is that they're a group made up of mostly up-perclassmen who say that they are in charge of school spirit and such."

"No, the short version is that they're hags from hell," Shaunee said.

"That's exactly what I said, Twin," Erin laughed.

"You two aren't helping," Damien told them. "Now, where was I?"

"School spirit and such," I prompted.

"That's right. Yeah, they're supposed to be this great, pro-school, pro-vamp organization. Also, it is assumed that their leader is being groomed to be a High Priestess, so she's supposed to be the heart, mind, and spirit of the school—as well as a future leader in vamp society, et cetera, et cetera, blah, blah. Think National Merit Scholar in charge of the Honor Society mixed with cheerleaders and band fags."

"Hey, isn't it disrespectful to your gayness to call them band fags?" Stevie Rae asked.

"I'm using the word as a term of endearment," Damien said.

"And football players—don't forget there are Dark Sons, too," Erin said.

"Uh-huh, Twin. It is truly a crime and a shame that such seriously hot young lads get sucked in—"

"And she does mean that literally," said Erin with a naughty grin.

"By hags from hell," concluded Shaunee.

"Hello! Like I would forget the boys? I just keep getting interrupted."

The three girls gave him apologetic smiles. Stevie Rae pantomimed zipping her lips shut and throwing away the key. Erin and Shaunee mouthed "dork" at her, but they stayed quiet so Damien could finish.

I noticed that they'd played with the word "sucked," making me think that the little scene I'd witnessed hadn't been too unusual.

"But what the Dark Daughters really are is a group of stuck-up bitches who get off on lording power over everyone else. They want everyone to follow them, to conform to their freaky ideas of what it means to become a vamp. Most of all, they hate humans, and if you don't feel the same they don't want shit to do with you."

"Except to give you a hard time," Stevie Rae added. I could tell from her expression that she must have firsthand knowledge about the "hard time" part, and I remembered how pale and scared she'd looked when Aphrodite had shown me to our room. I made a mental note to remember to ask her later about what had happened.

"Don't let them scare you, though," Damien said. "Just watch your back around them and—"

"Hello, Zoey. Nice to see you again so soon."

I didn't have any trouble recognizing her voice this time. I decided it was like honey—slick and too darn sweet. Everyone at the table jumped, including me. She was wearing a sweater like mine, except that over her heart was embroidered the silver silhouette of three goddess-like women, one of them holding what looked like a pair of scissors. She had on a *very* short pleated black skirt, black tights that had silver sparkles in them, and knee-high black boots. Two girls were standing behind her, dressed in much the same way. One was black, with impossibly long hair (must be a really good weave), and the other was yet another blonde (who, on closer inspection of her brows, was probably, I decided, as much a natural blonde as I am).

"Hello, Aphrodite," I said when everyone else seemed too shocked to speak.

"Hope I'm not interrupting anything," she said insincerely.

"You're not. We were just discussing the trash that needs to be taken out tonight," Erin said with a big, fake smile.

"Well, you would certainly know about that," she said with a sneer, and then purposefully turned her back on Erin, who was curling her fists and looking as if she might leap over the table at Aphrodite. "Zoey, I should have said something to you earlier, but I guess it just slipped my mind. I want to issue an invitation for you to join the Dark Daughters in our own private Full Moon Ritual tomorrow night. I know it's unusual for someone who hasn't been here long to take part in a ritual so soon, but your Mark has clearly shown that you're, well, different than the average fledgling." She looked down her perfect nose at Stevie Rae. "I've already mentioned it to Neferet, and she agrees that it would be good for you to join us. I'll give you the details later, when you're not so busy with . . . uh . . . *trash*." She gave the rest of the table her tight-lipped, sarcastic smile, flipped her long hair, and she and her entourage flitted off.

"Hag bitches from hell," Shaunee and Erin said together.

CHAPTER TEN

—

"I keep thinking that hubris is eventually going to bring Aphrodite down," Damien said.

"Hubris," Stevie Rae explained, "having godlike arrogance."

"I actually know that one," I said, still staring after Aphrodite and her mob. "We just finished reading *Medea* in English class. It's what brought Jason down."

"I'd love to knock the hubris right out of her bobble head," Erin said.

"I'll hold her for you, Twin," Shaunee said.

"No! Y'all know we've talked about this before. The penalty for fighting is bad. Really bad. It's not worth it."

I watched Erin and Shaunee pale at the same time and wanted to ask what could be so bad, but Stevie Rae went on talking, this time to me.

"Just be careful, Zoey. The Dark Daughters, and especially Aphrodite, can seem almost okay at times, and that's when they're most dangerous."

I shook my head. "Oh, nu uh. I'm not going to their full moon thing."

"I think you have to," Damien said softly.

"Neferet okayed it," Stevie Rae said as Erin and Shaunee nodded in agreement. "That means she'll expect you to go. You can't tell your mentor no."

"Especially when your mentor is Neferet, High Priestess of Nyx," Damien said.

"Can't I just say that I'm not ready for . . . for . . . whatever it is they want me to do, and ask Neferet if I can be—I dunno, what would you call it—excused from their full moon thingie this time?"

"Well, you could, but then Neferet would tell the Dark Daughters and they'd think that you're scared of them."

I thought about the major crap that had already passed between Aphrodite and me in such a short time. "Uh, Stevie Rae, I might already be scared of them."

"Don't ever let them know." Stevie Rae looked down at her plate, trying to hide her embarrassment. "That's worse than standing up to them."

"Honey," Damien said, patting Stevie Rae's hand, "stop beating yourself up about that."

Stevie Rae gave Damien a sweet, thank-you smile. Then she said to me, "Just go. Be strong and go. They won't do anything too awful at the ritual. It's here on campus; they wouldn't dare."

"Yeah, they do all their bad bullshit away from here, where it's harder for the vamps to catch them," Shaunee said. "Around here they pretend to be all sickeningly sweet so no one knows what they're really like."

"No one except us," Erin said, sweeping out her hand so that she included not just our little group, but everyone else in the room, too.

"I don't know, y'all, maybe Zoey will actually get along with some of them okay," Stevie Rae said without any touch of sarcasm or jealousy.

I shook my head. "Nope. I won't get along with them. I don't like their kind—the kind of people who try to control others and make them look bad just to feel better about themselves. And I don't want to go to their Full Moon Ritual!" I said firmly, thinking about my stepfather and his buddies, and how ironic it was that they seemed to have so much in common with a group of teenagers who called themselves the daughters of a goddess.

"I'd go with you if I could—any of us would—but unless you're one of the Dark Daughters you can only get in if you're invited," Stevie Rae said sadly.

"That's okay. I'll—I'll just deal with it." Suddenly I wasn't hungry anymore. I was just very, very tired, and I really wanted to change the subject. "So explain to me about the different symbols you wear here. You told me about ours—Nyx's spiral. Damien has a spiral, too, so that must mean he's a . . ." I paused to remember what Stevie Rae had called freshmen, "a third former. But Erin and Shaunee have wings, and Aphrodite had something else."

"You mean besides that cob stuck straight up her skinny anus?" Erin muttered.

"She means the three Fates," Damien interjected, beating Shaunee to whatever she was going to add. "The three Fates are children of Nyx. The sixth formers all wear the emblem of the Fates, with Atropos holding scissors to symbolize the end of school."

"And for some of us, the end of life," Erin added gloomily.

That shut everyone up. When I couldn't stand the uncomfortable silence anymore I cleared my throat and said, "So what about Erin and Shaunee's wings?"

"The wings of Eros, who is the child of Nyx's seed—"

"The *love* god," Shaunee said, adding a seated gyration of her hips.

Damien frowned at her and kept talking. "The golden wings of Eros are the fourth formers' symbol."

" 'Cause we're the *love* class," Erin sang, raising her arms over her head and shimmying her hips.

"Actually, it's because we're supposed to be reminded of Nyx's capacity to love, and the wings symbolize our continuous movement forward."

"What's the symbol for fifth formers?" I asked.

"Nyx's golden chariot pulling a trail of stars," Damien said.

"I think it's the prettiest of the four symbols," Stevie Rae said. "Those stars sparkle like crazy."

"The chariot shows that we continue on Nyx's journey. The stars represent the magic of the two years that have already passed."

"Damien, you are a good little student," Erin said.

"I told you we should have gotten him to help us study for the human mythology test," Shaunee said.

"I thought *I* told *you* we needed his help, and—"

"Anyway," Damien shouted over their bickering, "that's about all there is to the four symbols of the classes. Easy-peasy, really," he looked pointedly at the now silent Twins. "That is, if you pay attention in class instead of writing notes and staring at guys you think are cute."

"You're really prudey, Damien," Shaunee said.

"Especially for a gay boy," Erin added.

"Erin, your hair's looking kinda frizzy today. Not to be mean or anything, but maybe you should think about switching products. You can't be too careful about those kinds of things. The next thing you know you'll be getting split ends."

Erin's blue eyes got huge and her hand went automatically to her hair.

"Oh, no no no. I do not believe you just said that, Damien. You know how crazy she is about her hair." Shaunee started to puff up like a mocha-colored blowfish.

Damien, meanwhile, just smiled and returned to his spaghetti—the perfect picture of innocence.

"Uh, y'all," Stevie Rae said quickly, standing up and pulling me with her by the elbow. "Zoey looks beat. Y'all remember what it was like when you first got here. We're going to go back to our room. I have to study for that vamp sociology test, so I probably won't see you until tomorrow."

"Okay, see ya," Damien said. "Zoey, it was really nice to meet you."

"Yeah, welcome to Hell High," Erin and Shaunee said together before Stevie Rae pulled me out of the room.

"Thanks. I really am tired," I told Stevie Rae as we backtracked through a hall that I was happy to recognize as the one that would lead to the main entrance to the central school building. We paused while a sleek, silver-gray cat chased a smaller, harassed-looking tabby across the hall in front of us.

"Beelzebub! Leave Cammy alone! Damien is going to rip your fur out!"

Stevie Rae made a grab for the gray cat and missed, but he did stop chasing the tabby and instead streaked back down the hall the way we had just come. Stevie Rae was frowning after him.

"Shaunee and Erin need to teach that cat of theirs some manners; he's always up to something." She glanced at me as we left the building and walked out into the soft, pre-dawn darkness. "That cute little Cameron is Damien's cat. Beelzebub belongs to Erin and Shaunee; he chose both of them—together. Yep. It's as strange as it sounds, but after a little while you'll be like the rest of us and start thinking that they must really be twins."

"They seem nice, though."

"Oh, they're great. They bicker a lot, but they're totally loyal and will never let anyone talk about you." She grinned. "Okay, *they* might talk about you, but that's different, and it won't be behind your back."

"And I really like Damien."

"Damien's sweet, and really smart. I just feel bad for him sometimes, though."

"How come?"

"Well, he had a roommate when he first got here about six months ago, but as soon as the guy found out Damien was gay— hello, it's not like the boy tries to hide it—he complained to Neferet and said he wasn't going to room with a fag."

I grimaced. I can't stand homophobes. "And Neferet actually put up with that attitude?"

"No, she made it clear that the kid—oh, he changed his name to Thor after he got here"—she shook her head and rolled her eyes—"doesn't that just figure? Anyway, Neferet let it be known that Thor was way out of line, and she gave Damien the option of moving into another room by himself or staying with Thor. Damien chose to move. I mean, wouldn't you?"

I nodded. "Yep. No way would I room with Thor the Homophobe."

"That's what we all think, too. So Damien has been in a room by himself since then."

"Aren't there any other gay kids here?"

Stevie Rae shrugged. "There're a few girls who are lesbians and totally out, but even though a couple of them are cool and hang with the rest of us they mostly stick together. They're way into the religious aspect of Goddess worship and spend most of their time in Nyx's Temple. And, of course, there are the moronic party girls who think it's cool to make out with each other, but usually only if some cute guys are watching."

I shook my head. "You know, I've never understood why girls

think making out with each other is the way to catch a boyfriend. You'd think it would be counterproductive."

"Like I want a boyfriend who only thinks I'm hot when I'm kissing some girl? Bleck."

"What about gay guys?"

Stevie sighed. "There are a few besides Damien, but they're mostly too weird and girly for him. I feel bad for him. I think he gets pretty lonely. His parents don't write or anything."

"The whole vampyre thing freaked them out?"

"No, they didn't really care about that. Actually, don't say anything to Damien because it hurts his feelings, but I think they were relieved when he was Marked. They didn't know what to do with a son who is gay."

"Why did they have to *do* anything? He's still their son. He just likes guys."

"Well, they live in Dallas, and his dad is big into the People of Faith. I think he's some kind of minister or something—"

I held up my hand. "Stop. You don't have to say another word. I totally get it." And I did. I was way too acquainted with the narrow-minded, "our way is the only right way" ideas of the People of Faith. Even thinking about it made me feel exhausted and depressed.

Stevie Rae opened the door to the dorm. The living-room area was empty except for a few girls who were watching *That '70s Show* reruns. Stevie Rae waved absently at them.

"Hey, do you want a pop or something to take upstairs with us?"

I nodded and followed her through the living room and into a smaller room off to the side that had four refrigerators, a big sink, two microwaves, lots of cabinets, and a pretty white wooden table that sat in the middle of it—just like a regular kitchen, only this one was weirdly refrigerator-friendly. Everything was neat and clean. Stevie Rae opened one of the fridges. I peeked over her shoulder to see that it was filled with all kinds of drinks— everything from pop to lots of juices and that fizzy water that tastes nasty.

"What do you want?"

"Any brown pop is fine," I said.

"This stuff is for all of us," she said as she handed me two Diet Cokes and grabbed two Frescas for herself. "There're fruit and veggies and stuff like that in those two fridges, and lean meat for sandwiches in the other one. They're kept full all the time, but the vamps are pretty obsessed with us eating healthy, so you won't find bags of chips or Twinkies or stuff like that."

"No chocolate?"

"Yeah, there's some really expensive chocolate in the cabinets. The vamps say chocolate in moderation is good for us."

Okay, so who the hell wants to eat chocolate in moderation? I kept the thought to myself as we walked back through the living room and headed upstairs to our room.

"So the, uh, vamps"—I kinda stumbled over the word—"are big on healthy eating?"

"Well, yeah, but I think basically just fledglings eating healthy. I mean, you don't see fat vamps, but you also don't see them chewing on celery and carrots and picking at salads. Mostly they eat together in their own dining room, and rumor has it that they eat well." She glanced at me and lowered her voice. "I heard that they eat a lot of red meat. A lot of *rare* red meat."

"Eeesh," I said, not liking the bizarre visual image I suddenly got of Neferet gnawing on a bloody steak.

Stevie Rae shivered, and went on: "Sometimes someone's mentor will sit with a fledgling at dinner, but they usually have just a glass or two of wine and don't eat with us."

Stevie Rae opened the door and with a sigh I sat on my bed and pulled off my shoes. God, I was tired. Rubbing my feet I wondered about why the adult vamps didn't eat with us, and then I decided I didn't really want to think about that long. I mean, it brought to mind too many questions like what are they really eating? And what will I have to eat when/if I become an adult vamp? Ugh.

And, part of my brain whispered that it also made me remember my reaction to Heath's blood yesterday. Had that been only yesterday? And also my more recent response to the blood of that guy in the hall. No. I definitely didn't want to think about either of them—at all. So I quickly refocused on the healthy-diet issue.

"Okay, they don't particularly care about eating healthy, so what's the big obsession with us eating healthy?" I asked Stevie Rae.

She met my eyes, looking worried and more than a little scared.

"They want us to eat healthy for the same reason they make us exercise every day—so that our bodies are as strong as possible, because if you start getting weak or fat or sick, that's the first sign that your body is rejecting the Change."

"And then you die," I said quietly.

"And then you die," she agreed.

CHAPTER ELEVEN

—

I didn't think I'd sleep. I figured I'd lay there and miss home and think about the bizarre twist my life had taken. Disturbing flashes of the guy in the hall's eyes drifted through my mind, but I was so tired I couldn't focus. Even Aphrodite's psycho hatefulness was something else that seemed sleepily far away. Actually, my last worries before I could remember nothing else were about my forehead. Was it feeling sore again because of the Mark and the cut over my temple—or was it because I was getting a ginormic zit? And would my hair look okay for my first day of vamp school tomorrow? But as I curled up with my comforter and inhaled the familiar smell of down feathers and home, I felt unexpectedly safe and warm . . . and was totally out.

I didn't have a nightmare, either. Instead I dreamed about cats. Go figure. Hot boys? No. Cool new vampire powers? Of course not. Just cats. There was one in particular—a small orange tabby who had little tiny paws and a pot belly with a pouch that looked kinda marsupial. She kept yelling at me in an old lady's voice and asking what had taken me so long to get here. Then her cat voice changed to an annoying buzzing beeping sound and I . . .

"Zoey, come on! Turn that stupid alarm clock off!"

"Wha—, huh?" Oh, hell. I hate mornings. My hand flailed about trying to find the off switch of my annoying alarm clock.

Have I mentioned that I am totally, completely blind without my contacts? I grabbed my nerdy glasses and peeked at the time. Six thirty P.M., and I was just waking up. Talk about bizarre.

"Do you want to take a shower first, or do you want me to?" Stevie Rae asked sleepily.

"I will, if you don't care."

"I don't . . . ," She yawned.

" 'Kay."

"We should hurry, though, 'cause, I don't know about you, but I have to eat breakfast or I feel like I'm going to starve to death before lunch."

"Cereal?" I suddenly perked up. I seriously adore cereal, and have an I ♥ CEREAL shirt somewhere to prove it. I especially love Count Chocula—yet another vampyre irony.

"Yeah, there're always lots of those tiny boxes of cereal and bagels and fruit and hard-boiled eggs and stuff."

"I'll hurry." Suddenly I was starving. "Hey, Stevie Rae, does it matter what I wear?"

"Nope," she yawned again. "Just pick one of the sweaters or jackets that show our third former symbol and you'll be fine."

I did hurry, even though I was really nervous about not looking right and I wished I could take hours doing and redoing my hair and makeup. I used Stevie Rae's makeup mirror while she was in the shower, and decided that under-doing was probably a better choice than over-doing. It was weird how my Mark seemed to change the whole focus of my face. I've always had nice eyes—big and round and dark, with lots of lashes. So much that Kayla used to whine about how unfair it was that I had enough lashes for three girls and she only had short little blond ones. (Speaking of . . . I did miss Kayla, especially this morning as I was getting ready to go to a new school without her. Maybe I'd call her later. Or e-mail her. Or . . . I remembered the comment Heath had made about the party, and decided maybe not.) Anyway, the Mark somehow made my eyes look even bigger and darker. I lined them with a smoky black shadow that had little sparkly flecks of silver in it. Not heavily like those loser girls who think that plastering on black eyeliner makes them look cool. Yeah, *right*. They look like scary raccoons. I smudged the line, added mascara, brushed some bronzing power over my face, and put on lip gloss (to hide the fact that I'd been nervously picking at my lips).

Then I stared at myself.

Thankfully my hair was acting right, and even my weird widow's peak wasn't sticking all up crazily like it did sometimes. I still looked . . . umm . . . different, but the same. The effect my Mark had on my face hadn't faded. It made everything that was ethnic about my features stand out: the darkness of my eyes, my high Cherokee cheekbones, my proud, straight nose, and even the olive color of my skin that was like my grandma's. The sapphire Mark of the Goddess seemed to have flipped a switch and spotlighted those features; it had freed the Cherokee girl within me and allowed her to shine.

"Your hair looks great," Stevie Rae said as she came into the room toweling dry her short hair. "I wish mine would act right when it's long. It doesn't. It just frizzes out and looks like a horse's tail."

"I like your short hair," I said, moving out of her way and grabbing my cute sparkly black ballet flats.

"Yeah, well, it makes me a freak here. Everybody has long hair."

"I noticed, but I don't really get it."

"It's one of the things that happens while we're going through the Change. Vamps' hair grows abnormally fast, just like their fingernails."

I tried not to shudder as I remembered Aphrodite's fingernail slashing through jeans and skin.

Thankfully, Stevie Rae was oblivious to my thoughts, and kept on talking.

"You'll see. After a while you won't have to look at their symbols to know what year they are. Anyway, you'll learn all about that kind of stuff in Vamp Sociology class. Oh! That reminds me." She rifled through some papers on her desk until she found what she was looking for and handed it to me. "Here's your schedule. We have third hour and fifth hour together. And check out the list of electives you have for second hour. You can choose from any of them."

My name was at the top of the schedule, printed in bold letters, ZOEY REDBIRD, ENTERING THIRD FORMER, as well as the date, which was five (?!) days before the Tracker had Marked me.

1st hour—Vampyre Sociology 101. Rm. 215. Prof. Neferet
2nd hour—Drama 101. Performing Arts Center. Prof. Nolan
or
Sketching 101. Rm. 312. Prof. Doner
or
Intro to Music. Rm. 314. Prof. Vento
3rd hour—Lit 101. Rm. 214. Prof. Penthesilea
4th hour—Fencing. Gymnasium. Prof. D. Lankford

LUNCH BREAK

5th hour—Spanish 101. Rm. 216. Prof. Garmy
6th hour—Intro to Equestrian Studies. Field House. Prof. Lenobia

"No geometry?" I blurted, totally overwhelmed by the schedule, but trying to keep a positive attitude.

"No, thankfully. Next semester we'll have to take economics, though. But that couldn't be as bad."

"Fencing? Intro to Equestrian Studies?"

"I told you they like to keep us in shape. Fencing's okay, even though it's hard. I'm not very good at it, but you do get paired with upperclassmen a lot—kind of like peer instructors, and I'm just sayin', some of those boys are just plain hot! I'm not taking the horse class this semester—they put me in Tae Kwan Do. And I have to tell ya, I love it!"

"Really?" I said doubtfully. *Wonder what the horse class would be like?*

"Yep. Which elective are you going to pick?"

I glanced back down the list. "Which one are you taking?"

"Intro to Music. Professor Vento is cool, and I, uh . . ." Stevie Rae grinned and blushed. "I want to be a country music star. I mean, Kenny Chesney, Faith Hill, and Shania Twain are all vamps—and that's just three of them. Heck, Garth Brooks grew up right here in Oklahoma and you know he's the biggest vamp of them all. So I don't see why I can't be one, too."

"Makes perfect sense to me," I said. Why not?

"You want to take music with me?"

"That'd be fun if I could sing or play anything resembling an instrument. I can't."

"Oh, well, maybe not then."

"Actually, I was thinking about the drama class. I was in drama at SIHS, and I liked it okay. Do you know anything about Prof. Nolan?"

"Yeah, she's from Texas and has a major accent, but she studied drama in New York and everyone likes her."

I almost laughed out loud when Stevie Rae mentioned Prof. Nolan's accent. The girl twanged so bad she sounded like an ad for a trailer park, but no way was I gonna hurt her feelings by mentioning it.

"Well, then drama it is."

"Okay, grab your schedule and let's go. Hey," she said as we hurried out of the room and skipped down the stairs, "maybe you'll be the next Nicole Kidman!"

Well, I guess being the next Nicole Kidman wouldn't be bad (not that I plan on marrying and then divorcing a manic short guy). Now that Stevie Rae mentioned it, I hadn't really thought much about my future career since the Tracker had thrown my life into complete chaos, but now that I was actually thinking about it I still really wanted to be a veterinarian.

An obese long-haired black and white cat sprinted down the steps in front of us chasing a cat that looked like its clone. With all these cats you'd think that there would definitely be a need for vamp vets. (Hee hee . . . vamp vets . . . I could call my clinic Vamp Vets, and the ads would read: "We'll take your blood for free!")

The kitchen and living room were crowded with girls eating and talking and hurrying around. I tried to return some of the hellos I was getting as Stevie Rae introduced me to what seemed like an impossibly confusing stream of girls *and* keep my concentration on finding a box of Count Chocula. Just when I was starting to worry, I found it, hidden behind several massive boxes of Frosted Flakes (not a bad second choice, but, well, they're not chocolate and they don't have any yummy little marshmallows). Stevie Rae poured a quick bowl of Lucky Charms, and we perched at the kitchen table, eating fast.

"Hi, Zoey!"

That voice. I knew who it was before I saw Stevie Rae duck her head and stare into her cereal bowl.

"Hi, Aphrodite," I said, trying to sound neutral.

"In case I don't see you later I wanted to be sure you know where to go tonight. The Dark Daughters' Full Moon Ritual will start at four A.M., right after the school's ritual. You'll miss dinner, but don't worry about that. We'll feed you. Oh, it's in the rec hall over by the east wall. I'll meet you in front of Nyx's Temple before the school ritual so we can go in together, and then I can show you the way to the hall afterward."

"Actually, I already promised Stevie Rae that I'd meet her and we'd go to the school ritual together." I really hate pushy people.

"Yeah, sorry 'bout that." I was pleased to hear Stevie Rae lift her head and say.

"Hey, you know where the rec hall is, don't you?" I asked Stevie Rae in my most perkily clueless voice.

"Yep, I do."

"Then you can just show me how to get there, right? And that means Aphrodite doesn't have to worry about me getting lost."

"Anything I can do to help," Stevie Rae chirped, sounding like her old self.

"Problem solved," I said with a big smile at Aphrodite.

"Okay. Fine. I'll see you at four A.M. Don't be late." She twitched off.

"If she shakes her butt any more when she walks she's gonna break something," I said.

Stevie Rae snorted and almost spewed milk from her nose. Coughing, she said, "Don't do that while I'm eating!" Then she swallowed and smiled at me. "You didn't let her boss you around."

"Neither did you." I slurped the last spoonful of cereal. "Ready?"

"Ready. Okay, this'll be easy. Your first hour is right next to my first hour. All of the third former core classes are in the same hall. Come on—I'll point you in the right direction and you'll be set."

We rinsed off our dishes and stuffed them in one of the five dishwashers, then hurried outside into the darkness of a beautiful fall evening. Jeesh, it was weird going to school at night, even if my body was telling me that everything was normal. We followed the flow of students through one of the thick wooden doors.

"Third Former Hall is just over here," Stevie Rae said, guiding me around a corner and up a short flight of stairs.

"Is that a bathroom?" I asked as we hurried past water fountains situated between two doors.

"Yep," she said. "Here's my class, and there's yours right next door. See you after class!"

"Okay, thanks," I called.

At least the bathroom was close. If I had a case of raging nervous-stomach diarrhea I wouldn't have far to run.

CHAPTER TWELVE

—

"Zoey! Over here!"

I almost cried in relief when I heard Damien's voice and saw his hand waving at an empty desk next to him.

"Hi." I sat down and smiled gratefully at him.

"Are you ready for your first day?"

No.

I nodded. "Yep." I wanted to say more, but just then a bell gave five quick rings and as the echo of it died Neferet swept into the room. She was wearing a long black skirt slit up the side to show great stiletto boots, and a deep purple silk sweater. Over her left breast, embroidered in silver, was the image of a goddess with her arms upraised, hands cupping a crescent moon. Her auburn hair was pulled back into a thick braid. The series of delicate wavelike tattoos that framed her face made her look like an ancient warrior priestess. She smiled at us and I could see that the entire class was as caught as I was by her powerful presence.

"Good evening! I've been looking forward to beginning this unit. Delving into the rich sociology of the Amazons is one of my favorites." Then she gestured to me. "It is excellent timing that Zoey Redbird has joined us today. I am Zoey's mentor, so I'll expect my students to welcome her. Damien, would you please get Zoey a textbook? Her cabinet is next to yours. While you explain our locker system to her I want the rest of you to journal about what preconceived impressions you have of the ancient vampyre warriors who are known as the Amazons."

The typical paper rustling and student whispering commenced while Damien led me to the back of the classroom where there was a wall of cabinets. He opened one that had the number "12" in silver on it. The cabinet contained neat, wide shelves filled with textbooks and supplies.

"At the House of Night there aren't lockers, like at regular schools. Here, first hour is our homeroom and we each have a cabinet of our own. The room will always be open, so you come back here to get books and whatever, just like you would go to a locker in the hall. Here's the sociology book."

He handed me a thick leather book with the silhouette of a goddess stamped on the front of it along with the title, *Vampyre Sociology 101*. I grabbed a notebook and a couple of pens. When I shut the cabinet door I hesitated.

"Isn't there a lock or something?"

"No," Damien lowered his voice. "They don't need locks here. If someone steals something, the vamps know it. I don't even want to think about what would happen to someone stupid enough to do that."

We sat back down and I started to write about the only thing I knew about the Amazons—that they were warrior women who didn't have much use for men—but my mind wasn't on my work. Instead, I was wondering why Damien, Stevie Rae, and even Erin and Shaunee all freak out about getting in trouble. I mean, I'm a good kid—okay, not perfect, but still. I've only had detention once so far, and that wasn't my fault. Really. Some turd boy told me to suck his cock. What was I supposed to do? Cry? Giggle? Pout? *Umm . . . no . . .* So instead I bitch slapped him (although I prefer just using the word smacked), and *I* got detention for it.

Anyway, detention wasn't actually that bad. I got all my homework done and started the new Gossip Girls book. Clearly detention at the House of Night entailed more than going to a teacher's classroom for forty-five minutes of "quiet time" after school. I'd have to remember to ask Stevie Rae . . .

"First, what pieces of the Amazon tradition do we still practice at the House of Night?" Neferet asked, drawing my attention back to class.

Damien raised his hand. "The bow of respect, with our fist over our heart, comes from the Amazons, and so does the way we shake hands—by gripping forearms."

"Correct, Damien."

Huh. That explained the funny handshake.

"So, what preconceived notions do you have about the Amazon warriors?" she asked the class.

A blonde who sat on the other side of the room said, "The Amazons were heavily matriarchal, as are all vampyre societies."

Jeesh, she sounded smart.

"That's true, Elizabeth, but when people discuss the Amazons, legend tends to add an additional layer to history. What do I mean by that?"

"Well, people—especially humans—think that the Amazons were man-haters," said Damien.

"Exactly. What we know is that just because a society is matriarchal, as ours is, it does not automatically mean that it is anti-male. Even Nyx has a consort, the god Erebus, to whom she is devoted. The Amazons were unique, though, in that they were a society of vampyre women who chose to be their own warriors and protectors. As most of you already know, our society today is still matriarchal, but we respect and appreciate the Sons of Night, and consider them our protectors and consorts. Now, open your text to Chapter Three and let's look at the greatest of the Amazon warriors, Penthesilea, but be careful to keep legend and history separate in your mind."

And from there Neferet launched into one of the coolest lectures I'd ever heard. I had no idea an hour had passed; the ringing bell was a total surprise. I'd just shoved my sociology book back into my cubbie (okay, I know that Damien and Neferet called them *cabinets,* but come on—they totally remind me of the cubbies we used to have in kindergarten) when Neferet called my name. I grabbed a notebook and a pen and hurried over to her desk.

"How are you?" she asked, smiling warmly.

"I'm okay. I'm good," I said quickly.

She lifted an eyebrow at me.

"Well, I suppose I'm nervous and confused."

"Of course you are. It's a lot to take in, and changing schools is always difficult—let alone changing schools and lives." She glanced over my shoulder. "Damien, would you walk Zoey to Drama class?"

"Sure," Damien said.

"Zoey, I'll see you tonight at Ritual. Oh, and has Aphrodite issued a formal invitation for you to join the Dark Daughters in their private ceremony afterward?"

"Yes."

"I wanted to double-check with you and make sure that you feel fine about attending. I would, of course, understand your reticence, but I encourage you to go; I want you to take advantage of every opportunity here, and the Dark Daughters is an exclusive organization. It is a compliment that they already seem interested in you as a possible pledge."

"I'm fine with going." I forced my voice and my smile to be nonchalant. Obviously she expected me to go, and the last thing I wanted was for Neferet to be disappointed in me. Plus, no way in hell was I going to do anything that might make Aphrodite think I was scared of her.

"Well done," Neferet said with enthusiasm. She squeezed my arm and I automatically smiled at her. "If you need me my office is in the same wing as the infirmary." She glanced at my forehead. "I see the stitches have almost completely dissolved. That's excellent. Does your head still hurt?"

My hand automatically found its way up to my temple. I could only feel the prickle of a stitch or two today when there had been at least ten yesterday. Very, very weird. And, even weirder, I hadn't thought about the cut once this morning.

I also realized I hadn't thought about my mom or Heath or even Grandma Redbird. . . .

"No," I said, suddenly realizing Neferet and Damien were waiting for me to answer. "No, my head doesn't hurt at all."

"Good! Well, you two better go before you're late. I know you'll love Drama. I think Professor Nolan has just begun working on monologues."

I was halfway down the hall, hurrying to keep up with Damien when it hit me.

"How did she know I was going to take Drama? I just decided it this morning."

"Adult vamps know way too much sometimes," Damien whispered. "Scratch that. Adult vamps know way too much *all* the time, especially when that vamp is a High Priestess."

In light of what I hadn't been telling Neferet I didn't want to think about that too long.

"Hey, y'all!" Stevie Rae rushed up. "How was Vamp Soc? Did y'all start the Amazons?"

"It was cool." I was glad to change the subject from the too mysterious vampyres. "I had no idea they really cut off their right breasts to keep them out of the way."

"They wouldn't have had to if they'd been as flat as me," said Stevie Rae, looking down at her own chest.

"Or me," sighed Damien dramatically.

I was still giggling when they pointed me to the Drama room.

Professor Nolan didn't ooze power like Neferet. Instead she oozed energy. She had an athletic, but somehow pear-shaped body. Her brunet hair was long and straight. And Stevie Rae had been right—she had a serious Texas twang.

"Zoey, welcome! Have a seat anywhere."

I said hi and sat beside the Elizabeth girl I recognized from Vamp Soc. She looked friendly enough and I already knew she was smart. (It never hurts to sit next to a smart kid.)

"We're just about to begin choosing the monologues that each of you will present to the class sometime next week. But first, I thought you'd like to have a demonstration of how a monologue should be performed, so I asked one of our talented upperclassmen to stop by and recite the famous monologue from *Othello*, written by the ancient vampyre playwright, Shakespeare." Professor Nolan paused and glanced out of the window in the door. "Here he is now."

The door opened and *oh my dear sweet lord* I do believe my heart totally stopped beating. I'm positive my mouth flopped open like a moron. He was the most gorgeous young lad I had ever seen. He was tall and had dark hair that did that adorably perfect Superman curl thing. His eyes were an amazing sapphire blue and . . .

Oh. Hell! Hell! Hell! It was the guy from the hall.

"Come on in, Erik. As usual, your entrance timing is perfect. We are ready for your monologue." She turned back to the class. "Most of you already know fifth former, Erik Night, and are aware that he won last year's worldwide House of Night monologue competition, the finals of which were held in London. He is also already creating a buzz in Hollywood as well as on Broadway for his performance last semester as Tony in our production of *West Side Story*. The class is all yours, Erik." Prof Nolan beamed.

As if my body were suddenly on automatic, I clapped with the rest of the class. Smiling and confident, Erik stepped up on the little stage that was situated front and center in the large, airy classroom.

"Hi. How are you guys doing?"

He spoke directly to me. I mean, *directly* to me. I could feel my face getting really hot.

"Monologues seem intimidating, but the key is to get your lines down, and then to imagine that you're actually acting *with* a full cast of actors. Trick yourself into thinking you're not up here all alone, like this . . ."

And he began the monologue from *Othello*. I don't know much about the play, except that it's one of Shakespeare's tragedies, but Erik's performance was amazing. He was a tall guy, probably at least six feet, but as he began to speak he seemed to get bigger and older and more powerful. His voice deepened and he took on an accent I couldn't place. His incredible eyes darkened and narrowed into slits, and when he said Desdemona's name it was like he was praying. It was obvious he loved her, even before he spoke the concluding lines:

> She loved me for the dangers I had passed,
> And I loved her that she did pity them.

As he said the last two lines his eyes locked with mine and, just like in the hall the day before, it seemed as if there was no one else in the room—no one else in the world. I felt a shiver deep inside of something very much like what I'd felt the two times I'd smelled blood since I'd been Marked, only no blood had been spilled in the room. There was only Erik. And then he smiled, touched his lips to his fingers as though he was sending me a kiss, and bowed. The whole class clapped like crazy, including me. Really. I couldn't help it.

"Now, that's how it's done," Professor Nolan said. "So, there are copies of monologues in the red bookshelves at the rear of the class. Each of you take several books and begin looking through them. What you're trying to find is a scene that means something to you—that touches some part of your soul. I'll be circulating and can answer any questions you have about individual monologues. Once you've chosen your pieces, I'll go through the steps you'll need to take as you prepare your own presentation." With an energetic smile and nod, she motioned for us to start looking through the zillions of monologue books.

I still felt flushed and short of breath, but I got up with the rest of the class, even though I couldn't help peeking at Erik over my shoulder. He was (unfortunately) leaving the room, but not before he turned and caught me gawking at him. I blushed (again). He met my eyes and smiled directly at me (again). And then he was gone.

"He's so f-ing hot," someone whispered in my ear. I turned and, shockingly, Ms. Perfect Student Elizabeth was staring after Erik and fanning herself.

"Doesn't he have a girlfriend?" I blurted like an idiot.

"Only in my dreams," Elizabeth said. "Actually, word has it that he and Aphrodite used to be hooked up, but I've been here for a few months and it's been over between them at least that long. Here ya go," she tossed a couple of monologue books at me. "I'm Elizabeth, no last name."

My face was a question mark.

She sighed. "My last name was Titsworth. Can you imagine? When I got here a few weeks ago and my mentor explained that I could change my name to whatever I wanted it to be, I knew I was going to get rid of the Titsworth part, but then the whole issue of picking a new last name just stressed me too much. So I decided I'd keep my first name and not hassle with a last name." Elizabeth No Last Name shrugged.

"Well, hi," I said. There were really some odd kids here.

"Hey," she said as we went back to our desks. "Erik was looking at you."

"He was looking at everyone," I said, even though I could feel my stupid face getting all hot and red again.

"Yeah, but he was *really* looking at you." She grinned and added, "Oh, I think your colored-in Mark is cool."

"Thanks." It probably looked weird as hell on my beet-red face.

"Any questions about choosing a monologue, Zoey?" Professor Nolan asked, making me jump.

"No, Professor Nolan. I've done them before in drama at SIHS."

"Very good. Let me know if I can clarify setting or character for you." She patted me on the arm and kept moving around the room. I opened up the first book and started to flip through the pages, trying (unsuccessfully) to forget about Erik and concentrate on monologues.

He *had* been looking at me. But why? He must have known that it had been me in the hall. So what kind of interest in me was he showing? And did I want a guy to like me who had been getting a blow job from the hateful Aphrodite? I probably shouldn't. I mean, I definitely wasn't going to take up where she left off. Or maybe he was just curious about my freakishly colored-in Mark, like practically everybody else was.

But it hadn't seemed like it . . . it had seemed like he'd been looking at *me*. And I'd liked it.

I glanced down at the book I'd been ignoring. The page was open to the subchapter: Dramatic Monologues for Women. The first monologue on the page was from *Always Ridiculous* by Jose Echegaray.

Well, hell. It was probably a sign.

CHAPTER THIRTEEN

—

I actually found my way to Lit class by myself. Okay, so it was just on the other side of Neferet's room, but still I felt a little more confident when I didn't have to ask to be led around like the helpless idiot new kid.

"Zoey! We saved a desk for ya!" Stevie Rae yelled the instant I got to class. She was sitting beside Damien, and practically hopping up and down with excitement. She looked like a happy puppy again, which made me smile. I was really glad to see her. "So, so, so! Tell me everything! How was Drama? Did you like it? Do you like Professor Nolan? Isn't her tattoo cool? It reminds me of a mask—kinda."

Damien grabbed Stevie Rae's arm. "Breathe and let the girl answer."

"Sorry," she said sheepishly.

"I guess Nolan's tattoos are cool," I said.

"You guess?"

"Well, I was distracted."

"What?" she said. Then her eyes narrowed. "Did someone embarrass you about your Mark? I swear people are just plain rude."

"No, that wasn't it. Actually that Elizabeth No Last Name girl said she thought it was cool. I was distracted because, well . . ." I was feeling my face get hot again. I'd decided that I was going to ask them about Erik, but now that I'd started talking I wondered whether I should say anything. Should I tell them about the hall?

Damien perked up. "I feel a juicy tidbit coming on. Come on, Zoey. You were distracted *becauuuuse?*" He drew the word out into a question.

"Okay, okay. I can sum it up in two words: Erik Night."

Stevie Rae's mouth dropped open and Damien did a little pretend swoon, which he had to straighten up from right away because at that moment the bell rang and Professor Penthesilea swept into the room.

"Later!" Stevie Rae whispered.

"Absolutely!" Damien mouthed.

I smiled innocently. If nothing else I was sure that I would love the fact that mentioning Erik would drive them crazy all hour.

Lit class was an experience. First of all, the classroom itself was totally different than any I'd ever seen. There were bizarrely interesting posters and paintings and what looked like original art work filling every inch of wall space. And hanging from the ceiling were wind chimes and crystals—lots of them. Professor Penthesilea (whose name I now recognized from Vamp Soc class as belonging to the most revered of all the Amazons, and who everyone called Prof P) was like something out of the movies (well, the ones on the Sci-Fi Channel). She had seriously long reddish-blond hair, big hazel eyes, and a curvy body that probably made all the guys drool (not that it's very hard to make teenage boys drool). Her tattoos were thin, pretty Celtic knots that traced their way down her face and around her cheekbones, making them look high and dramatic. She was wearing expensive-looking black slacks and a moss-colored silk cardigan sweater set that had the same goddess figure embroidered over her breast as Neferet had been wearing. And, now that I thought about it (and not Erik), I realized Prof

Nolan's blouse had the goddess embroidered on the breast pocket of her blouse, too. Hmmm . . .

"I was born in April of year 1902," Professor Penthesilea said, instantly grabbing our attention. I mean, please, she barely looked thirty. "So I was ten years old in April of 1912, and I remember the tragedy very well. About what am I speaking? Do any of you have any idea?"

Okay, I knew exactly what she was talking about, but it wasn't because I'm a hopeless history nerd. It's because when I was younger I thought I was in love with Leonardo DiCaprio, and my mom got me the entire DVD collection of his movies for my twelfth birthday. This particular movie I watched so many times I still have most of it memorized (and I can not tell you how many times I snot cried when he slipped off that board and floated away like an adorable Popsicle).

I looked around. No one else seemed to have a clue, so I sighed and raised my hand.

Prof P smiled and called on me, "Yes, Miss Redbird."

"The *Titanic* sank in April of 1912. It was struck by the iceberg late on Sunday night, the fourteenth, and sank just a few hours later on the fifteenth."

I heard Damien suck air beside me, and Stevie Rae's little *huh.* Jeesh, had I really been acting so stupid that they were shocked to hear me answer a question correctly?

"I do love it when a new fledgling knows something," Professor Penthesilea said. "Absolutely correct, Miss Redbird. I was living in Chicago at the time of the tragedy, and I will never forget the newsies shouting the tragic headlines from the street corners. It was a horrid event, especially because the loss of lives was so preventable. It also signaled the end of one age and the beginning of another, as well as bringing about many much-needed changes in shipping laws. We are going to study all of this, plus the deliciously melodramatic events of the night, in our next piece of literature, Walter Lord's meticulously researched book, *A Night to Remember*. Although Lord was not a vampyre—and it's really a shame he wasn't," she added under her breath, "I still find his take on the night compelling and his writing style and tone interesting and very readable. Okay, let's get started! The last person in each row, get books for the people in your row from the long cabinet in the back of the room."

Well, cool! This was definitely more interesting than reading *Great Expectations* (Pip, Estella, *who cares?!*). I settled in with *A Night to Remember* and my notebook opened to take, well, notes. Prof P started to read Chapter One aloud to us, and she was actually a good reader. Three class hours almost over and I'd liked all of them. Was it possible that this vamp school would actually be more than a boring place I went to every day because I had to and, besides that, all my friends were there? Not that *all* of the classes at SIHS had been boring, but we didn't get to study the Amazons and the *Titanic* (from a teacher who'd been alive when it sank!).

I glanced around at the other kids while Prof P read. There were about fifteen of us, which seemed about the average in my other classes, too. All of them had their books open and were paying attention.

Then my eye was caught by something red and bushy on the other side of the room near the rear of the class. I'd spoken too soon—not all of the kids were paying attention. This one had his head down on his arms and he was sound asleep, which I knew because his chubby, way-too-white-and-freckled face was turned in my direction. His mouth was open, and I think he might have been drooling a little. I wondered what Prof P would do to the kid. She didn't seem like the kind of teacher who would be cool with some slug sleeping in the back of the room, but she just kept on with her reading, interspersed with interesting firsthand facts about the early twentieth century, which I really liked (I loved hearing about the flappers—I would definitely have been a flapper if I'd lived in the 1920s). It wasn't until the bell was about to ring and Prof P had assigned the next chapter as homework, and then told us we could talk quietly amongst ourselves, that she acted as if she noticed the sleeping kid at all. He'd started to stir, finally lifting up his head to display the bright red sleeping circle that was on the side of his forehead and looked bizarrely out of place beside his Mark.

"Elliott, I need to see you," Prof P said from behind her desk.

The kid took his time getting up and then dragged his feet, scuffing his untied shoes, over to her desk.

"Yeah?"

"Elliott, you are, of course, failing Lit. But what's more important, you're failing life. Vampyre males are strong, honorable, and unique. They have been our warriors and protectors for countless generations. How do you expect to make the Change into a being who is more warrior than man if you do not practice the discipline it takes even to stay awake in class?"

He shrugged his soft-looking shoulders.

Her expression hardened. "I shall give you one opportunity to make up the zero for class participation you received today by writing a short paper on any issue that was important in America in the early twentieth century. The paper is due tomorrow."

Without saying anything, he started to turn away.

"Elliott," Prof P's voice had dropped and, thick with irritation, it made her sound way scarier than she'd seemed while she had been reading and lecturing. I could feel the power radiating from her, and it made me wonder why she would ever need a male anything to protect her. The kid stopped and turned back to face her.

"I did not excuse you. What is your decision about doing the work to make up today's zero?"

The kid just stood there without saying anything.

"That question calls for an answer, Elliott. Now!" The air around her crackled with the command, making the skin on my arms tingle.

Seemingly unaffected, he shrugged again. "I probably won't do it."

"That says something about your character, Elliott, and it's not something good. You're not only letting yourself down, but you're letting down your mentor, too."

He shrugged again and absently picked his nose. "The Dragon already knows how I am."

The bell rang and Prof P, with a disgusted look on her face, motioned for Elliott to leave the room. Damien, Stevie Rae, and I had just stood up and were starting to walk out the door when Elliott slouched by us, moving more quickly than I believed possible for someone so sloth-like. He bumped into Damien, who was ahead of us. Damien made an *oops* sound and stumbled a little.

"Fucking faggot, get outta my way," the loser kid snarled, pushing Damien with his shoulder so he could get through the door before him.

"I should smack the crap out of that jerk!" Stevie Rae said, hurrying up to Damien, who was waiting for us.

He shook his head. "Don't worry about it. That Elliott kid has major problems."

"Yeah, like having poopie for brains," I said, staring down the hall at the slug's back. His hair was certainly unattractive.

"*Poopie* for brains?" Damien laughed and linked one arm through mine and one through Stevie Rae's, leading us down the hall *Wizard of Oz* fashion. "That's what I like about our Zoey," he said. "She has such a way with vulgar language."

"Poopie's not vulgar," I said defensively.

"I think that's his point, honey," Stevie Rae laughed.

"Oh." I laughed, too, and I really, really liked how it sounded when he'd said "our" Zoey . . . like I belonged . . . like I might be home.

CHAPTER FOURTEEN

—

Fencing was totally cool, which was a surprise. Class was held in a huge room off the gym that looked like a dance studio, complete with a floor-to-ceiling wall of mirrors. Hanging from the ceiling along one side were weird life-sized manikins that reminded me of three-dimensional shooting targets. Everyone called Professor Lankford Dragon Lankford, or just Dragon. It didn't take me long to figure out why. His tattoo represented two dragons whose bodies, serpent-like, wrapped down over his jaw line. Their heads were over his brows and their mouths were open, breathing fire at the crescent moon. It was amazing and hard not to stare at. Plus, Dragon was the first male adult vampyre I'd seen up close. At first he confused me. I guess if you'd asked me what I expected from a male vampyre I would have said his opposite. Honestly, I had the movie-star vampyre stereotype in mind—tall, dangerous, handsome. You know, like Vin Diesel. Anyway, Dragon is short, has long blondish hair that he pulls back in a low ponytail, and (except for the fierce looking dragon tattoo) has a cute face with a warm smile

It was only when he began leading the class through its warm-up exercises that I began to realize his power. From the instant he held the sword (which I later found out was called an épée) in the traditional salute he seemed to become someone else—someone who moved with unbelievable quickness and grace. He feinted and lunged and effortlessly made the rest of the class—even the kids who were pretty good, like Damien—look like awkward puppets. When he finished leading the warm-ups, the Dragon paired everyone off and had them work on what he called "the standards." I was relieved when he motioned for Damien to be my partner.

"Zoey, it's good to have you join the House of Night," Dragon said, shaking my hand in the traditional Amazon vampyre greeting. "Damien can explain the different parts of the fencing uniform to you, and I'll get you a handout to study over the next few days. I am assuming you've had no previous instruction in the sport?"

"No, I haven't," I said, and then added nervously, "but I'd like to learn. I mean, the whole idea of using a sword is just cool."

Dragon smiled. "Foil," he corrected, "you'll be learning how to use a foil. It's the lightest weight of the three types of weapons we have here, and an excellent choice for women. Did you know that fencing is one of the very few sports where women and men can compete on entirely equal terms?"

"No," I said, instantly intrigued. How cool would it be to kick a guy's butt at a sport?!

"This is because the intelligent and focused fencer can successfully compensate for any perceived deficiencies he or she may have, and may even be able to turn those deficiencies—such as strength or reach—into assets. In other words, you may not be as strong or as fast as your opponent, but you could be smarter or able to remain focused better, which will tip the scales in your favor. Right, Damien?"

Damien grinned. "Right."

"Damien is one of the most focused fencers I've had the privilege to coach in decades, which makes him a dangerous opponent."

I snuck a sideways glance at Damien, who flushed with pride and pleasure.

"For the next week or so I'll have Damien drill you in the opening maneuvers. Always remember, fencing requires a mastery of skills that are sequential and hierarchical in nature. If one of the skills is not acquired, subsequent skills will be very difficult to master and the fencer will be at a permanent and serious disadvantage."

"Okay, I'll remember," I said. Dragon smiled warmly again before he moved off to work his way among each practicing pair.

"What he means is don't get discouraged or bored if I make you do the same exercise over and over."

"So what you're really saying is that you're going to be annoying, but there's a purpose behind it?"

"Yep. And part of that purpose will help lift that cute little butt of yours," he said sassily, tapping me with the side of his foil.

I slapped at him and rolled my eyes, but after twenty minutes of lunging and settling back into the beginning stance and lunging—over and over again—I knew he was right. My butt would be killing me tomorrow.

We took quick showers after class (thankfully, there were separate curtain-draped stalls for each of us in the girls' locker room and we didn't have to barbarically and tragically shower in a huge open area like we were prison inmates or whatever) and then I hurried with the rest of the crowd to the lunch room—better known as the dining hall. And I do mean hurry. I was starving.

Lunch was a huge build-your-own salad buffet, which included everything from tuna salad (eesh) to those weird mini-corns that are so confusing, and don't even taste like corn. (What exactly are they? Baby corn? Midget corn? Mutant corn?) I piled my plate high and got a big hunk of what looked and smelled like freshly baked bread, and slid into the booth beside Stevie Rae, with Damien following close behind me. Erin and Shaunee were already arguing over something to do with whose essay for their Lit class was better, even though they'd both gotten 96 on their papers.

"So, Zoey, give. What about Erik Night?" Stevie Rae asked the instant I'd forked a big bite of salad into my mouth. Stevie Rae's words immediately shut up the Twins and focused the entire table's attention on me.

I'd thought about what I was going to say about Erik, and decided that I wasn't ready to tell anyone about the unfortunate blow-job scene. So I just said, "He kept looking at me." When they frowned at me I realized that through my salad mouth what I'd really said was "He keffft looookn at mmm." I swallowed and tried again. "He kept looking at me. In Drama class. It was just, I dunno, confusing."

"Define 'looking at me,'" Damien said.

"Well, it happened the second he came into class, but it was especially noticeable when he was giving us an example of a monologue. He did this thing from *Othello*, and when he said the line about love and such, he stared straight at me. I would have thought it was just an accident or something, but he looked at me before he started the monologue, and then again as he was leaving the room." I sighed and squirmed a little, uncomfortable with their way too piercing looks. "Never mind. It was probably just part of his act."

"Erik Night is the hottest damn thing at this entire school," Shaunee said.

"Forget that—he's the hottest damn thing on this planet," Erin said.

"He's not hotter than Kenny Chesney," Stevie Rae said quickly.

"Okay, just please with your country obsession!" Shaunee frowned at Stevie Rae before turning her attention back to me. "Do *not* let this opportunity pass you by."

"Yeah," Erin echoed. "Do *not.*"

"Pass me by? What am I supposed to do? He didn't even say anything to me."

"Uh, Zoey honey, did you smile back at the boy?" Damien asked.

I blinked. Had I smiled back at him? Ah, crap. I bet I hadn't. I bet I just sat there and stared like a moron and maybe even drooled. Okay, well, I might not have drooled, but still. "I dunno," I said instead of the sad truth, which didn't fool Damien at all.

He snorted. "Next time smile at him."

"And maybe say hi," Stevie Rae said.

"I thought Erik was a just pretty face," Shaunee said.

"And body," Erin added.

"Until he dumped Aphrodite," Shaunee continued. "When he did that I realized the boy might have something going on upstairs."

"We can already tell he has it going on downstairs!" Erin said, waggling her eyebrows.

"Uh-huh!" Shaunee said, licking her lips like she was contemplating eating a big piece of chocolate.

"You two are gross," Damien said.

"We only meant that he has the cutest butt in town, Miss Priss," Shaunee said.

"As if you haven't noticed," Erin said.

"If you started talking to Erik it would really piss off Aphrodite." Stevie Rae said.

Everyone turned and stared at Stevie Rae as if she'd just parted the Red Sea or something.

"It's true," Damien said.

"Very true," Shaunee said while Erin nodded.

"So the rumor is he used to go out with Aphrodite," I said.

"Yep," Erin said.

"The rumor is grotesque but true," Shaunee said. "Which makes it even better that now he likes you!"

"Guys, he was probably just staring at my weird Mark," I blurted.

"Maybe not. You're really cute, Zoey," Stevie Rae said with a sweet smile.

"Or maybe your Mark made him look, and then he thought you were cute so he kept looking," Damien said.

"Either way, his looking will definitely piss Aphrodite off," Shaunee said.

"Which is a good thing," Erin said.

Stevie Rae waved away their comments. "Just forget about Aphrodite and your Mark and all that other stuff. Next time he smiles at you, say hi. That's all."

"Easy," Shaunee said.

"Peasy," Erin said.

"Okay," I mumbled and went back to my salad, wishing desperately that the whole Erik Night issue was as easy-peasy as they thought it was.

One thing about lunch at the House of Night was the same as lunch at SIHS or any other school I'd ever eaten at—it was over too soon. And then Spanish class was a blur. Profesora Garmy was like a little Hispanic whirlwind. I liked her right away (her tattoos looked oddly like feathers, so she reminded me of a little Spanish bird), but she ran the class speaking entirely in Spanish. Entirely. I should probably mention here that I haven't had Spanish since eighth grade, and I freely admit to not paying much attention to it then. So I was pretty lost, but I wrote down the homework and promised myself that I'd study the vocab words. I hate being lost.

Intro to Equestrian Studies was held in the Field House. It was a long, low brick building over by the south wall, attached to a huge indoor riding arena. The whole place had that sawdusty, horsey smell that mixed with leather to form something that was pleasant, even though you know that part of the "pleasant" scent was poopie—horse poopie.

I stood nervously with a small group of kids just inside the corral where a tall, stern-faced upperclassman had directed us to wait. There were only about ten of us, and we were all third formers. Oh, (great) that annoying redheaded Elliott kid was slouching against the wall kicking at the sawdust floor. He raised enough dust to make the girl standing closest to him sneeze. She threw him a dirty look and moved a few steps away. God, did he irritate *everyone*? And why couldn't he use some product (or perhaps a comb) on that nappy hair?

The sound of hooves drew my attention from Elliott and I looked up in time to see a magnificent black mare pounding into the corral at full gallop. She slid to a stop a couple feet in front of us. While we all gawked like fools, the mare's rider dismounted gracefully. She had thick hair that reached to her waist and was so blond it was almost white, and eyes that were a weird shade of slate gray. Her body was tiny, and the way she stood reminded me of those girls who obsessively take dance classes so that even when they're not in ballet they stand like they have something stuck way up their butts. Her tattoo was an intricate series of knots entwined around her face—within the sapphire design I was sure I could see plunging horses.

"Good evening. I am Lenobia, and *this*," she pointed at the mare and gave our group a contemptuous look before finishing the sentence, "is a horse." Her voice rang against the walls. The black mare blew through her nose as if to punctuate her words. "And you are my new group of third formers. Each of you has been chosen for my class because we believe you might possibly have an aptitude for riding. The truth is that less than half of you will last the semester, and less than half of those who last will actually develop into decent equestrians. Are there any questions?" She didn't pause long enough for anyone to ask anything. "Good. Then follow me and you shall begin." She turned and marched back into the stable. We followed.

I wanted to ask who the "we" were who thought I might have an aptitude for riding, but I was scared to say anything and just scrambled after her like everyone else. She came to a halt in front of a row of empty stalls. Outside of them were pitchforks and wheelbarrows. Lenobia turned to face us.

"Horses are not big dogs. Nor are they a little girl's romanticized dream image of a perfect best friend who will always understand you."

Two girls standing beside me fidgeted guiltily and Lenobia skewered them with her gray eyes.

"Horses are work. Horses take dedication, intelligence, and time. We'll begin with the work part. In the tack room down this hall you'll find mucking boots. Choose a pair quickly, while we all get gloves. Then each of you take your own stall and get busy."

"Professor Lenobia?" said a chubby girl with a cute face, who raised her hand nervously.

"Lenobia will do. The name I chose in honor of the ancient vampyre queen needs no other title."

I didn't have a clue who Lenobia was, and made a mental note to look it up.

"Go on. You have a question, Amanda?"

"Yeah, uh, yes."

Lenobia raised one brow at the girl.

Amanda swallowed noisily. "Get busy doing what, Profes—, I mean, Lenobia, ma'am?"

"Cleaning out stalls, of course. The manure goes in the wheelbarrows. When your barrow is full you can dump it in the compost area on the wall side of the stables. There is fresh sawdust in the storage room beside the tack room. You have fifty minutes. I'll be back in forty-five to inspect your stalls."

We all blinked at her.

"You may commence. Now."

We commenced.

Okay. Really. I know it's going to sound weird, but I didn't mind cleaning out my stall. I mean, horse poopie just isn't that gross. Especially because it was obvious that these stalls were cleaned out like every other instant of the day. I grabbed the mucking boots (which were big rubber galoshes—totally ugly, but they did cover my jeans all the way up to my knees) and a pair of gloves and got to work. There was music playing through excellent loudspeakers— something that I was pretty sure was Enya's latest CD (my mom used to listen to Enya before she married John, but then he decided that it might be witch music so she quit, which is why I'll always like Enya). So I listened to the haunting Gaelic lyrics and pitch-forked up poopie. It didn't seem that hardly any time had passed when I was dumping the wheelbarrow and then filling it with clean sawdust. I was just smoothing it around the stall when I got that prickly feeling that someone was watching me.

"Good job, Zoey."

I jumped and whirled around to see Lenobia standing just outside my stall. In one hand she was holding a big, soft curry brush. In the other she was holding the lead rope of a doe-eyed roan mare.

"You've done this before," Lenobia said.

"My grandma used to have a really sweet gray gelding I named Bunny," I said before I realized how stupid I sounded. Cheeks hot, I hurried on, "Well, I was ten, and his color reminded me of Bugs Bunny, so I started calling him that and it stuck."

Lenobia's lips tilted up in the barest hint of a smile. "It was Bunny's stall you cleaned?"

"Yeah. I liked to ride him, and Grandma said that no one should ride a horse unless they clean up after one." I shrugged. "So I cleaned up after him."

"Your grandmother is a wise woman."

I nodded.

"And did you mind cleaning up after Bunny?"

"No, not really."

"Good. Meet Persephone," Lenobia nodded her head at the mare beside her. "You've just cleaned her stall."

The mare came into the stall and walked straight up to me, sticking her muzzle in my face and blowing gently, which tickled and made me giggle. I rubbed her nose and automatically kissed the warm velvet of her muzzle.

"Hi there, Persephone, you pretty girl."

Lenobia nodded in approval as the mare and I got to know each other.

"There are only about five minutes left before the bell rings for school to end, so it is not necessary that you stay as part of today's class, but if you'd like, I believe you have earned the privilege of brushing Persephone."

Surprised, I looked up from patting the horse's neck. "No problem, I'll stay," I heard myself saying.

"Excellent. You can return the brush to the tack room when you've finished. I'll see you tomorrow, Zoey." Lenobia handed me the brush, patted the mare, and left us alone in the stall.

Persephone stuck her head in the metal rack that held fresh hay, and got to work chewing, while I got to work brushing. I'd forgotten how relaxing it was to groom a horse. Bunny had died of a sudden and very scary heart attack two years ago, and Grandma had been too upset to get another horse. She'd said that "the rabbit" (which is what she used to call him) couldn't be replaced. So it had been two years since I'd been around a horse, but it came back to me instantly—all of it. The smells, the warm, soothing sound of a horse eating, and the gentle *shoosh* the curry brush made as it slid over the mare's slick coat.

At the edge of my attention I vaguely heard Lenobia's voice, sharp and angry, as she totally chewed out a student I guessed was the annoying redheaded kid. I peeked over Persephone's shoulder and took a quick look down the stall line. Sure enough, the red-headed kid was slouched in front of his stall. Lenobia stood beside him, hands on her hips. Even from the side view I could see she was mad as hell. Was it that kid's mission to piss off every teacher here? And his mentor was Dragon? Okay, the guy looked nice, un-til he picked up a sword—uh, I mean *foil*—then he shifted from nice guy to deadly-dangerous-vampyre-warrior-guy.

"That redheaded slug kid must have a death wish," I told Persephone as I returned to her grooming. The mare twitched an ear back at me and blew through her nose. "Yep, I knew you'd agree. Wanta hear my theory about how my generation could single-handedly wipe out slugs and loser kids from America?" She seemed receptive, so I launched into my Don't Procreate with Losers speech. . . .

"Zoey! There you are!"

"Ohmygod! Stevie Rae! You scared the poo out of me!" I pat-ted and reassured Persephone, who had shied when I'd squealed.

"What in the world are ya doin'?"

I waggled the curry brush in her direction. "What does it look like I'm doing, Stevie Rae, getting a pedicure?"

"Stop messing around. The Full Moon Ritual is gonna start in like two minutes?"

"Ah, hell!" I gave Persephone one more pat and hurried out of the stall to the tack room.

"You forgot all about it, didn't you?" Stevie Rae said, holding my hand to help me balance while I kicked my feet out of the rubber boots and put my cute little ballet slippers back on.

"No," I lied.

Then I realized that I'd also forgotten all about the Dark Daughters' ritual afterward.

"Ah, *hell!*"

CHAPTER FIFTEEN

—

About halfway to Nyx's Temple I realized that Stevie Rae was being unusually quiet. I glanced sideways at her. Was she also looking pale? I got a creepy walk-over-your-grave feeling.

"Stevie Rae, is something wrong?"

"Yeah, well, it's sad and kinda scary."

"What is? The Full Moon Ritual?" My stomach started to hurt.

"No, you'll like that—or at least you'll like this one." I knew she meant, versus the Dark Daughters' ritual I had to go to afterward, but I didn't want to talk about that. Stevie Rae's next words made the whole issue of the Dark Daughters seem like a small, secondary problem. "A girl died last hour."

"What? How?"

"How they all die. She didn't make the Change, and her body just . . ." Stevie Rae paused, shuddering. "It happened near the end of Tae Kwan Do class. She'd been coughing, like she was short of breath at the beginning of our warmup exercises. I didn't think anything of it. Or maybe I did, but I put it out of my mind."

Stevie Rae gave me a small, sad smile and she looked ashamed of herself.

"Is there any way to save a kid? After, you know, they start—" I broke off and made a vague, uncomfortable gesture.

"No. There's no way you can be saved if your body starts to reject the Change."

"Then don't feel bad about not wanting to think about the girl who was coughing. There's nothing you could have done anyway."

"I know. I just . . . it was awful. And Elizabeth was so nice."

I felt a sharp jolt somewhere in the middle of my body. "Elizabeth No Last Name? She's the girl who died?"

Stevie Rae nodded, blinking hard and obviously trying not to cry.

"That's horrible," I said, my voice so weak it was almost a whisper. I remembered how considerate she'd been about my Mark, and how she'd noticed Erik looking at me. "But I just saw her in Drama class. She was fine."

"That's how it happens. One second the kid sitting next to you looks perfectly normal. The next . . ." Stevie Rae shivered again.

"And everything's going to go on like normal? Even though someone at the school just died?" I remembered that last year, when a group of sophomores from SIHS had been in a car accident one weekend and two of them had been killed, extra counselors had been called in to school on Monday and all the athletic events had been cancelled for that week.

"Everything goes on like normal. We're supposed to get used to the idea that it might happen to anyone. You'll see. Everyone will act like nothing happened, especially upperclassmen. It's just third formers and good friends of Elizabeth, like her roommate, who will show any reaction at all. The third formers—that's us—are supposed to act right and get over it. Elizabeth's roommate and best friends will probably keep to themselves for a couple days, but then they'll be expected to get it together." She lowered her voice, "Truthfully, I don't think the vamps think of any of us as *real* until we actually Change."

I thought about this. Neferet didn't seem to treat me like I was temporary—she'd even said that it was an excellent sign that my Mark was colored in already, not that I was as confident as she seemed to be about my future. But I absolutely was not going to say anything that might sound as if Neferet was giving me special treatment. I didn't want to be "the weird one." I just wanted to be Stevie Rae's friend and fit in with my new group.

"That's really awful," was all I said.

"Yeah, but at least if it happens, it happens fast."

Part of me wanted to know the details, and part of me was too scared even to ask the question.

Thankfully, Shaunee interrupted before I could make myself ask what I was really too freaked out to want to know.

"Just please with the taking so long," Shaunee called from the front steps of the temple. "Erin and Damien are already inside saving a place in the circle for us, but you know that once the ritual starts they won't let anyone else in. Hurry up!"

We rushed up the steps, and with Shaunee leading us, hurried into the temple. Sweet, smoky incense engulfed me as I entered the dark arched foyer of Nyx's Temple. Automatically, I hesitated. Stevie Rae and Shaunee turned to me.

"It's okay. There's nothing to be nervous or scared about." Stevie Rae met my eyes and added, "At least nothing in there."

"The Full Moon Ritual is great. You'll like it. Oh, when the vamp traces the pentagram on your forehead and says 'blessed be' all you have to do is say 'blessed be' back to her," Shaunee explained. "Then follow us over to our place in the circle." She smiled reassuringly at me and hurried ahead into the dimly lit interior room.

"Wait." I grabbed Stevie Rae's sleeve. "I don't want to sound stupid, but isn't a pentagram a sign of evil or something like that?"

"That's what I thought, too, until I got here. But all that evil stuff is bull that the People of Faith want you to believe so that . . . Heck," she said with a shrug, "I'm not even sure why they're so set on people—well, humans that is—believing that it's an evil sign. The truth is that for like a zillion years the pentagram has stood for wisdom, protection, perfection. Good stuff like that. It's just a five-pointed star. Four of the points stand for the elements. The fifth, the one that points up, stands for the spirit. That's all it is. No boogieman there."

"Control," I muttered, glad we had a reason to quit talking about Elizabeth and death.

"Huh?"

"The People of Faith want to control everything, and part of that control is that everyone has to always believe exactly the same. That's why they want people to think the pentagram is bad." I shook my head in disgust. "Never mind. Come on. I'm readier than I thought I was. Let's go in."

We walked deeper into the foyer and I heard running water. We passed a beautiful fountain, and then the entryway curved gently to the left. Within a thick, arched stone doorway stood a vampyre I didn't recognize. She was dressed entirely in black—a long skirt and a silky, bell-sleeved blouse. The only decoration she had on was the silver embroidered goddess figure over her breast. Her hair was long and the color of wheat. Sapphire-colored spirals radiated from her crescent moon tattoo to down around her flawless face.

"That's Anastasia. She teaches the Spells and Rituals class. She's also Dragon's wife," Stevie Rae whispered quickly before she stepped up to the vampyre and respectfully placed her fist over her heart.

Anastasia smiled and dipped her finger in a rock bowl she was holding. Then she traced a five-pointed star on Stevie Rae's forehead.

"Blessed be, Stevie Rae," she said.

"Blessed be," Stevie Rae responded. She gave me an encouraging look before she disappeared into the smoky room beyond.

I took a deep breath and made a conscious decision to put all thoughts of Elizabeth and death and what-ifs out of my mind— at least during this ritual. I moved purposefully into the space in front of Anastasia. Mimicking Stevie Rae, I placed my closed fist over my heart.

The vampyre dipped her finger in what I could now see was oil. "Merry meet, Zoey Redbird, welcome to the House of Night and your new life," she said as she traced the pentagram on my forehead over my Mark. "And blessed be."

"Blessed be," I murmured, surprised at the electric shiver that passed through my body when the damp star had taken form on my forehead.

"Go on in and join your friends," she said kindly. "There's no need to be nervous, I believe the Goddess is already looking after you."

"Th-thank you," I said, and hurried into the room. There were candles everywhere. Huge white ones suspended from the ceiling in iron chandeliers. Big candle trees held more of them and were lined along the walls. In the temple, sconces didn't burn oil tamely in lanterns, like in the rest of the school. Here the sconces were *real*. I knew that this place used to be a People of Faith church dedicated to St. Augustine, but it looked like no church I'd ever seen before. Besides being lit only by candlelight, there were no pews. (And, by the way, I really dislike pews—could they be any more uncomfortable?) Actually, the only furniture in the big room was an antique wooden table situated in the center that was kinda like the one in the dining hall—only this one wasn't just loaded with food and wine and such. This one also held a marble statue of the Goddess, arms upraised and looking a lot like the embroidered design the vamps wore. There was a huge candelabrum on the table, its fat white candles burning brightly, as well as several thick sticks of smoking incense.

Then my eyes were caught by the open flame burning from out of a recess in the stone floor. It flickered wildly, its yellow fire almost waist high. It was beautiful, in a controlled danger kind of a way, and it seemed to draw me forward. Thankfully, Stevie Rae's waving hands snagged my attention before I could follow my impulse to approach the flame, and then I noticed, wondering how I could have failed to see this from the beginning, that there was a huge circle of people—students as well as adult vamps—stretching around the edges of the room. Feeling nervous and awestruck at the same time, I made my feet move so I could take my place in the circle beside Stevie Rae.

"Finally," Damien said under his breath.

"Sorry we're late," I said.

"Leave her alone. She's nervous enough as it is," Stevie Rae told him.

"*Sssh!* It's starting," Shaunee hissed.

Four forms seemed to materialize from within the darkened corners of the room to become women who made their way to four spots just within the living circle, like the directions on a compass. Two more entered from the doorway through which I'd just come. One was a tall man—well, scratch that—male vampyre (all of the adults were vamps), and, ohmygod, he was hot. Now, here was an excellent example of the stereotype of the gorgeous vamp guy, up close and personal. He was over six feet tall and looked like he belonged on the big screen.

"And *there* is the only reason I'm taking that damn Poetry elective," Shaunee whispered.

"I'm with you there, Twin," Erin breathed dreamily.

"Who is he?" I asked Stevie Rae.

"Loren Blake, Vamp Poet Laureate. He's the first male Poet Laureate in two hundred years. Literally," she whispered. "*And* he's only like twenty-something, and that's in real years, not just in looks."

Before I could say anything else, he started to speak and my mouth was too busy flopping open at the sound of his voice for me to do anything but listen.

She walks in beauty, like the night
Of cloudless climes and starry skies . . .

As he spoke he moved slowly toward the circle. As if his voice was music, the woman who had entered the room with him began to sway, and then to dance gracefully around the outside of the living circle.

And all that's best of dark and bright
Meet in her aspect and her eyes . . .

The dancing woman had everyone's attention. With a jolt I realized that it was Neferet. She was wearing a long silk dress that had tiny crystal beads sewn all over it, so that the candlelight caught each of her movements and made her shimmer like the star-filled night sky. Her movements seemed to call alive the words of the old poem (at least my mind was still working well enough that I recognized it as Lord Byron's "She Walks in Beauty").

Thus mellowed to that tender light
Which heaven to gaudy day denies.

Somehow both Neferet and Loren managed to end up in the center of the circle as he finished reciting the stanza. Then Neferet took a goblet from the table and lifted it, as if offering a drink to the circle.

"Welcome Nyx's children to the Goddess's celebration of the full moon!"

The adult vamps chorused, "Merry meet."

Neferet smiled and put the goblet back on the table and picked up a long white taper that was already lit and sitting in a single candlestick holder. Then she walked across the circle to face a vamp I didn't know who was standing at what must be the head of the circle. The vamp saluted her, hand over breast, before turning around so that her back was to Neferet.

"*Psst!*" Stevie Rae whispered. "We all face each of the four directions as Neferet evokes the elements and casts Nyx's circle. East and air come first."

Then everyone, including me even though I was kinda slow, turned to face east. Out of the corner of my eye I could see Neferet raise her arms over her head as her voice rang against the stone walls of the temple.

"From the east I summon air and ask that you carry to this circle the gift of knowledge that our ritual will be filled with learning."

The instant Neferet began speaking the invocation I felt the air change. It moved around me, ruffling my hair and filling my ears with the sound of wind sighing through leaves. I looked around, expecting to see that everyone else had been caught in a mini-whirlwind, but didn't notice anyone else's hair getting messed up. Weird.

The vamp who was standing in the east pulled a thick yellow candle from the folds of her dress, and Neferet lit it. She lifted it into the air, and then placed it, flickering, at her feet.

"Turn to the right, for fire," Stevie Rae whispered again.

We turned and Neferet continued. "From the south I summon fire and ask that you light in this circle the gift of strength of will, so that our ritual will be binding and powerful."

The wind that had been blowing softly against me was replaced by a sensation of heat. It wasn't exactly uncomfortable; it was more like the flush you feel when you step into a hot tub, but it was warm enough to make a light sweat break out over my body. I glanced at Stevie Rae. She had her head raised slightly and her eyes were closed. There was no sign of sweat on her face. The intensity of the heat suddenly jumped up a notch, and I looked back at Neferet. She had lit a large red candle that Penthesilea was holding. Then, as the east-facing vamp had done, Penthesilea lifted it up in offering before placing it by her feet.

This time I didn't need Stevie Rae's nudging to turn again to my right and face west. Somehow, I knew not just that we needed to turn, but that the next element to be summoned would be water.

"From the west I summon water and ask that you wash this circle in compassion, that the light of the full moon can be used to bestow healing to our group as well as understanding."

Neferet lit the west-facing vamp's blue candle. The vamp lifted it, and placed it at her feet as the sound of waves filled my ears and the salty scent of the sea filled my nose. Eagerly, I completed the circle by facing north and knew I'd be embracing earth.

"From the north I summon earth and ask that you grow within this circle the gift of manifestation, that the wishes and prayers from tonight will come to fruition."

Suddenly I could feel the softness of a grassy meadow under my feet, and I smelled hay and heard birdsong. A green candle was lit and placed at "earth"'s feet.

I should have probably been afraid of the odd sensations breaking over me, but they filled me with an almost unbearable lightness—*I felt good!* So good that when Neferet faced the flame that burned in the middle of the room and the rest of us turned to the interior of the circle I had to press my lips tightly together to keep from laughing out loud. The drop-dead gorgeous poet was standing across the fire from Neferet and I could see that he was holding a big purple candle in his hands.

"And last, I summon spirit to complete our circle and ask that you fill us with connection, so that as your children we may prosper together."

Unbelievably, I felt my own spirit leap, like there were bird wings fluttering around inside my chest, as the poet lit the candle from the huge flame and then placed it on the table. Then Neferet began to move around within the circle, speaking to us, meeting our eyes, including us in her words.

"This is the time of the fullness of the moon. All things wax and wane, even Nyx's children, her vampyres. But on this night the powers of life, of magick, and of creation are at their brightest—as is our Goddess's moon. This is the time of building . . . of doing."

My heart was beating hard as I watched Neferet speak, and I realized with a little start that she was actually giving a sermon. This was a worship service, but the casting of the circle and Neferet's words coupled to touch me like no other sermon had ever even begun to do. I glanced around. Maybe it was the setting. The room was misty with incense and magical in the flickering candlelight. Neferet was everything a High Priestess should be. Her beauty was a flame of its own, and her voice was a magic that held everyone's attention. No one was slumped down in a pew sleeping or sneakily doing sudoku.

"This is a time when the veil between the mundane world and the strange and beautiful realms of the Goddess become thin indeed. On this night may one transcend the boundaries of the worlds with ease, and know the beauty and enchantment of Nyx."

I could feel her words wash against my skin and close my throat. I shivered and the Mark on my forehead suddenly felt warm and tingly. Then the poet began to speak in his deep, powerful voice.

"This is a time for weaving the ethereal into being, of spinning the strands of space and time to bring forth Creation. For life is a circle as well as a mystery. Our Goddess understands this, as does her consort, Erebus."

As he spoke I felt better about Elizabeth's death. Suddenly it didn't seem so scary, so horrible. It seemed more like a part of the natural world, a world that we all had a place in.

"Light . . . dark . . . day . . . night . . . death . . . life . . . all is tied together by spirit and the touch of the Goddess. If we keep the balance and look to the Goddess we can learn to weave a spell of moonlight and fashion with it a fabric of pure magical substance to keep with us all the days of our lives."

"Close your eyes, Children of Nyx," Neferet said "and send a secret desire to your Goddess. Tonight, when the veil between the worlds is thin—when magic is afoot within the mundane—perhaps Nyx will grant your petitions and dust you with the gossamer mist of dreams fulfilled."

Magic! They actually were praying for magic! Would it work—could it work? Was there *really* magic in this world? I remembered the way my spirit had been able to see words and how the Goddess had called me with her visible voice down into the crevasse and then kissed my forehead and changed my life forever. And how, just moments ago, I'd felt the power of Neferet's calling of the elements. I hadn't imagined it—I *couldn't* have imagined it.

I closed my eyes and thought about the magic that seemed to surround me, and then I sent up my wish into the night. *My secret wish is that I belong . . . that I have finally found a home no one can take away from me.*

Despite the unusual warmth of my Mark, my head felt light and unimaginably happy as Neferet called for us to open our eyes and, in a voice that was at the same time soft and powerful—woman and warrior combined—she continued the ritual.

"This is a time of traveling unseen in the full moonlight. A time to listen for music not fashioned by human or vampyre hands. It is a time for oneness with the winds that caress us"—Neferet bowed her head slightly to the east—"and the bolt of lightning that mimics the spark of first life." She tilted her head to the south. "It is a time to revel in the eternal sea and the warm rains that soothe us, as well as the verdant land that surrounds and keeps us." She acknowledged the west and north in turn.

And each time Neferet named an element it felt as though a jolt of sweet electricity sizzled through my body.

Then the four women who personified the elements moved as one to the table. With Neferet and Loren, each of them lifted a goblet.

"All hail, O Goddess of Night and the full moon!" Neferet said. "All hail Night, from whom our blessings come. On this night we give thanks to thee!"

Still holding the goblets, the four women scattered back to their places in the circle.

"In the mighty name of Nyx," Neferet said.

"And of Erebus," the poet added.

"We ask from within your sacred circle that you give us the knowledge to speak the language of the wilds, to fly with the freedom of the bird, to live the power and grace of the feline, and to find an ecstasy and joy in life that would stir the very heights of our being. Blessed be!"

I couldn't stop grinning. I'd never heard stuff like this in church before, and I sure as hell had never felt so energized there, either!

Neferet drank from the goblet she held, and then she offered it to Loren, who drank from it and said "blessed be." Mirroring their actions, the four women moved quickly around the circle, allowing each person, fledgling and adult, to drink from a goblet. When it was my turn I was happy to see the familiar face of Penthesilea offer me a drink and a blessing. The wine was red and I expected it to be bitter, like the sip of my mom's hidden Cabernet I tried once (and definitely did not like), but it wasn't. It was sweet and spicy and it made my head feel even lighter.

When everyone had been given a drink, the goblets were returned to the table.

"Tonight I want each of us to spend at least a moment or two alone in the light of the full moon. Let its light refresh you and help you to remember how extraordinary you are . . . or you are becoming." She smiled at some of the fledglings, including me. "Bask in your uniqueness. Revel in your strength. We stand separate from the world because of our gifts. Never forget that, because you may be sure the world never will. Now let us close the circle and embrace the night."

In reverse order, Neferet thanked each element and sent them away as each candle was blown out, and as she did so I felt a little twinge of sadness, like I was saying good-bye to friends. Then she completed the ritual by saying, "This rite is ended. Merry meet and merry part and merry meet again!"

The crowd echoed: "Merry meet and merry part and merry meet again!"

And that was it. My first ritual of the Goddess was over.

The circle broke up quickly—more quickly than I would have liked it to. I wanted to stand there and think about the amazing things I had felt, especially during the calling of the elements, but that was impossible. I was carried out of the temple on a tide of chatter. I was glad that everyone was so busy talking that no one noticed how quiet I was; I didn't think I could explain to them what had just happened to me. Hell! I couldn't even explain it to myself.

"Hey, you think they'll have Chinese food again tonight? I just loved it last full moon when they had that yummy moo goo stuff afterward," Shaunee said. "Not to mention, my fortune cookie said 'You will make a name for yourself,' which is way cool."

"I'm so starved I don't care what they feed us as long as they feed us," Erin said.

"Me too," Stevie Rae said.

"For once we are in perfect agreement," Damien said, linking arms with Stevie Rae and me. "Let's eat."

And suddenly, that reminded me. "Uh, guys." That nice tingly feeling the ritual had given me was gone. "I can't go. I have to—"

"We're morons." Stevie Rae thumped herself on the forehead hard enough to make a smacking sound. "We totally forgot."

"Ah, crap!" Shaunee said.

"The hags from hell," Erin said.

"Want me to save you a plate of something?" Damien asked sweetly.

"No. Aphrodite said they're going to feed me."

"Probably raw meat," Shaunee said.

"Yeah, from some poor kid she caught in her nasty spider web," Erin said.

"By that she means the one between her legs," Shaunee explained.

"Stop, you're freaking Zoey out," Stevie Rae said as she started nudging me toward the door. "I'll show her where the rec hall is, then I'll meet you guys at our table."

Outside I said, "Okay, tell me that they're kidding about the raw meat."

"They're kidding?" Stevie Rae said unconvincingly.

"Great. I don't even like my steak rare. What am I going to do if they really do try to feed me raw meat?" I refused to think about what kind of raw meat it might be.

"I think I have a Tums somewhere in my purse. Do you want it?" Stevie Rae asked.

"Yeah," I said, already feeling nauseous.

CHAPTER SIXTEEN

—

"That's it." Stevie Rae had stopped, looking uncomfortable and apologetic in front of the steps that led to a round brick building situated on a little hill overlooking the eastern part of the wall surrounding the school. Huge oaks wrapped it in darkness within darkness, so I could barely make out flickers of either gas or candles lighting up the entrance. Not one speck of light was coming from the darkened windows that were long and arched and seemed to be made of stained glass.

"Okay, well, thanks for the Tums." I tried to sound brave. "And save a place for me. This really can't take that long. I should be able to get done here and join you guys for dinner."

"Don't rush. Really. You might meet someone you like and want to hang out. Don't worry about it if you do. I won't be mad and I'll just tell Damien and the Twins that you're reconnoitering."

"I'm not going to become one of them, Stevie Rae."

"I believe you," she said, but her eyes looked suspiciously big and round.

"So I'll see you soon."

" 'Kay. See you soon," she said, and started to follow the sidewalk back to the main building.

I didn't want to watch her walk away—she looked all forlorn and spanked puppylike. Instead I climbed up the steps and told myself that this was going to be no big deal—nothing worse than the time my Barbie sister talked me into going to cheerleading camp with her (I don't know what the hell I'd been thinking). At least this fiasco wouldn't last a week. They'll probably cast another circle, which was actually very cool, do some unusual praying like Neferet did, and then break for dinner. That would be my cue to smile nicely and slip out. Easy-peasy.

The torches on either side of the thick wooden door were lit by gas and not the raw flame sconces used in Nyx's Temple. I reached my hand toward the heavy iron knocker, but, with a sound that was disturbingly like a sigh, it opened away from my touch.

"Merry meet, Zoey."

Oh. My. God. It was Erik. He was wearing all black, and his dark, curly hair and his insanely blue eyes reminded me of Clark Kent—well, okay, without the dorky glasses and the nerdy slicked-back hair . . . so . . . I supposed that would mean he actually reminded me (again) of Superman—well, without the cape or tights or the big S . . .

Then the babble in my mind totally shut itself up when his oil-dampened finger slid over my forehead, tracing the five points of the pentagram.

"Blessed be," he said.

"Blessed be," I replied, and would be eternally grateful that my voice didn't croak or crack or squeak. Ah, man, he smelled *good*, but I couldn't place what he smelled like. It wasn't any of the tired, overused colognes guys apply by the gallon. He smelled like . . . he smelled like . . . the forest at night just after it's rained . . . something earthy and clean and . . .

"You can come on in," he was saying.

"Oh, uh, thanks," I said brilliantly. I stepped inside. And then I stopped. The interior was all one big room. The circular-shaped walls were draped in black velvet, totally blocking the windows and the silver moonlight. I could see that under the heavy curtains there were weird shapes, which started to freak me out until I realized that—hello—it's a rec room. They must have shoved the TVs and game stuff to the sides of the room and covered them so everything would look, well, creepier. Then my attention was captured by the circle itself. It was situated in the middle of the room and made up entirely of candles in tall red glass containers, like the prayer candles you can buy in the Mexican foods section of the grocery store that smell like roses and old ladies. There must have been more than a hundred of them and they lit up the kids who were standing in a loose circle behind them talking and laughing with a ghostly light that was tinted red. The kids were all wearing black and I noticed right away that none of them were wearing any embroidered rank insignias, but each had a thick silver chain that glittered around their necks from which an odd symbol dangled. It looked like two crescent moons positioned back to back against a full moon.

"There you are, Zoey!"

Aphrodite's voice slid across the room just ahead of her body. She was wearing a long black dress that flashed with onyx beading, reminding me weirdly of a dark version of Neferet's beautiful gown. She had on the same necklace as the others, but hers was bigger and outlined in red jewels that might have been garnets. Her blond hair was loose and draped around her like a gold veil. She was entirely too pretty.

"Erik, thanks for making Zoey welcome. I can take it from here." She sounded normal, and she even rested her manicured fingertips on Erik's arm for a second in what the uninformed might think of as just a friendly gesture, but her face told a different story. It was set and cold, and her eyes seemed to blaze into his.

Erik barely gave her a look, and he definitely moved his arm away from her touch. Then he gave me a quick smile and, without glancing at Aphrodite again, walked away.

Great. Exactly what I didn't need was to get in the middle of a nasty breakup. But I couldn't seem to help the fact that my eyes followed him across the room.

Stupid me. Again. Sigh.

Aphrodite cleared her throat, and I tried (unsuccessfully) not to look like I'd been caught doing something I shouldn't have been doing. Her slick, mean smile said there was absolutely no doubt that she'd noticed my interest in Erik (and his interest in me). And, again, I wondered if she knew it had been me in the hall the day before.

Well, it wasn't like I could ask her.

"You need to hurry, but I brought something for you to change into." Aphrodite was talking quickly as she motioned for me to follow her to the girls' restroom. She threw me a disgusted look over her shoulder. "It's not like you can come to a Dark Daughters' ritual dressed like that." Once we were in the bathroom she brusquely handed me a dress that had been hanging from one of the partitions and kinda pushed me into the stall. "You can put your clothes on the hanger and carry them back to the dorm like that."

There didn't seem to be any arguing with her and, anyway, I felt like an outsider enough as it was. Being dressed differently made me feel like I'd shown up at a party dressed like a duck, but no one had told me it wasn't a costume party so everyone else was wearing jeans.

I quickly got out of my clothes and slid the black dress over my head, sighing with relief when it fit. It was simple but flattering. The material was the soft clingy stuff that never wrinkles. It had long sleeves and a round neckline that showed most of my shoulders (good thing I'd worn my black bra). All around the neckline, the edge of the long sleeves, and the hem, which was right above my knee, were sewn little red sparkly beads. It really was pretty. I slipped my shoes back on thinking, happily, that a nice pair of ballet flats can go with just about any outfit, and stepped out of the stall.

"Well, at least it fits." I said.

But I noticed Aphrodite wasn't looking at the dress. She was looking at my Mark, which bugged the crap out of me. Okay, my Mark is colored in—get over it already! I didn't say anything, though. I mean, this was her "party" and I was a guest. Translation: I was totally outnumbered, so I better be good.

"I'll be leading the ritual, of course, so I'm gonna be too busy to hold your hand through it."

Okay, I should've just kept my mouth shut, but she was wearing on my last nerve. "Look, Aphrodite, I don't need you to hold my hand."

Her eyes narrowed and I braced myself for another psycho girl scene. Instead she smiled a totally non-nice smile that made her look like a snarling dog. Not that I was calling her a bitch, but the analogy seemed scarily accurate.

"Of course you don't need your hand held. You'll just breeze right through this little ritual like you've breezed through everything else here. I mean, after all, you *are* Neferet's new favorite."

Wonderful. On top of the Erik issue and the weirdness over my Mark issue, she was jealous that Neferet was my mentor.

"Aphrodite, I don't think I'm Neferet's new favorite. I'm just new." I tried to sound reasonable, and I even smiled.

"Whatever. So, are you ready?"

I gave up trying to reason with her and nodded, wishing this whole ritual thing would hurry up and be over.

"Fine. Let's go." She led me out of the rest room and over to the circle. I recognized the two girls we walked up to as two of the "hags from hell" who had followed her around in the cafeteria. Only instead of wearing pursed-face, I-just-ate-a-lemon expressions, they were smiling warmly at me.

No. I wasn't fooled. But I made my face smile, too. When in enemy territory it's best to blend in and look inconspicuous and/or stupid.

"Hi, I'm Enyo," said the taller of the two. She was, of course, blonde, but her long, flowing locks were more the color of waving wheat than gold. Although in the candlelight it was hard to be sure which cliché was a more appropriate description. And I still didn't believe she was a natural blonde.

"Hi," I said.

"I'm Deino," said the other girl. She was obviously mixed and had a gorgeous combination of really pretty, coffee-with-lots-of-cream skin and excellent thick, curly hair, which probably had never had the nerve to nap up on her for an instant, no matter the humidity.

The two of them were freakishly perfect.

"Hi," I said again. Feeling more than a little claustrophobic, I moved into the space they'd created between them.

"You three enjoy the ritual," Aphrodite said.

"Oh, we will!" Enyo and Deino said together. The three of them shared a look that made my skin crawl. I turned my attention away from them before my better judgment won out over my pride and I bolted from the room.

I had a good view of the inner area of the circle now, and again it was similar to the one in Nyx's Temple, except this one had a chair pulled up beside the table and there was someone sitting in it. Well, kinda sitting. Actually, the whoever was slumped down with the hood of a cloak covering his or her head.

Well . . . hmmm . . .

Anyway, the table was draped with the same black velvet as the walls, and there was a Goddess statue on it, a bowl of fruit and bread, several goblets, and a pitcher. And a knife. I squinted to be sure I was seeing right. Yep. It was a knife—it had a bone handle and a long, wicked curving blade that looked entirely too sharp to be used for cutting fruit or bread safely. A girl I thought I recognized from the dorm was lighting several fat sticks of incense that sat in ornately carved incense holders on the table, and totally ignoring whoever was slumped in the chair. Jeesh, was the kid asleep?

Immediately the air began to fill with smoke that I swear was green-tinged and curled, ghostlike, around the room. I expected it to smell sweet, like the incense at Nyx's Temple, but when a feathery wisp of smoke reached me and I breathed it in I was surprised by its bitterness. It was kinda familiar and I frowned, trying to figure out what it reminded me of . . . crap, what was it? It was almost like bay leaf, with a clovey middle. (I had to remember to thank Grandma Redbird later for teaching me about spices and their smells.) I sniffed again, intrigued, and my head felt a little woozy. Weird. Okay, the incense was odd. It seemed to change as it filled the room, like expensive perfume that changes with each person who wears it. I breathed in again. Yep. Clove and bay, but there was something at the end of it; something that made the scent finish tangy and bitter . . . dark and mystic and alluring in its . . . naughtiness.

Naughtiness? Then I knew.

Well, hell! They were filling the room with pot smoke mixed with spices. Unbelievable. I'd stood up to peer pressure and for years said no to even the most polite offers to try one of those gross-looking homemade joints that get passed around at parties and whatnot. (I mean, please. Is that even sanitary? And just exactly why would I want to do a drug that made me want to obsessively eat fattening snack foods?) And now here I stood, immersed in pot smoke. Sigh. Kayla would never believe it.

Then, feeling paranoid (probably another side effect of the pot invasion) I looked around the circle, sure I'd see a professor who was ready to leap in and haul us all away to . . . to . . . I dunno, something unspeakably horrid, like the boot camp Maury sends all of his troubled teen guests to.

But, thankfully, unlike the circle in Nyx's Temple, there were no adult vamps here, and only about twenty kids. They were talking quietly and acting like the totally illegal marijuana incense was no big deal. (Pot heads.) Trying to breathe shallowly, I turned to the girl to my right. When in doubt (or panic), make small talk.

"So . . . Deino is a, well, different name. Does it mean something special?"

"Deino means terrible," she said, smiling sweetly.

From my other side the tall blonde chimed in perkily, "And Enyo means warlike."

"Huh," I said, trying hard to be polite.

"Yeah, Pemphredo, which means wasp, is the one lighting the incense," explained Enyo. "We got the names from Greek mythology. They were the three sisters of the Gorgon and Scylla. Myth says they were born as hags who shared an eye, but we decided that was probably just bullshit male-dominant propaganda written by human men who wanted to keep strong women down."

"Really?" I didn't know what else to say. Really.

"Yeah," Deino said. "Human men suck."

"They should all die," Enyo said.

On that lovely thought the music suddenly started, making it impossible (thankfully) to talk.

Okay, the music was disturbing. It had a deep, pulsing beat that was ancient as well as modern. Like someone had mixed one of those nasty bootie-humping songs with a tribal mating dance. And then, much to my shock, Aphrodite began to dance her way around the circle. Yes, I suppose you could say she was hot. I mean, she had a good body and she moved like Catherine Zeta-Jones in *Chicago*. But somehow it didn't work for me. And I don't mean because I'm not gay (even though I'm not gay). It didn't work because it seemed like a crude imitation of Neferet's dance to "She Walks in Beauty." If this music was a poem it would be more like "Some Ho Grinds Her Bootie."

During Aphrodite's crotch-flailing display everyone was, naturally, staring at her, so I looked around the circle, pretending that I wasn't really looking for Erik, until . . . oh, crap . . . I found him almost directly opposite me. And he was the one kid in the room not watching Aphrodite. He was watching me. Before I could figure out whether I should look away, smile at him or wave or whatever (Damien had said to smile at the kid, and Damien was a self-proclaimed expert on guys), the music stopped and I looked from Erik to Aphrodite. She was standing in the middle of the circle in front of the table. Purposefully, she picked up a big purple pillar candle in one hand, and the knife in another. The candle was lit, and she carried it, holding it in front of her like a beacon, to the side of the circle where I now noticed one yellow candle nestled amongst the red ones. I didn't need any prodding from Warlike or Terrible (yeesh) to turn to the east. As wind ruffled my hair, from the corner of my vision I could see that she had lit the yellow candle and now she raised the knife, slashing a pentagram in the air as she spoke:

O winds of storm, in Nyx's name I do call thee forth,
cast thy blessing, I do ask,
upon the magic which shall be worked here!

I will admit that she was good. Though not as powerful as Neferet, it was obvious that she'd practiced voice control and the silky sound of her words carried easily. We turned to the south and she approached the large red pillar candle among the other red ones, and I could feel what I was already recognizing as the power of the fire and the magic circle wash over my skin.

O fire of lightning, in Nyx's name I do call thee forth,
bringer of storms and power of magic,
I ask your aid in the spell I do here work!

We turned again and, along with Aphrodite, I felt flushed and unexpectedly drawn to the blue candle that nestled within the red ones. Even though it thoroughly freaked me out, I had to keep myself from stepping from circle and joining her in the invocation of water.

O torrents of rain, in Nyx's name I do call thee forth.
Join me with your drowning strength, in performing this
most powerful of rituals!

What in the hell was wrong with me? I was sweating and instead of feeling just a little warm, like during the earlier ritual, the Mark on my forehead was hot—burning hot—and I swear I could hear the roar of the sea in my ears. Numbly, I turned again to the right.

O earth, deep and damp, in Nyx's name I do call thee forth,
that I may feel the earth herself move in the roar of the storm
   of power
which doth come when you aid me in this rite!

Aphrodite sliced the air again, and I could feel the palm of my right hand tingle, as if it ached to hold the knife and cut the air.

I smelled cut grass and heard the cry of a whippoorwill, like it was nesting invisibly in the air beside me. Aphrodite moved back to the center of the circle. Placing the still-burning purple candle back on its place in the middle of the table she completed the casting.

O spirit, wild and free, in Nyx's name I do call thee to me!
Answer me! Stay with me during this mighty ritual
and grant me thy Goddess's power!

And somehow I knew what she was going to do next. I could hear the words inside my mind—inside my own spirit. When she raised the goblet and began walking around the circle I felt her words, and even though she didn't have the poise and power of Neferet what she said ignited within me, like I was burning from the inside out.

"This is the time of the fullness of our Goddess's moon. There is magnificence to this night. The ancients knew the mysteries of this night, and used them to strengthen themselves . . . and to split the veil between worlds and have adventures we only dream about today. Secret . . . mysterious . . . magical . . . true beauty and power in vampyre form—not tainted by human rules or law. We are *not* humans!" With this, her voice did ring against the walls, very much as Neferet's had earlier. "And all your Dark Daughters and Sons ask tonight in this rite is what we have petitioned each full moon for the past year. Free the power within us so that, like the mighty felines of the wild, we know the lithe suppleness of our animal brethren and we are not bound by human chains or caged by their ignorant weaknesses."

Aphrodite had stopped right in front of me. I knew I was flushed and breathing hard, just as she was. She raised the goblet and offered it to me.

"Drink, Zoey Redbird, and join us in asking Nyx for what is ours by the right of blood and body and the Mark of the great Change—the Mark that she has already touched you with."

Yes, I know. I should have probably said no. But how? And suddenly I didn't want to. I definitely didn't like or trust Aphrodite, but wasn't what she was saying basically true? My mother and stepfather's reactions to my Mark came back hard and clear in my memory, along with Kayla's look of fear and Drew's and Dustin's revulsion. And how no one had called me, or even text-messaged me, since I'd been gone. They'd just let me be dumped here to deal with a new life all on my own.

It made me sad, but it also made me mad.

I grabbed the goblet from Aphrodite and took a big drink. It was wine, but it didn't taste like the wine in the other moon ritual. This one was sweet, too, but there was a spice to it that tasted like nothing I'd ever experienced before. It caused an explosion of sensation in my mouth that traveled with a hot, bittersweet trail down my throat and filled me with a dizzy desire to drink more and more and more of it.

"Blessed be," Aphrodite hissed at me as she jerked the goblet from me, sloshing some of the red liquid over my fingers. Then she gave me a tight, triumphant smile.

"Blessed be," I replied automatically, head still reeling with the taste of the wine. She moved to Enyo, offering her the goblet, and I couldn't stop myself from licking my fingers to get one more taste of the wine that had spilled there. It was beyond delicious. And it smelled . . . it smelled familiar . . . but through the whoosh of dizziness in my head I couldn't concentrate enough to figure out where I'd smelled something that incredible before.

It hardly took any time for Aphrodite to travel around the circle, giving each of the kids a taste from the goblet. I watched her closely, wishing I could have more as she returned to the table. She lifted the goblet again.

"Great and magical Goddess of Night and of the full moon, she who rides through the thunder and the tempest, leading the spirits and the Elder Ones, beautiful and awesome one, who even those most ancient must obey, aid us in what we ask. Fill us with your power and magic and strength!"

Then she upended the goblet, and I watched, jealously, as she drank until she drained the last drops. When she finished drinking, the music started up again. In time with it she made her way back around the circle, dancing and laughing as she blew out each candle and told each element good-bye. And somehow, as she was moving around the circle, my vision got all screwed up because her body rippled and changed and it suddenly seemed as if I was watching Neferet again—only now she was a younger, rawer version of the High Priestess.

"Merry meet and merry part and merry meet again!" she finally said. We all responded while I blinked my vision clear and the weird image of Aphrodite-as-Neferet faded, as did the burning of my Mark. But I could still taste the wine on my tongue. It was way strange. I don't like alcohol. Seriously. I just don't like the way it tastes. But there was something about this wine that was delicious beyond . . . well, beyond even Godiva dark chocolate truffles (I know, it's hard to believe). And I still couldn't figure out why it somehow seemed familiar.

Then everyone started to talk and laugh as the circle broke up. The gaslights came on overhead, making us blink from their brightness. I looked across the circle, trying to see if Erik might still be watching me, and a movement at the table caught my eye. The person who had been slumped and motionless during the entire ritual was finally moving. He kinda jerked around, awkwardly pulling himself more into a sitting position. The hood on the dark cloak fell back, and I was shocked to see bright orange-red, bushy, unattractive hair and a pudgy too-white and freckled face.

It was that annoying Elliott kid! Very, very odd that he was here. What could the Dark Daughters and Sons want with him? I looked around the room again. Yep, as I'd suspected, there wasn't one ugly, dorky-looking kid present. Everyone, and I do mean everyone, except Elliott was attractive. He definitely didn't belong.

He was blinking and yawning and looked like he'd been sniffing way too much of the incense. He lifted his hand to wipe something off his nose (probably one of the boogers he liked to go spelunking after) and I saw the white of thick bandages that were wrapped around his wrists. What the . . . ?

A terrible, crawly feeling worked its way up my spine. Enyo and Deino were standing not far from me, talking animatedly to the girl they'd called Pemphredo. I walked over to them and waited till there was a lull in the conversation. Pretending that my stomach wasn't trying to squeeze itself to death, I smiled and nodded in the general direction of Elliott.

"What's that kid doing here?"

Enyo glanced at Elliott and then rolled her eyes. "He's nothing. Just the refrigerator we used tonight."

"What a loser," Deino said, dismissing Elliott with a sneer.

"He's practically *human*," Pemphredo said in disgust. "No wonder all he's good for is a snack bar."

My stomach felt like it was being turned inside out. "Wait, I don't get it. Refrigerator? Snack bar?"

Deino the Terrible turned her haughty, chocolate-colored eyes on me. "That's what we call humans—refrigerators and snack bars. You know—breakfast, lunch, and dinner."

"Or any of the meals in between," warlike Enyo practically purred.

"I still don't—" I started, but Deino interrupted me.

"Oh, come on! Don't pretend that you couldn't tell what was in the wine, and that you didn't *love* the taste of it."

"Yeah, admit it, Zoey. It was obvious. You would have downed the whole thing—you wanted it even more than we did. We saw you licking it off your fingers," Enyo said, leaning forward all into my personal space as she stared at my Mark. "That makes you some kind of freak, doesn't it? Somehow you're fledgling and vamp, all in one, and you wanted more of that kid's blood than just a taste."

"Blood?" I didn't recognize my own voice. The word "freak" kept echoing round and round in my head.

"Yes, *blood*," Terrible said.

I felt hot and cold at once and looked away from their knowing faces, and right into Aphrodite's eyes. She was standing across the room from me talking to Erik. Our eyes locked and slowly, purposefully, she smiled. She was holding the goblet again, and she raised it in an almost imperceptible salute to me before taking a drink from it and turning back to laugh at something Erik had just said.

Holding myself together, I made a lame excuse to Warlike, Terrible, and the Wasp, and walked calmly from the room. The instant I closed the thick wooden door of the rec hall behind me I ran like a crazy blind person. I didn't know where I was going, except that I wanted to be away.

I drank blood—that horrid Elliott kid's blood—and I'd liked it! And worse, the delicious smell had been familiar because I'd smelled it before when Heath's hands had been bleeding. It hadn't been a new cologne I'd been drawn to; it had been his blood. And I'd smelled it again in the hall yesterday when Aphrodite had slit Erik's thigh and I had wanted to lick up his blood, too.

I was a freak.

Finally, I couldn't breathe and I collapsed against the cool stone of the school's protective wall, gasping for air and puking my guts up.

CHAPTER SEVENTEEN

—

Shakily, I wiped the back of my hand across my mouth and then stumbled away from the puke spot (I refused to even consider what I puked up and how it must have looked) until I came to a giant oak that had grown so close to the wall that half of its branches hung over the other side of it. I leaned against the tree, concentrating on not getting sick again.

What had I done? What was happening to me?

Then, from somewhere in the limbs of the oak I heard a meow. Okay, it wasn't really your normal, average, catlike meow. It was more like a grumpy, "me-eeh-uf-me-eef-uf-*snort.*"

I looked up. Perched on a limb that was resting against the wall was a small orange cat. She was staring at me with huge eyes and she definitely looked disgruntled.

"How did you get up there?"

"Me-uf," she said, sneezed, and inched her way along the branch, clearly trying to get closer to me.

"Well, come on kitty-kitty-kitty," I coaxed.

"Me-eeh-uf-ow," she said, creeping forward about half one of her little paw lengths.

"That's it, come on, baby girl. Move your little tiny paddies this way." Yes, I was displacing my freak-out and channeling it into saving the cat, but the truth was that I couldn't think about what had just happened. Not now. It was too soon. Too fresh. So the cat was an excellent distraction. Plus, she looked familiar. "Come on baby girl, come on . . ." I kept up a conversation with her as I hooked the toe of my flats into the rough brick of the wall and managed to pull myself up far enough so I could grab onto the lowest part of the branch the cat was on. Then I was able to use the branch as a kind of rope to climb farther up the wall, the whole time talking to the cat, while she kept complaining at me.

Finally I got within touching range of her. We stared at each other for a long time, and I started to wonder if she knew about me. Could she tell that I'd just tasted (and liked) blood? Did I have blood puke breath? Did I look different? Had I grown fangs? (Okay, that last question was ridiculous. Adult vamps don't have fangs, but still.)

She "me-eeh-uf-owed" at me again, and moved a little closer. I reached out and scratched the top of her head so that her ears went down and she closed her eyes, purring.

"You look like a little lioness," I told her. "See how much nicer you are when you're not complaining?" Then I blinked in surprise, realizing why she seemed so familiar. "You were in my dream." And a little happiness pushed through the wall of sickness and fear inside me. "You're my cat!"

The cat opened her eyes, yawned, and sneezed again, as if to comment on why it had taken me so long to figure it out. With a grunt of effort I scrambled up so that I was sitting on the wide top of the wall beside the branch where the cat was perched. With a kitty sigh, she jumped delicately off the branch, onto the top of the wall, and walked on tiny white paws over to me to crawl into my lap. There didn't seem to be anything for me to do except to scratch her on the head some more. She closed her eyes and purred loudly. I petted the cat and tried to still the tumult in my mind. The air smelled like it might rain, but the night was unusually warm for the end of October, and I put my head back, breathing deeply and letting the silver moonlight that peeked through the clouds calm me.

I looked at the cat. "Well, Neferet said that we should sit in the moonlight. I glanced up at the night sky again. "It would be better if the stupid clouds would blow away, but still . . ."

I had only just spoken the words and a gust of wind whistled around me, suddenly blowing away the wispy clouds.

"Well, thanks," I called aloud to nothing in particular. "That was a very convenient wind." The cat muttered, reminding me that I'd had the nerve to quit scratching her ears. "I think I'll call you Nala because you are a little lioness," I told her, resuming my scratching. "You know, baby girl, I'm so glad I found you today; I really needed something good to happen to me after the night I've had. You would not believe—"

A weird smell drifted up to me. It was so odd that I broke off what I was saying. What was that? I sniffed and wrinkled my nose. It was a dry, old smell. Like a house that had been closed up for too long, or somebody's scary old basement. It wasn't a good smell, but it also wasn't so gross that it made me want to gag. It was just wrong. Like it didn't belong out here in the open at night.

Then something caught at the corner of my eyesight. I looked down the long, winding brick wall. Standing there, half turned away from me like she wasn't sure which way she wanted to go, was a girl. The light from the moon, and my new and improved fledgling ability to see well at night, let me see her even though there were no outside lights near this part of the wall. I felt myself tense. Had one of those hateful Dark Daughters followed me? No way did I feel like dealing with any more of their crap tonight.

I must have actually voiced the frustrated groan I thought I had made in my mind, because the girl looked up toward where I was sitting on top of the wall.

I gasped in shock and felt fear skitter through me.

It was Elizabeth! The Elizabeth No Last Name kid who was supposed to be dead. When she saw me her eyes, which were a weird, glowing red, widened and then she made an odd shrieking sound before whirling around and disappearing with inhuman speed into the night.

At the same instant, Nala arched her back and hissed with such ferocity that her little body shook.

"It's okay! It's okay!" I said over and over, trying to calm the cat and me. Both of us were shaking and Nala was still growling low in her throat. "It couldn't have been a ghost. It couldn't have been. It was just . . . just . . . a weird kid. I probably scared her and she—"

"Zoey! Zoey! Is that you?"

I jumped and almost fell off the wall. It was too much for Nala. She gave another tremendous hiss and leaped neatly from my lap to the ground. Completely and utterly freaked out, I grabbed the branch for balance and squinted out into the night.

"Who—who is it?" I called over the pounding of my heart. Then I was blinded by the beams of two flashlights aimed directly at me.

"Of course it's her! Like I couldn't recognize my own best friend's voice? Jeesh, she hasn't been gone *that* long!"

"Kayla?" I said, trying to shield my eyes from the glare of the flashlights with my hand, which was shaking like crazy.

"Well, I told you we'd find her," a guy's voice said. "You always want to give up too soon."

"Heath?" Maybe I was dreaming.

"Yep! Whoo-hoo! We found ya, baby!" Heath yelled, and even in the awful flashlight glare I could see him hurl himself at the wall and then start to scramble up like a tall, blond, football-playing monkey.

Incredibly relieved it was him and not a boogie monster, I called down to him, "Heath! Be careful. If you fall you're going to break something." Well, unless he landed on his head—then he'd probably be okay.

"Not me!" he said, pulling himself up and over so that he was sitting beside me, straddling the wall. "Hey, Zoey, check it out— look at me; I'm king of the world!" He yelled, throwing out his arms, grinning like a total fool, and breathing alcohol-scented air all over me.

No wonder I'd refused to go out with him.

"Okay, there's no need to *forever* make fun of my unfortunate *ex*-infatuation with Leonardo." I glared at him, feeling more like myself than I had in hours. "Actually, it's kinda like my unfortunate *ex*-infatuation with you. Only it didn't last as long, and you didn't make a bunch of cheesy but cool movies."

"Hey, you're not still mad about Dustin and Drew are you? Forget them! They're retards." Heath said, giving me his puppy-dog look, which used to be really cute when he was in eighth grade. Too bad the cuteness had stopped working for him about two years ago. "And, anyway, we came all the way over here to bust you out."

"What?" I shook my head and squinted at him. "Wait. Turn those flashlights off. They're killing my eyes."

"If we turn them off we can't see," Heath said.

"Fine. Then turn them away. Uh, point them out there or something," I gestured out away from the school (and me). Heath turned the beam of the one he'd been clutching out into the night, and so did Kayla. I was able to drop my hand, which I was pleased to see had quit shaking, and stop squinting. Heath's eyes widened when he saw my Mark.

"Check it out! It's colored in now. Wow! It's like . . . like . . . on TV or something."

Well, it was nice to see that some things never change. Heath was still Heath—cute, but not the brightest Crayola in the pack.

"Hey! What about me? I'm here too, ya know!" Kayla called. "Someone help me get up there, but be careful. Let me put my new purse down. Oh, and I better take off these shoes. Zoey, you would not believe the sale you missed yesterday at Bakers. All of their summer shoes totally on closeout. I mean, *serious* closeout. Seventy percent off. I got five pairs for . . ."

"Help her up," I told Heath. "Now. It's the only way she'll stop talking."

Yep. Some things just didn't change.

Heath scooted around till he was on his belly, and then leaned down to offer his hands to Kayla. Giggling, she grabbed them and let him haul her up on top of the wall with us. And it was while she was giggling and he was hauling that I saw it—the unmistakable way Kayla grinned and giggled and blushed at Heath. I knew it as well as I knew I would never be a mathematician. Kayla liked Heath. Okay, not liked. She *liked* Heath.

Suddenly Heath's guilty comment about messing around on me at the party I'd missed made perfect sense.

"So how's Jared?" I asked abruptly, totally stopping K-babble's giggles.

"Okay, I guess," she said without meeting my eyes.

"You guess?"

She moved her shoulders and I saw that under her very cute leather jacket she was wearing the tiny little cream lace cami we used to call the Boob Shirt, because not only did it show a lot of cleavage, but it was the color of skin, so it looked like it was showing even more than it actually was.

"I dunno. We haven't really talked much the past couple days or so."

She still wouldn't look at me, but she did glance at Heath, who looked clueless—but that was really his only look. So my best friend was going after my boyfriend. Now that pissed me off, and for a second I wished it wasn't such a nice warm night. I wished it was cold and Kayla would freeze her over-developed boobies right off.

From the north the wind whipped around us suddenly, viciously, bringing an almost frightening chill.

Trying not to look obvious, Kayla pulled her jacket closed and giggled again, this time nervously instead of flirtatiously, and I got another big whiff of beer, and something else. Something that had been so recently imprinted into my senses that I was surprised I hadn't smelled it right away.

"Kayla you've been drinking *and* smoking?"

She shivered and blinked at me like a very slow rabbit. "Just a couple. Beers, I mean. And, well, um, Heath had one little bitty joint and I was really, really scared to come here, so I just had a couple tiny hits off it."

"She needed some fortification," Heath said, but he's never been good with words over two syllables, so it sounded like fort-fi-ka-shun.

"Since when have you started smoking pot?" I asked Heath.

He grinned. "It's no big deal, Zo. I just have a joint once in a while. They're safer than cigarettes."

I really hated it when he called me Zo.

"Heath," I tried to sound patient. "They are not safer than cigarettes, and even if they are that's not saying much. Cigarettes are disgusting and they kill you. And, seriously, the biggest losers at school smoke pot. Besides the fact that you really can not afford to kill any more brain cells." I almost added "or sperms," but I didn't want to go there. Heath would definitely get the wrong idea if I made a reference to his man parts.

"Nu uh," Kayla said.

"What Kayla?"

She was still clutching her jacket against the chill. Her eyes had changed from pitiful rabbit to sly, tail-twitchy cat. I recognized the change. She did it constantly with people she didn't consider part of her girlfriend group. It used to drive me crazy and I would yell at her and tell her she shouldn't be so mean. Now she was turning that crap on me?

"I said nu uh because not just losers smoke—at least not just once in a while. You know those two really hot running backs who play for Union, Chris Ford and Brad Higeons? I saw them at Katie's party the other night. They smoke."

"Hey, they're not that hot," Heath said.

Kayla ignored him and kept talking. "And Morgan smokes sometimes."

"Morgan, as in Morgie who's a Tigette?" Yes, I was pissed at K, but good gossip is good gossip.

"Yeah. She also just got her tongue and her"—K broke off and mouthed the word "clit"—"pierced. Can you imagine how much that must have hurt?"

"What? What did she get pierced?" Heath said.

"Nothing," K and I said together, for a moment sounding eerily like the best friends we used to be.

"Kayla, you're not staying on subject. Again. The Union football players have always been drug-happy. Hello! Please recall their steroid use, which is why it took sixteen years for us to beat them."

"Go, Tigers! Yeah, we kicked Union's ass!" Heath said.

I rolled my eyes at him.

"And Morgan has clearly begun losing her mind, which is why she's piercing her . . ." I glanced at Heath and reconsidered. "Her body *and* smoking. Tell me someone normal who's smoking."

K thought for a second. "Me!"

I sighed. "Look, I just don't think it's smart."

"Well, you don't always know *everything*." The hateful glint was back in her eyes.

I looked from her to Heath, and then back to her again. "Clearly, you're right. I don't know *everything*."

Her mean look turned startled and then flattened out to mean again, and I suddenly couldn't help comparing her to Stevie Rae, who, even though I'd only known for a couple days, I was absolutely, totally sure would not ever go after my boyfriend, whether he was an almost-ex or not. I also didn't think she would run away from me and treat me like I was a monster when I needed her the most.

"I think you should leave," I said to Kayla.

"Fine," she said.

"It's probably not a good idea for you to come back again, either."

She shrugged one shoulder so that her jacket fell open and I could see the thin strap of the cami slip down her shoulder, making it clear she wasn't wearing a bra.

"Whatever," she said.

"Help her get down, Heath."

Heath was generally pretty good at following simple directions, so he hoisted Kayla down. She grabbed the flashlight and looked back up at us.

"Hurry up, Heath. I'm getting really cold." Then she spun around and started marching off toward the road.

"Well . . . ," Heath said a little awkwardly. "It did get cold all of a sudden."

"Yeah, it can quit now," I said absently, and didn't pay much attention when the wind suddenly stopped.

"Hey, uh, Zo. I really did come to bust you out."

"No."

"Huh?" Heath said.

"Heath, look at my forehead."

"Yeah, you have that half moon thing. And it's colored in, which is weird because it wasn't colored in before."

"Well, it is now. Okay, Heath, focus. I've been Marked. That means that my body is going through the Change to become a vampyre."

Heath's eyes went from my Mark and traveled down my body. I saw them hesitate at my boobs and then my legs, which made me realize that they were showing all naked almost up to my crotch because my skirt had hiked up when I climbed on top of the wall.

"Zo, whatever's happening to your body is cool with me. You look seriously hot. You've always been beautiful, but now you look like a real goddess." He smiled at me and touched my cheek gently, reminding me why I've liked him so much for such a long time. Despite his faults, Heath could be really sweet, and he always made me feel completely beautiful.

"Heath," I said softly. "I'm sorry, but things have changed."

"Not with me they haven't." Taking me completely by surprise he leaned forward, slid a hand up over my knee and kissed me.

I jerked back and grabbed his wrist. "Stop it Heath! I'm trying to talk to you."

"How about you talk, and I kiss?" he whispered.

I started to tell him no again.

Then I felt it.

His pulse under my fingers.

It was beating hard and fast. I swear I could hear it, too. And as he leaned into me to kiss me again I could see the vein that ran along his neck. It moved, beating strong as the blood pumped through his body. Blood . . . His lips touched mine and I remembered the taste of the blood in the goblet. That blood had been cold and mixed with wine, and from a weak, loser kid who was a nothing. Heath's blood would be hot and rich . . . sweet . . . sweeter than Elliott the Refrigerator. . . .

"Ow! Damn, Zoey. You scratched me!" He jerked his wrist from my hand. "Shit, Zo, you made me bleed. If you didn't want me to kiss you, all you had to do was say so."

He lifted his bleeding wrist to his mouth and sucked at the drop of blood that was glistening there. Then he raised his eyes to meet mine, and he froze. He had blood on his lips. I could smell it—it was like the wine, only better, worlds better. The scent of it wrapped around me and made the hair on my arms rise.

I wanted to taste it. I wanted to taste it more than anything I'd ever wanted in my life.

"I want . . ." I heard myself whisper in a voice I didn't know.

"Yes . . . ," Heath answered like he was in a trance. "Yes . . . whatever you want. I'll do whatever you want."

This time I leaned into him and touched my tongue to his lip, taking the drop of blood into my mouth where it exploded—heat, sensation, and a rush of pleasure I'd never known.

"More," I rasped.

Like he'd lost the ability to speak and could only nod, Heath lifted his wrist to me. It was barely bleeding, and when I licked the tiny scarlet line Heath moaned. The touch of my tongue seemed to do something to the scratch, because instantly it started dripping blood, faster . . . faster . . . My hands were shaking as I raised his wrist to my mouth and pressed my lips against his warm skin. I shivered and moaned in pleasure and—

"Oh my *God!* What are you doing to him!" Kayla's voice was a scream that pierced through the scarlet fog in my brain.

I dropped Heath's wrist as though it had burned me.

"Get away from him!" Kayla was shrieking. "Leave him alone!"

Heath didn't move.

"Go," I told him. "Go and don't ever come back."

"No," he said, looking and sounding oddly sober.

"Yes. Get out of here."

"Let him go!" Kayla yelled.

"Kayla, if you don't shut up I'll fly down there and suck every last bit of blood from your stupid cheating cow body!" I spit the words at her.

She squealed and took off. I turned back to Heath, who was still staring at me.

"Now you need to go, too."

"I'm not scared of you, Zo."

"Heath, I'm scared of me enough for both of us."

"But I don't mind what you did. I love you, Zoey. More now than I ever have."

"Stop it!" I didn't mean to yell, but I caused him to flinch at the power that had filled my words. I swallowed hard and calmed my voice. "Just go. Please." Then, searching for some way to make him leave I added, "Kayla's probably going to get the cops right now. Neither of us needs that."

"Okay, I'll go. But I won't stay away." He kissed me hard and quick. I felt a white-hot stab of pleasure when I tasted the blood that was still on our lips. Then he slid down the wall and disappeared into the darkness until all I could see of him was the little dot of light from his flashlight, and then, finally, not even that.

I wouldn't let myself think. Not yet. Moving methodically, like a robot, I used the branch to steady myself as I climbed down. My knees were shaking so badly that I was able to walk only the couple of feet to the tree where I sank down on the ground, pressing my back against the security of its ancient bark. Nala materialized, hopping into my lap as if she'd been my cat for years instead of minutes, and as my sobs started she crawled from my lap to my chest to press her warm face against my wet cheek.

After what seemed like a long time my sobs turned to hiccups and I wished I hadn't run out of the rec hall without my purse. I could really use a Kleenex.

"Here. You look like you need this."

Nala complained as I jumped in surprise at the voice, and blinked up through my tears to see someone handing me a tissue.

"Th-thanks," I said, taking it and wiping my nose.

"No problem," Erik Night said.

CHAPTER EIGHTEEN

—

"Are you okay?"

"Yeah, I'm okay. Totally. Fine." I lied.

"You don't look fine," Erik said. "Mind if I sit down?"

"No, go ahead," I said listlessly. I knew my nose was bright red. I'd definitely been snotting on myself when he walked up, and I had the sneaking suspicion he'd witnessed at least part of the nightmare between Heath and me. The night was just getting worse and worse. I glanced at him and decided, *What the hell, I might as well continue the trend.* "In case you didn't realize it, it was me who saw that little scene between you and Aphrodite in the hall yesterday."

He didn't even hesitate. "I know, and I wish you hadn't. I don't want you to get the wrong idea about me."

"And what idea would that be?"

"That there's more going on between Aphrodite and me than there really is."

"Not my business," I said.

He shrugged. "I just want you to know that she and I are not going out anymore."

I almost said that it sure looked like Aphrodite wasn't aware of that, but then I thought about what had just happened between

Heath and me, and with a sense of surprise I realized that maybe I shouldn't judge Erik too harshly.

"Okay. You guys aren't going out," I said.

He sat quietly beside me for a little while, and when he spoke again I thought he sounded almost angry. "Aphrodite didn't tell you about the blood in the wine."

He hadn't said it like a question, but I answered anyway. "Nope."

He shook his head and I saw his jaw tighten. "She told me she was going to. She said she'd let you know while you were changing your clothes so that if you weren't okay with it you could skip drinking from the goblet."

"She lied."

"Not a big surprise," he said.

"Ya think?" I could feel my own anger building inside me. "This whole thing has just been wrong. I get pressured into going to the Dark Daughters' ritual where I'm tricked into drinking blood. Then I meet up with my almost-ex-boyfriend who just happens to be one hundred percent human, and no-damn-body bothered to explain to me that the tiniest speck of his blood would turn me into . . . into . . . a monster." I bit my lip and held on to my anger so I wouldn't start crying again. I also decided I wouldn't say anything about thinking I saw Elizabeth's ghost—that was too much weird to admit for one night.

"No one explained it to you because it's something that shouldn't have started to effect you until you were a sixth former," he said quietly.

"Huh?" I was back to being dazzlingly articulate.

"Bloodlust doesn't usually begin until you're a sixth former and you're almost completely Changed. Once in a while you'll hear about a fifth former who has to deal with it early, but that doesn't happen very often."

"Wait—what are you saying?" My mind felt like bees were buzzing around in it.

"You start having classes about bloodlust and other things mature vamps have to deal with during your fifth form, and then, in your final year, that's mostly what school focuses on—that and whatever you've decided to major in."

"But I'm a third former—barely I mean, I've only been Marked a few days."

"Your Mark is different; *you're* different," he said.

"I don't want to be different!" I realized I was shouting and got my voice under control. "I just want to figure out how to get through this like everybody else."

"Too late, Z," he said.

"So what now?"

"I think you'd better talk to your mentor. It's Neferet, isn't it?"

"Yeah," I said miserably.

"Hey, cheer up. Neferet's great. She hardly ever takes on fledglings to mentor anymore, so she must really believe in you."

"I know, I know. It's just that this makes me feel . . ." How *did* I feel about talking to Neferet about what had happened tonight? Embarrassed. Like I was twelve years old again and I had to tell our male gym teacher that I'd started my period and had to go to the locker room to change my shorts. I peeked sideways at Erik. There he sat, gorgeous and attentive and perfect. Hell. I couldn't tell him that. So instead I blurted, "Stupid. It makes me feel stupid." Which wasn't actually a lie, but mostly what it made me feel, besides embarrassed and stupid, was scared. I didn't want this thing that made it impossible for me to fit in.

"Don't feel stupid. You're actually way ahead of the rest of us."

"So . . . ," I hesitated, then took a deep breath and barreled on, "did you like the way the blood in the goblet tasted tonight?"

"Well, here's the deal with that: My first Full Moon Ritual with the Dark Daughters was at the end of my third former year. Except for the 'refrigerator' that night, I was the only third former there—just like you tonight." He gave a small, humorless laugh. "They only invited me because I'd finaled in the Shakespeare soliloquy contest and was being flown to London for the competition the next day." He glanced at me and looked a little embarrassed. "No one from this House of Night had ever made it to London. It was a big deal." He shook his head self-mockingly. "Actually, I thought *I* was a big deal. So the Dark Daughters invited me to join them, and I did. I knew about the blood. I was given the opportunity to turn it down. I didn't."

"But did you like it?"

This time his laugh was real. "I gagged and puked my guts up. It was the most disgusting thing I'd ever tasted."

I groaned. My head dropped forward and I put my face in my hands. "You're not helping me."

"Because you thought it was good?"

"Better than good," I said, my face still in my hands. "You say it was the most disgusting thing you'd ever tasted? I thought it was the most delicious. Well, the most delicious until I—" I stopped, realizing what I had been about to say.

"Until you tasted fresh blood?" he asked gently.

I nodded my head, afraid to speak.

He tugged at my hands, making me unbury my face. Then he put his finger under my chin and forced me to look straight at him.

"Don't be embarrassed or ashamed. It's normal."

"Loving the taste of blood is *not* normal. Not for me."

"Yes, it is. All vampyres have to deal with their lust for blood," he said.

"I am not a vampyre!"

"Maybe you're not—yet. But you're also definitely not the

average fledgling, and there's nothing wrong with that. You're special, Zoey, and special can be amazing."

Slowly, he took his finger from my chin and, as he had earlier that night, he traced the shape of a pentagram softly over my darkened Mark. I liked the way his finger felt against my skin—warm and a little rough. I also liked that being near him didn't set off all the weird reactions I'd had to being close to Heath. I mean, I couldn't hear Erik's blood beating or see the pulse in his neck jumping. Not that I'd mind if he kissed me. . . .

Hell! Was I becoming a vampyre slut? What was next? Would no male of any species (which might even include Damien) be safe around me? Maybe I should avoid all guys until I figured out what was going on with me and knew I could control myself.

Then I remembered that I had been trying to avoid everyone, which is why I was out here in the first place.

"What are you doing out here, Erik?"

"I followed you," he said simply.

"Why?"

"I figured I knew what Aphrodite had pulled in there and I thought you might need a friend. You're rooming with Stevie Rae, right?"

I nodded.

"Yeah, I thought about finding her and sending her out here to you, but I didn't know if you'd want her to know about . . ." He paused and made a vague gesture back in the direction of the rec hall.

"No! I—I don't want her to know." I stumbled over the words, I said them so fast.

"That's what I thought. So, that's why you're stuck with me." He smiled and then looked kinda uncomfortable. "I really didn't mean to listen in between you and Heath. Sorry about that."

I focused on petting Nala. So, he'd watched Heath kiss me, and then saw the whole blood thing. God, how embarrassing... Then a thought struck me and I glanced up at him, smiling ironically. "I guess that makes us even. I didn't mean to listen in between you and Aphrodite, either."

He smiled back at me. "We're even. I like that."

His smile made my stomach do funny things. "I wouldn't really have flown down and sucked Kayla's blood," I managed to say.

He laughed. (He had a really nice laugh.) "I know that. Vampyres can't fly."

"It freaked her out, though," I said.

"From what I saw, she deserved it." He waited a beat and then said, "Can I ask you something? It's kinda personal."

"Hey, you've seen me drink blood from a cup and like it, puke, kiss a guy, lick his blood like I'm a puppy, and then bawl my eyes out. And I've seen you turn down a blow job. I think I can manage to answer a kinda personal question."

"Was he really in a trance? He looked like it and he sounded like it."

I squirmed uncomfortably and Nala complained at me till I petted her quiet.

"It seemed like he was," I finally managed to say. "I don't know if it was a trance or not—and I totally didn't mean to put him under my power or anything freaky like that—but he did change. I dunno. He'd been smoking and drinking. He might have just been high." I heard Heath's voice again, rising from my memory like a cloying mist: *Yes ... whatever you want ... I'll do whatever you want.* And I saw that intense look he'd given me. Hell, I hadn't even known Heath the Jock was capable of that kind of intensity (at least off the football field). I knew for sure he couldn't spell the word (intensity, not football).

"Had he been like that the whole time, or just after you . . . um . . . started to—"

"Not the whole time. Why?"

"Well, that rules out two things that could have been making him act weird. One—if he was just high then he would have been like that the whole time. Two—he might have been acting like that because you're really pretty, and that alone could make a guy feel like he's in a trance around you."

His words made something flutter low in my stomach again—something that no guy had made me feel before. Not Heath the Jock, or Jordon the Sloth, or Jonathan the Stupid Band Kid (my dating history isn't long, but it's colorful).

"Really?" I said like a moron.

"Really." He smiled very unmoronically.

How could this guy like me? I'm a blood-drinking dork.

"But that wasn't it either, because he should have noticed how hot you look even before you kissed him, and what you're saying is that he didn't seem entranced until after blood came into the picture."

(*Entranced*—hee hee—he actually said *entranced*.) I was too busy grinning stupidly at his use of complex vocab to think before I answered him. "Actually, it happened when I started to hear his blood."

"Say again?"

Ah, crap. I hadn't meant to say that. I cleared my throat. "Heath started to change when I heard the blood pounding through his veins."

"Only adult vamps can hear that." He paused and then, with a quick smile added, "And Heath sounds like the name of a gay soap opera star."

"Close. He's BA's star quarterback."

Erik nodded and looked amused.

"Uh, by the way, I like what you changed your name to. Night is a cool last name," I said, trying to hold up my end of the conversation and say something even slightly insightful.

His smile widened. "I didn't change it. Erik Night is the name I was born with."

"Oh, well. I like it." Why didn't someone just shoot me?

"Thanks."

He glanced at his watch and I could see that it was almost six thirty—in the A.M., which still seemed freaky.

"It'll be getting light soon," he said.

Guessing that this was our cue for us to go our separate ways, I started to gather my feet under me and get a better hold on Nala so I could stand up, and I felt Erik's hand under my elbow, steadying me. He helped me up and then just stood there, so close that Nala's tail was brushing against his black sweater.

"I'd ask if you wanted to get something to eat, but the only place serving food right now is the rec hall, and I don't think you want to go back there."

"No, definitely not. But I'm not hungry anyway." Which, I realized as soon as I said it, was a big lie. At the mention of food I was suddenly starving.

"Well, do you mind if I walk you back to your dorm?" he asked.

"Nope," I said, trying to be nonchalant.

Stevie Rae, Damien, and the Twins would totally die if they saw me with Erik.

We didn't say anything as we started walking, but it wasn't an awkward, uncomfortable silence. Actually, it was nice. Once in a while our arms would brush against each other and I thought about how tall and cute he was and how much I'd like him to hold my hand.

"Oh," he said after a while, "I didn't finish answering your question before. The first time I tasted blood at one of the Dark Daughters' rituals I hated it, but it got better and better each time. I can't say I think it's delicious, but it's grown on me. And I definitely like the way it makes me feel."

I looked sharply at him. "Dizzy and kinda weak-kneed? Like you're drunk, only you're not."

"Yeah. Hey, did you know it's impossible for a vamp to get drunk?" I shook my head. "It's something about what the Change does to our metabolism. It's even tough for fledglings to get wasted."

"So drinking blood is the way vamps get wasted?"

He shrugged. "I suppose. Anyway, drinking human blood is forbidden for fledglings."

"Well then why hasn't anyone clued the teachers in on what Aphrodite's up to?"

"She's not drinking human blood."

"Uh, Erik, I was there. Blood was definitely in the wine and it came from that Elliott kid." I shuddered. "And what a gross choice he was, too."

"But he's not human," Erik said.

"Wait—it's forbidden to drink human blood," I said slowly. (Oh, hell! That's what I'd just done.) "But it's okay to drink another fledgling's blood?"

"Only if it's consensual."

"That makes no sense."

"Sure it does. It's normal for our bloodlust to develop as our bodies Change, so we need an outlet. Fledglings heal quickly, so there's no real chance of someone getting hurt. And there aren't any aftereffects, like when a vamp feeds off a living human."

What he was saying was banging through my head like the annoying, too-loud music that blared in Wet Seal, and I grasped the first thing I could think clearly about. "*Living* human?" I squeaked. "Tell me you don't mean versus feeding off a corpse." I was feeling a little nauseous again.

He laughed. "No, I mean versus drinking blood harvested from the vamps' blood donors."

"Never heard of such a thing."

"Most humans haven't. You won't learn about it until you're a fifth former."

Then some more of what he'd said broke through the confusion that was my mind. "What did you mean by aftereffects?"

"We just started learning about it in Vamp Sociology 312. Seems that when an adult vampyre feeds from a living human, there can be a very strong bond formed. It's not always on the part of the vamp, but humans become infatuated pretty easily. It's dangerous for the human. I mean, think about it. The blood loss alone isn't a good thing. Then add that to the fact that we outlive humans by decades, sometimes even centuries. Look at it from a human's point of view; it would really suck to be totally in love with someone who never seems to age while you get old and wrinkled and then die."

Again I thought about the dazed but intense way Heath had looked at me, and I knew that, no matter how hard it might be, I'd have to tell Neferet everything.

"Yep, that would suck," I said faintly.

"Here we are."

I was surprised to see that we'd stopped in front of the girl's dorm. I looked up at him.

"Well, thanks for following me—I think," I said, with a wry smile.

"Hey, any time you want someone to butt in when he's not invited, I'm the guy for you."

"I'll keep that in mind," I said. "Thanks." I hefted Nala up on my hip and started to open the door.

"Hey, Z," he called.

I turned back.

"Don't give back the dress to Aphrodite. By her including you in the circle tonight she formally offered you a position in the Dark Daughters, and it's tradition that the High Priestess in training gives a gift to the new member on her first night. I don't imagine you'll want to join, but you still have the right to keep the dress. Especially because you look so much better in it than she ever did." He reached forward and took my hand (the one that wasn't clutching my cat), and turned it over so that my wrist faced up. Then he took his finger and traced the vein that was close to the surface there, making my pulse jump crazily.

"And you should also know that I'm the guy for you if you decide you might like to try another sip of blood. Keep that in mind, too."

Erik bent and, still looking in my eyes, he lightly bit the pulse point at my wrist before kissing the spot softly. This time the fluttery feeling in my stomach was more intense. It made the inside of my thighs tingle and my breathing deepen. His lips still on my wrist he met my eyes and I felt a shiver of desire pass through my body. I knew he could feel me tremble. He let his tongue flick against my wrist, which made me shiver again. Then he smiled at me and walked away into the pre-dawn light.

CHAPTER NINETEEN

—

My wrist was still tingling from Erik's totally unexpected kiss (and bite and lick), and I wasn't sure I could speak yet, so I was relieved that there were only a few girls in the big entry room, and they did little more than glance at me before they went back to watching what sounded like *America's Next Top Model.* I hurried into the kitchen and plunked Nala down on the floor, hoping she wouldn't run off while I made a sandwich. She didn't; actually she followed me around the room like a little orange dog, complaining at me in her weird non-meow. I kept telling her "I know" and "I understand" because I figured she was yelling at me about what a moron I'd been tonight, and, well, she was right. Sandwich made, I grabbed a bag of pretzels (Stevie Rae had been right, I couldn't find any decent junk food in any of the cabinets), some brown pop (I don't really care what kind, just so that it's brown and not diet—eesh), and my cat, and I slipped up the stairs.

"Zoey! I've been so worried about you! Tell me everything." Curled up in bed with a book, Stevie Rae was obviously waiting up for me. She was wearing her pajamas that had cowboy hats all over the drawstring cotton pants, and her short hair was sticking out on one side as if she'd fallen asleep on it. I swear she looked about twelve years old.

"Well," I said brightly. "Looks like we have a pet." I turned so that Stevie Rae could see Nala squished against my hip. "Here, help me before I drop something. If it's the cat she'll probably never stop complaining."

"She's adorable!" Stevie Rae leaped up and rushed over to try to take Nala from me, but the cat clung to me as though someone would kill her if she let go, so Stevie Rae took my food instead and set it on my bedside table.

"Hey, that dress is amazing."

"Yeah, I changed before the ritual." Which reminded me that I was going to have to give it back to Aphrodite. Fine. I was not keeping the "gift," even though Erik had said I should. Anyway, returning it seemed like a good time to "thank" her for "forgetting" to clue me in about the blood. Hag bitch.

"So . . . how was it?"

I sat on my bed and gave Nala a pretzel, which she promptly started batting around (at least she'd stopped complaining), then I took a big bite of sandwich. Yes, I was hungry, but I was also buying time. I didn't know what I should tell Stevie Rae, and what I shouldn't. The blood thing was just so confusing—and so gross. Would she think I was awful? Would she be scared of me?

I swallowed and decided to steer the conversation to a safer topic. "Erik Night walked me home."

"Get out!" She bobbed up and down on the bed like a country jack-in-the-box. "Tell me *everything*."

"He kissed me," I said, crinkling my eyebrows at her.

"You have got to be kidding! Where? How? Was it good?"

"He kissed my hand." I decided quickly to lie. I didn't want to explain the whole wrist/pulse/blood/bite thing. "It was when he said good night. We were right in front of the dorm. And, yes, it was good." I grinned at her around another mouthful of sandwich.

"I'll bet Aphrodite shit puppies when you left the rec hall with him."

"Well, actually, I left before him and he caught up with me. I'd, uh, gone for a walk along the wall, which is where I found Nala," I scratched the cat's head. She curled up next to me, closed her eyes, and started purring. "Actually, I think *she* found *me*. Anyway, I had climbed up on the wall because I thought she needed rescuing, and then—and you will *not* believe this—I saw something that looked like Elizabeth's ghost, and then my almost-ex-boyfriend from SIHS, Heath, and my ex–best friend showed up."

"What? Who? Slow down. Start with Elizabeth's ghost."

I shook my head and chewed. Through bites of sandwich I explained. "It was really creepy and really weird. I was sitting up there on the wall petting Nala, and something caught my attention. I looked down and there was this girl standing not too far away from me. She looked up at me, with red glowing eyes, and I swear it was Elizabeth."

"No way! Were you totally freaked?"

"Totally. The second she saw me she gave this horrible shriek and then ran off."

"I would have been scared shitless."

"I was, only I hardly had time to think about it when Heath and Kayla showed up."

"What do you mean? How could they be here?"

"No, not *here,* they were outside the wall. They must have heard me trying to settle Nala down after she completely freaked at Elizabeth's ghost, because they came running up."

"Nala saw her, too?"

I nodded.

Stevie Rae shivered. "Then she must have really been there."

"Are you sure she's dead?" My voice was almost a whisper.

"There couldn't have been some mistake made and she's still alive but wandering around the school?" It sounded ridiculous, but not much more ridiculous than me seeing an actual ghost.

Stevie Rae swallowed hard. "She's dead. I saw her die. Everyone in class did."

She looked like she was going to cry and the whole subject was creeping me out, so I shifted to a less scary topic. "Well, I could be wrong. Maybe it was just some kid with weird eyes who looked like her. It was dark, and then Heath and Kayla were suddenly there."

"What was that all about?"

"Heath said they came to 'bust me out.' " I rolled my eyes. "Can you imagine?"

"Are they stupid?"

"Apparently. Oh, and then Kayla, my ex–best friend, made it obvious that she's after Heath!"

Stevie Rae gasped. "Slut!"

"No kidding. Anyway, I told them to leave and not come back, and then I got upset, which is when Erik found me."

"Aww! Was he sweet and romantic?"

"Yeah, he was, kinda. And he called me Z."

"Ooooh, a nickname is a seriously good sign."

"That's what I thought."

"So then he walked you back to the dorm?"

"Yeah, he said that he'd take me to get something to eat, but the only thing that was still open was the rec hall, and I didn't want to go back there." Ah, crap. I knew right away that I shouldn't have said that much.

"Were the Dark Daughters awful?"

I looked at Stevie Rae with her big deer-like eyes, and knew I couldn't tell her about drinking blood. Not yet. "Well, you know how Neferet was sexy and beautiful *and* classy?"

Stevie Rae nodded.

"Aphrodite did basically what Neferet did, but she looked like a ho."

"I've always thought that she was really nasty," Stevie Rae said, shaking her head in disgust.

"Tell me about it." I looked at Stevie Rae and blurted, "Yesterday, right before Neferet took me here to the dorm I saw Aphrodite trying to give Erik a blow job."

"No way! Jeesh, she's disgusting. Wait, you said she was *trying* to do it. What's up with that?"

"He was telling her no and pushing her away. He said he didn't want her anymore."

Stevie Rae giggled. "I'll bet that made her lose what little of her mind she has left."

I remembered how she'd been all over him, even when he was clearly telling her no. "Actually, I would have felt sorry for her if she hadn't been so . . . so . . ." I struggled to put it into words.

"Hag from hell–like?" Stevie Rae offered helpfully.

"Yeah, I guess that's it. She has this attitude, like it's her right to be as mean and nasty as she wants to be, and we should all just bow down and accept her."

Stevie Rae nodded. "That's how her friends are, too."

"Yeah, I met the awful triplets."

"You mean Warlike, Terrible, and Wasp?"

"Exactly. What were they thinking when they took those horrid names?" I said, popping pretzels in my mouth.

"They were thinking exactly what that entire group of hers thinks—that they are better than everyone else and untouchable because nasty Aphrodite is going to be the next High Priestess."

I spoke the next words as they whispered through my mind. "I don't think Nyx will allow that."

"What do you mean? They are already the 'in' group, and

Aphrodite has been leader of the Dark Daughters since her affinity became obvious during her fifth former year."

"What's her affinity?"

"She gets visions, like of future tragedies," Stevie Rae scowled.

"Do you think she fakes them?"

"Oh, heck no! She's amazingly accurate. What I think, and Damien and the Twins agree with me, is that she only tells about the visions if she has one when she's around people outside her little group."

"Wait, are you saying she knows about bad things that are going to happen in time to stop them, but she doesn't do anything about it?"

"Yep. Last week she had a vision during lunch, but the hags closed ranks around her and started leading her out of the dining hall. If Damien hadn't run right into them because he was late and hurrying in to lunch, making them scatter so that he could see that Aphrodite was in the middle of a vision, no one would ever have known. And a whole plane full of people would probably be dead."

I choked on a pretzel. Between coughs I sputtered, "A plane full of people! What the hell?"

"Yeah, Damien could tell Aphrodite was having a vision, so he got Neferet. Aphrodite had to tell her the vision, which was seeing a jet crash just after takeoff. Her visions are so clear that she could describe the airport and read the numbers on the tail of the plane. Neferet took that info and contacted the Denver airport. They double-checked the plane and found some problem that they hadn't noticed before, and said that if they hadn't fixed it the plane would have crashed immediately after takeoff. But I know darn well Aphrodite wouldn't have said a word if she hadn't been caught, even though she made up a big lie about her friends leading her from the dining hall because they knew she'd want to be taken to Neferet right away. Total b.s."

I started to say that I couldn't believe that even Aphrodite and her hags would purposefully allow the death of hundreds of people, but then I remembered the hateful stuff they'd said that night— *Human men suck . . . They should all die*—and I realized they hadn't just been talking; they'd been serious.

"So why didn't Aphrodite lie to Neferet? You know, tell her a different airport or switch the numbers of the plane around or something?"

"Vamps are almost impossible to lie to, especially when they ask you a direct question. And, remember, Aphrodite wants to be a High Priestess more than anything. If Neferet believed she was as twisted as she is, it would seriously hurt her future plans."

"Aphrodite has no business being a High Priestess. She's selfish and hateful, and so are her friends."

"Yeah, well, Neferet doesn't think so, and she was her mentor."

I blinked in surprise. "You've got to be kidding! And she doesn't see through Aphrodite's crap?" That couldn't be right; Neferet is way smarter than that.

Stevie Rae shrugged. "She acts different around Neferet."

"But still . . ."

"And she does have a powerful affinity, which has to mean that Nyx has special plans for her."

"Or she's a demon from hell, and she gets her power from the dark side. *Hello!* Has no one seen *Star Wars*? It was hard to believe Anakin Skywalker would turn, and look what happened there."

"Uh, Zoey. That's like total fiction."

"Still, I think it makes a good point."

"Well, try telling that to Neferet."

I chewed my sandwich and thought about it. Maybe I should. Neferet did seem way too smart to fall for Aphrodite's games. She probably already knew something was up with the hags. Maybe all she needed was someone to stand up and say something to her.

"So, has anyone ever tried to tell Neferet about Aphrodite?" I asked.

"Not that I know of."

"Why not?"

Stevie Rae looked uncomfortable. "Well, I think it seems kinda tattletale-like. Anyway, what would we tell Neferet? That we *think* Aphrodite *might* hide her visions, but that the only proof we have is that she's a hateful bitch." Stevie Rae shook her head. "No, I can't see that going over very well with Neferet. Plus, if by some miracle she believed us, what would Neferet do? It's not like she's going to kick her out of the school so she can cough herself to death on the streets. She'd still be here with her pack of hags and all those guys who would do anything for her if she snapped her little clawed fingers at them. I guess it's just not worth it."

Stevie Rae had a point, but I didn't like it. I really, really didn't like it.

Things might be different if a more powerful fledgling took Aphrodite's place as leader of the Dark Daughters.

I jumped guiltily, and covered it by taking a big gulp of pop. What was I thinking? I wasn't power hungry. I didn't want to be a High Priestess or get caught up in a pain-in-the-ass battle with Aphrodite and half the school (the more attractive half, at that). I just wanted to find a place for myself in this new life, a place that felt like home—a place where I fit in and was like the rest of the kids.

Then I remembered the electric jolts I'd felt during the casting of both circles, and how the elements had seemed to sizzle through my body, and also how I had had to force myself to stay in the circle and not join Aphrodite in the casting.

"Stevie Rae, when a circle's being cast, do you feel anything?" I asked abruptly.

"What do you mean?"

"Well, like when fire's called to the circle. Do you ever feel hot?"

"Nah. I mean, I really like the circle stuff, and sometimes when Neferet is praying I feel a zap of energy traveling through the circle itself, but that's it."

"So you've never felt a breeze when wind's called, or smelled rain with water, or felt grass under your feet with earth?"

"No way. Only a High Priestess with a major affinity for the elements would—" She broke off suddenly and her eyes got huge. "Are you saying that *you* felt that stuff? Any of that stuff?"

I squirmed. "Maybe."

"Maybe!" she squeaked. "Zoey! Do you have any idea what this could mean?"

I shook my head.

"Just last week in Soc class we were studying about the most famous vamp High Priestesses in history. There hasn't been a priestess with an affinity for all four of the elements for hundreds of years."

"Five," I said miserably.

"All five! You felt something with spirit, too!"

"Yeah, I think so."

"Zoey! This is amazing. I don't think there's ever been a High Priestess who felt all five of the elements." She nodded at my Mark. "It's that. It means you're different, and you really are."

"Stevie Rae, can we just keep this between us for a while? I mean, not even tell Damien or the Twins? I just—I just want to try to figure this out on my own a little. I feel like everything's happening too fast."

"But Zoey, I—"

"And I might be wrong," I interrupted quickly. "What if I was just excited and nervous because I'd never been in a ritual before? Do you know how embarrassed I'd be if I told people 'hey, I'm the only fledgling ever to have an affinity for all the elements' and it turned out to be nerves?"

Stevie Rae chewed her cheek. "I dunno, I still think you should tell someone."

"Yeah, then Aphrodite and her herd could be right there to gloat if it turned out that I was imagining things."

Stevie Rae paled. "Oh, man. You're totally right. That would be really awful. I won't say anything till you're ready. Promise."

Her reaction reminded me. "Hey, what is it Aphrodite did to you?"

Stevie Rae looked down at her lap, clasped her hands together, and hunched her shoulders as if she suddenly felt a chill. "She invited me to a ritual. I hadn't been here very long, only about a month or so, and I was kinda excited that the 'in' group wanted me." She shook her head, still not looking at me. "It was stupid of me, but I didn't really know anyone very well yet, and I thought maybe they would be my friends. So I went. But they didn't want me to be one of them. They wanted me to be a—a—blood donor for their ritual. They even called me 'refrigerator,' like I wasn't good for anything except holding blood for them. They made me cry and when I said no they laughed at me and kicked me out. That's how I met Damien, and then Erin and Shaunee. They were hanging out together and they saw me run out of the rec hall, so they followed me and told me not to worry about it. They've been my friends ever since." She finally looked up at me. "I'm sorry. I would have said something to you before, except I knew they wouldn't try that with you. You're too strong, and Aphrodite is too curious about your Mark. Plus, you're beautiful enough to be one of them."

"Hey, so are you!" I felt sick to my stomach thinking about Stevie Rae being slumped in the chair like Elliott . . . about drinking Stevie Rae's blood.

"No, I'm just kinda cute. I'm not them."

"I'm not them, either!" I yelled, causing Nala to wake up and mutter restlessly at me.

"I know you're not. That's not what I meant. I just meant that I knew they would want you in their group, so they wouldn't try to use you like that."

No, they managed to trick me and tried their best to freak me out. But why? Wait! I knew what they'd been up to. Erik said that the first time he drank blood he'd hated it, and had run out puking. I'd been here only two days. They'd wanted to do something that would disgust me so badly that I'd be scared away from them and their ritual forever.

They didn't want me to be part of the Dark Daughters, but they also didn't want to tell Neferet they didn't want me. Instead, they wanted *me* to refuse to join *them*. For whatever twisted reason, bully Aphrodite wanted to keep me out of the Dark Daughters. Bullies have always pissed me off, which meant, unfortunately, I knew what I had to do.

Ah, crap. I was going to join the Dark Daughters.

"Zoey, you're not mad at me, are you?" Stevie Rae said in a small voice.

I blinked, trying to clear my thoughts. "Of course not! You were right; Aphrodite didn't try to get me to do anything like giving blood." I popped the last bite of sandwich into my mouth, chewing fast. "Hey, I'm really beat. Do you think you could help me find a litter box for Nala so that I can get some sleep?"

Stevie Rae instantly brightened, and hopped off the bed with her usual perkiness. "Check this out." She practically skipped to the side of the room and held up a big green bag that had FELICIA'S SOUTHERN AGRICULTURE STORE, 2616 S. HARVARD, TULSA printed in bold white letters across it. From it she dumped onto the floor a litter box, food and water dishes, a box of Friskies cat food (with extra hairball protection), and a sack of kitty litter.

"How did you know?"

"I didn't. It was sitting in front of our door when I got back from dinner." She reached into the bottom of the bag and pulled out an envelope and an adorable pink leather collar that had miniature silver spikes all around it.

"Here, this is for you."

She handed me the envelope, which I could now see had my name printed on it, while she coaxed Nala into her collar. Inside, written in a beautiful, flowing script on expensive bone-colored stationery was one line.

Skylar told me she was coming.

It was signed with a single letter: N.

CHAPTER TWENTY

—

I was going to have to talk to Neferet. I thought about it as Stevie Rae and I rushed through breakfast the next morning. I didn't want to tell her anything about my supposed strange reaction to the elements—I mean, I hadn't been lying to Stevie Rae. I could have imagined the entire thing. What if I tell Neferet and she makes me take some kind of weird affinity test (in this school, who knew?) and she finds out that I don't have anything other than an overactive imagination? No way did I want to go through something like that. I'd just keep my mouth shut until I knew more about it. I also didn't want to say anything to her about thinking I might have seen Elizabeth's ghost. Like I wanted Neferet to think I was psycho? Neferet was cool, but she was an adult, and I could almost hear the "it was just your imagination because you'd been through so many changes" lecture I would get if I admitted to seeing a ghost. But I did need to talk to her about the bloodlust thing. (Yeesh—if I liked it so much why did the thought of it still make me feel queasy?)

"Ya think she's going to follow you to class?" Stevie Rae said, pointing to Nala.

I looked down at my feet where the cat lay curled, purring contentedly. "Can she?"

"Do you mean, is she allowed?"

P. C. CAST and KRISTIN CAST

I nodded.

"Yeah, cats can go anywhere they want."

"Huh," I said, reaching down to scratch the top of her head. "I guess she might follow me around all day then."

"Well, I'm glad she's yours and not mine. From what I saw when the alarm when off, she's a serious pillow-hogger."

I laughed. "You're right about that. How such a petite girl could push me off my own pillow, I do not know." I gave her head one more scratch. "Let's go. We're gonna be late."

I stood up with my bowl in my hand, and almost ran smack into Aphrodite. She was, as usual, flanked by Terrible and War-like. Wasp was nowhere to be seen (maybe she'd taken a shower this morning and melted when the water touched her—hee hee). Aphrodite's nasty smile reminded me of a piranha I'd seen at the Jenks Aquarium when my biology class went there last year on a field trip.

"Hi, Zoey. Gosh, you left in such a hurry last night I didn't get a chance to say bye. Sorry you didn't have a good time. It's too bad, but the Dark Daughters isn't for everyone." She glanced at Stevie Rae and curled her lip.

"Actually, I had a great time last night, and I absolutely love the dress you gave me!" I gushed. "Thank you for inviting me to join the Dark Daughters. I accept. Totally."

Aphrodite's feral smile flattened. "Really?"

I grinned like an utterly clueless fool. "Really! When's the next meeting or ritual or whatever—or should I just ask Neferet? I'm going to see her this morning. I know she'll be happy to hear how welcome you made me feel last night and that I'm now a Dark Daughter."

Aphrodite hesitated for just a moment. Then she smiled again and matched my clueless tone of voice perfectly "Yes, I bet Neferet will be glad to hear you've joined us, but I am the leader of the Dark Daughters and I know our schedule by heart, so there's no need to bother her with silly questions. Tomorrow is our Samhain celebration. Wear *your* dress," she emphasized the word, and my smile widened. I'd meant to get to her and I had. "And meet at the rec hall right after dinner, four thirty A.M., sharp."

"Great. I'll be there."

"Good, what a nice surprise," she said slickly. Then, followed by Terrible and Warlike (who looked vaguely shell-shocked), the three of them left the kitchen.

"Hags from hell," I muttered under my breath. I glanced at Stevie Rae, who was staring at me with a stricken expression frozen on her face.

"You're joining them?" she whispered.

"It's not what you think. Come on, I'll tell you on the way to class." I put our breakfast dishes in a dishwasher and herded the too quiet Stevie Rae out of the dorm. Nala padded after us, occasionally hissing at any cat who dared wander too close to me on the sidewalk. "I'm reconnoitering, just like you said last night," I explained.

"No. I don't like it," she said, shaking her head so hard she made her short hair bounce crazily.

"Have you never heard of the old saying 'keep your friends close and your enemies closer'?"

"Yeah, but—"

"That's all I'm doing. Aphrodite gets away with too much crap. She's mean. She's selfish. She can't be what Nyx wants for a High Priestess."

Stevie Rae's eyes got huge. "You're going to stop her?"

"Well, I'm gonna try." And as I spoke I felt the sapphire crescent moon on my forehead tingle.

* * *

"Thanks for the cat things you got for Nala," I said.

Neferet looked up from the paper she was grading and smiled. "Nala—that's a good name for her, but you should thank Skylar, not me. He's the one who told me she was coming." Then she glanced at the orange ball of fur that was impatiently twining between my legs. "She's really attached to you." Her eyes lifted again to meet mine. "Tell me, Zoey, do you ever hear her voice inside your head, or know exactly where she is, even when she's not in the same room as you?"

I blinked. Neferet thought I might have an affinity for cats! "No, I—I don't hear her in my head. But she does complain at me a lot. And I wouldn't know about whether or not I know where she is when she's not with me. She's always with me."

"She is delightful." Neferet crooked a finger at Nala and said, "Come to me, child."

Instantly, Nala padded over and jumped up on Neferet's desk, scattering papers everywhere.

"Oh, gosh, I'm sorry, Neferet." I grabbed for Nala, but Neferet waved me away. She scratched Nala's head, and the cat closed her eyes and purred.

"Cats are always welcome, and papers are easily reorganized. Now, what is it you really wanted to speak with me about, Zoey-bird?"

Her use of my grandma's nickname for me made my heart hurt, and I suddenly missed her with an intensity that had me blinking tears from my eyes.

"Are you missing your old home?" Neferet asked softly.

"No, not really. Well, except for Grandma, but I've been so busy that I guess I just now realized it," I said guiltily.

"You don't miss your mother and father."

It wasn't like she'd said it as a question, but I felt that I needed to answer her. "No. Well, I don't really have a dad. He left us when I was little. My mom remarried three years ago and, well . . ."

"You can tell me. I give you my word that I will understand," Neferet said.

"I hate him!" I said with more anger than I'd expected to feel. "Since he joined our *family*"—I said the word sarcastically—"nothing has been right. My mom totally changed. It's like she can't be his wife and my mother anymore. It hasn't been my home for a long time."

"My mother died when I was ten years old. My father did not remarry. Instead, he began to use me as his wife. From the time I was ten until Nyx saved me by Marking me when I was fifteen, he abused me." Neferet paused and let the shock of what she was saying settle into me before she continued. "So you see, when I say that I understand what it is to have your home become an unbearable place I am not just spouting platitudes."

"That's awful." I didn't know what else to say.

"It was then. Now it is simply another memory. Zoey, humans in your past, and even in your present and future, will become less and less important to you until, eventually, you will feel very little for them. You'll understand this more as you continue to Change."

There was a cold flatness to her voice that made me feel odd, and I heard myself saying, "I don't want to stop caring about my grandma."

"Of course you don't." She was back to being warm and caring again. "It's only nine P.M., why don't you call her? You can be late to Drama class; I'll let Professor Nolan know that you are excused."

"Thank you, I'd like that. But it's not what I wanted to talk to you about." I took a deep breath. "I drank blood last night."

Neferet nodded. "Yes, the Dark Daughters often mix fledgling blood with their ritual wine. It's something the young like to do. Did it upset you greatly, Zoey?"

"Well, I didn't know about it until afterward. Then, yes, it did upset me."

Neferet frowned. "It wasn't ethical of Aphrodite not to tell you before. You should have had a choice about partaking. I'll speak with her."

"No!" I said a little too quickly, and then I forced myself to sound calmer. "No, there's really no need. I'll take care of it. I've decided to join the Dark Daughters, so I don't want to start off by looking like I set out to get Aphrodite in trouble."

"You're probably right. Aphrodite can be rather temperamental, and I trust that you can take care of it yourself, Zoey. We do like to encourage fledglings to solve the problems they have with each other among themselves whenever possible." She studied me, concern obvious in her face. "It's normal for the first few tastes of blood to be less than appetizing. You'd know that if you had been with us longer."

"It's not that. It—it tasted really good. Erik told me that mine was an unusual reaction."

Neferet's perfect brows shot up. "It is, indeed. Did you also feel dizzy or exhilarated?"

"Both," I said softly.

Neferet glanced at my Mark. "You are unique, Zoey Redbird. Well, I think it would be best to pull you out of this section of Sociology, and move you into a Sociology 415.

"I'd really rather you didn't do that," I said quickly. "I already feel like enough of a freak with everyone staring at my Mark and watching to see if I'll do something weird. If you move me into a class with kids who have been here for three years, they'll really think I'm bizarre."

Neferet hesitated, scratching Nala's head while she considered.

"I understand what you mean, Zoey. I haven't been a teenager for over one hundred years, but vampyres have long, accurate memories, and I do recall what it was like to go through the Change." She sighed. "Okay, how about a compromise? I'll allow you to stay in the third former Soc class, but I want to give you the text we use in the upper-level class, and have you agree to read a chapter a week, and promise that you'll discuss any questions you have with me."

"Deal," I said.

"You know, Zoey, as you Change, you literally are becoming an entirely new being. A vampyre is not a human, although we are humane. It may sound reprehensible to you now, but your desire for blood is as normal for your new life as your desire for"—she paused and smiled—"brown pop has been in your old life."

"Jeesh! Do you know everything?"

"Nyx has gifted me generously. Besides my affinity for our lovely felines and my abilities as a healer, I am also an intuitive."

"You can read my mind?" I asked nervously.

"Not exactly. But I can pick up bits and pieces of things. For instance, I know that there's something else you need to tell me about last night."

I drew a deep breath. "I was upset after I found out about the blood, so I ran out of the rec hall. That's how I found Nala. She was in a tree that was real close to the school's wall. I thought she was stuck up there, so I climbed up on the wall to get her and, well, while I was talking to her two kids from my old school found me."

"What happened?" Neferet's hand had stilled; she was no longer petting Nala, and I had all of her attention.

"It wasn't good. They—they were wasted, high and drunk." Okay, I hadn't meant to blurt that!

"Did they try to hurt you?"

"No, nothing like that. It was my ex–best friend and my almost-ex-boyfriend."

Neferet raised her brow at me again.

"Well, I'd quit going out with him, but he and I still had a thing for each other."

She nodded as though she understood. "Go on."

"Kayla and I kinda fought. She sees me differently now and I guess I see her differently, too. Neither one of us likes the new view." As I said it I realized it was true. It wasn't that K had changed—actually, she'd been exactly the same. It was just that the little things I used to ignore, like her nonsensical babble and her mean side, were now suddenly too irritating to deal with. "Anyway, she left and I was alone with Heath." I stopped there, not sure how to say the rest of it.

Neferet's eyes narrowed. "You experienced bloodlust for him."

"Yes," I whispered.

"Did you drink his blood, Zoey?" Her voice was sharp.

"I just tasted a drop of it. I'd scratched him. I hadn't meant to, but when I heard his pulse pounding it—it made me scratch him."

"So you didn't actually drink from the wound?"

"I started to, but Kayla came back and interrupted us. She totally freaked, and that's how I finally got Heath to leave."

"He didn't want to?"

I shook my head. "No. He didn't want to." I felt like I was going to cry again. "Neferet, I'm so sorry! I didn't mean to. I didn't even know what I was doing until Kayla screamed."

"Of course you didn't realize what was happening. How could a newly Marked fledgling be expected to know about bloodlust?" She touched my arm in a reassuring, mom-like gesture. "You probably didn't Imprint with him."

"Imprint?"

"It's what often happens when vampyres drink directly from humans, especially if there is a bond that has been established between them prior to the blood-letting. This is why it is forbidden for fledglings to drink the blood of humans. Actually, it's strongly discouraged for adult vampyres to feed from humans, too. There's an entire sect of vampyres who consider it morally wrong and would like to make it illegal," she said.

I watched her eyes darken as she talked. The expression in them suddenly made me very nervous and I shivered. Then Neferet blinked and her eyes changed back to normal. Or had I just imagined their weird darkness?

"But that's a discussion best left for my sixth form sociology class."

"What do I do about Heath?"

"Nothing. Let me know if he tries to see you again. If he calls you, don't answer. If he began Imprinting even the sound of your voice will effect him and work as a lure to draw him to you."

"It sounds like something out of *Dracula*," I muttered.

"It's nothing like that wretched book!" she snapped. "Stoker vilified vampyres, which has caused our kind endless petty troubles with humans."

"I'm sorry, I didn't mean—"

She waved her hand dismissively. "No, I shouldn't have taken out my frustration about that old fool's book on you. And don't worry about your friend Heath. I'm sure he'll be fine. You said that he was smoking and drinking? I assume you mean marijuana?"

I nodded. "But I don't smoke," I added. "Actually, he didn't used to and neither did Kayla. I don't get what's happening to them. I think they're hanging with some of those druggie football players from Union, and none of them have enough sense to just say no."

"Well, his reaction to you might have had more to do with his level of intoxication than a possible Imprint." She paused, pulling a scratch pad out of her desk drawer, and handing me a pencil. "But just in case, why don't you write down your friends' full names and where they live. Oh, and add the names of the Union football players, too, if you know them."

"Why would you need all of their names?" I felt my heart fall into my shoes. "You're not going to call their parents, are you?"

Neferet laughed. "Of course not. The misbehavior of human teenagers is no concern of mine. I only ask so that I can focus my thoughts on the group and perhaps pick up any vestiges of a possible Imprint among them."

"What happens if you do? What happens to Heath?"

"He's young and the Imprint will be weak, so time and distance should make it fade eventually. If he actually Imprinted in full, there are ways to break it." I was about to say that maybe she should just go ahead and do whatever she did to break an Imprinting when she continued. "None of the ways are pleasant."

"Oh, okay."

I wrote the names and addresses for Kayla and Heath. I didn't have a clue where the Union guys lived, but I did remember their names. Neferet got up and went to the back of the classroom to retrieve a thick textbook whose title in silver letters read *Sociology 415*.

"Begin with Chapter One and work your way through this entire book. Until you've finished it, let's consider it your homework instead of the work I assign to the rest of the Soc 101 class."

I took the book. It was heavy and the cover felt cool in my hot, nervous grip.

"If you have any questions, any at all, come see me right away. If I'm not here you can come to my apartment in Nyx's Temple. Go in the front door and follow the stairs on your right. I am the only priestess at the school right now, so the entire second floor belongs to me. And don't worry about disturbing me. You're my fledgling—it's your job to disturb me," she said with a warm smile.

"Thank you, Neferet."

"Try not to worry. Nyx has touched you and the goddess cares for her own." She hugged me. "Now, I'm going to go tell Professor Nolan what's been keeping you. Go ahead and use the phone at my desk to call your grandma." She hugged me again and then closed the classroom door gently behind her as she left.

I sat down at her desk and thought about how great she was, and how long it'd been since my mom had hugged me like that. And for some reason, I started to cry.

CHAPTER TWENTY-ONE

—

"Hi Grandma, it's me."

"Oh! My Zoeybird! Are you okay, honey?"

I smiled into the phone and wiped my eyes. "I'm good, Grandma. I just miss you."

"Little bird, I miss you, too." She paused and then said, "Has your mom called you?"

"No."

Grandma sighed. "Well, honey, maybe she doesn't want to bother you while you're settling into your new life. I did tell her that Neferet had explained to me that your days and nights will be flip-flopped."

"Thanks, Grandma, but I don't think that's why she hasn't called me."

"Maybe she has tried and you just missed her call. I called your cell yesterday, but I only got your voicemail."

I felt a twinge of guilt. I hadn't even checked my phone for messages. "I forgot to plug my cell phone in. It's back in the room. Sorry I missed your call, Grandma." Then, to make her feel better (and to get her to quit talking about it), I said, "I'll check my phone when I get back to my room. Maybe Mom did call."

"Maybe she did, honey. So, tell me, how is it there?"

"It's good. I mean, there are a lot of things I like about it.

My classes are cool. Hey, Grandma, I'm even taking fencing and an equestrian class."

"That's wonderful! I remember how much you liked to ride Bunny."

"And I got a cat!"

"Oh, Zoeybird, I'm so glad. You've always loved cats. Are you making friends with the other kids?"

"Yeah, my roommate, Stevie Rae, is great. And I already like her friends, too."

"So, if everything is going so well, why the tears?"

I should have known I couldn't hide anything from my grandma. "It's just . . . just that some of the things about the Change are really hard to deal with."

"You're well, aren't you?" Worry was thick in her voice. "Is your head okay?"

"Yeah, it's nothing like that. It's—" I stopped. I wanted to tell her; I wanted to tell her so bad I could explode, but I didn't know how. And I was afraid—afraid she wouldn't love me anymore. I mean, Mom had quit loving me, hadn't she? Or, at the very least, Mom had traded me in for a new husband, which in some ways was worse than quitting loving me. What would I do if Grandma walked away from me, too?

"Zoeybird, you know you can tell me anything," she said gently.

"It's hard, Grandma." I bit my lip to keep from crying.

"Then let me make it easier. There is nothing you could say that would make me stop loving you. I'm your Grandma today, tomorrow, and next year. I'll be your Grandma even after I join our ancestors in the spirit world, and from there I'll still love you, Little Bird."

"I drank blood and I liked it!" I blurted.

Without any hesitation, Grandma said, "Well, honey, isn't that what vampyres do?"

"Yeah, but I'm not a vampyre. I'm just a few-days-old fledgling."

"You're special, Zoey. You always have been. Why should that change now?"

"I don't feel special. I feel like a freak."

"Then remember something. You're still you. Doesn't matter that you've been Marked. Doesn't matter that you're going through the Change. Inside, your spirit is still *your* spirit. On the outside you might look like a familiar stranger, but you need only look inside to find the you you've known for sixteen years."

"The familiar stranger . . . ," I whispered. "How did you know?"

"You're my girl, Honey. You're daughter of my spirit. It's not hard to understand what you must be feeling—it's very much like what I imagine I'd be feeling."

"Thank you, Grandma."

"You are welcome, *u-we-tsi-a-ge-ya.*"

I smiled, loving how the Cherokee word for daughter sounded—so magical and special, like it was a Goddess-given title. Goddess-given . . .

"Grandma, there's something else."

"Tell me, Little Bird."

"I think I feel the five elements when a circle is cast."

"If that is the truth, you have been given great power, Zoey. And you know that with great power comes great responsibility. Our family has a rich history of Tribal Elders, Medicine Men, and Wise Women. Have a care, Little Bird, to think before you act. The Goddess would not have granted you special powers on a whim. Use them carefully, and make Nyx, as well as your ancestors, look down and smile on you."

"I'll try my best, Grandma."

"That's all I would ever ask of you, Zoeybird."

"There's a girl here who also has special powers, too, but she's

221

awful. She's a bully and she lies. Grandma, I think . . . I think . . ."
I took a deep breath and said what had been brewing in my mind
all morning. "I think I'm stronger than she is and I think that
maybe Nyx Marked me so that I can get her out of the position
she's in. But—but that would mean that I have to take her place,
and I don't know if I'm ready for that, not now. Maybe not ever."

"Follow what your spirit tells you, Zoeybird." She hesitated,
then said, "Honey, do you remember the purification prayer of
our people?"

I thought about it. I couldn't count the times I'd gone with her
to the little stream behind Grandma's house and watched her
bathe ritualistically in the running water and speak the purification prayer. Sometimes I stepped into the stream with her and
said the prayer, too. The prayer had been entwined throughout
my childhood, spoken at the change of seasons, in thanks for the
lavender harvest, or in preparation for the coming winter, as well
as whenever Grandma was faced with hard decisions. Sometimes
I didn't know why she purified herself and spoke the prayer.
It simply had always been.

"Yes," I said. "I remember it."

"Is there running water inside the school grounds?"

"I don't know, Grandma."

"Well, if there isn't then get something to use as a smudge stick.
Sage and lavender mixed together are best, but you can even use
fresh pine if you have no other choice. Do you know what to do,
Zoeybird?"

"Smudge myself, starting at my feet and working my way up
my body, front and back," I recited, as if I was a small child again
and Grandma was drilling me in the ways of our people. "And
then face the east and speak the purification prayer."

"Good, you do remember. Ask for the Goddess's help, Zoey.

I believe that she will hear you. Can you do this before sunrise tomorrow?"

"I think so."

"I will perform the prayer, too, and add a grandmother's voice to ask the Goddess to guide you."

And suddenly I felt better. Grandma was never wrong about these sorts of things. If she believed it would be okay, then it really would be okay.

"I'll speak the purification prayer before dawn. I promise."

"Good, Little Bird. Now this old woman had better let you go. You are in the middle of a school day right now, aren't you?"

"Yeah, I'm on my way to Drama class. And, Grandma, you'll never be old."

"Not as long as I can hear your young voice, Little Bird. I love you, *u-we-tsi-a-ge-ya.*"

"I love you, too, Grandma."

Talking to Grandma had lifted a terrible weight from my heart. I was still scared and freaked out about the future, and I wasn't wild about the thought of bringing down Aphrodite. Not to mention that I really didn't have a clue how to go about it. But I did have a plan. Okay, maybe it wasn't a "plan," but at least it was something to do. I'd complete the purification prayer, and then . . . well . . . then I'd figure out what to do after that.

Yeah, that would work. Or at least that's what I kept telling myself through my morning classes. By lunch I'd decided on the place for my ritual—under the tree by the wall where I'd found Nala. I thought about it while I made my way through the salad bar behind the Twins. Trees, especially oaks, were sacred to the Cherokee people, so that seemed to be a good choice. Plus, it was secluded and easy to get to. Sure, Heath and Kayla had found me over there, but I wasn't planning on sitting on top of the wall again, and I couldn't imagine Heath showing up at dawn two days in a row, whether he had been Imprinted or not. I mean, this was the guy who slept till two in the afternoon in the summer, *every day*. It took two alarm clocks and his mother shrieking at him to get him up for school. The kid was not going to be up at pre-dawn again. It would probably take him months to recover from yesterday. No, actually, he'd probably snuck out of the house and met K (sneaking out had always been easy for her, her parents were totally clueless), and they'd been up all night. Which meant that he'd missed school *and* would be playing sick and sleeping in for the next two days. Anyway, I wasn't worried about him showing up.

"Don't you think baby corns are scary? There's just something wrong about their midget bodies."

I jumped and almost dropped the ladle of ranch dressing into the vat of white liquid, and looked up into Erik's laughing blue eyes.

"Oh, hi," I said. "You scared me."

"Z, I think I'm making a habit of sneaking up on you."

I giggled nervously, very aware that the Twins were watching every move we made.

"You look like you've recovered from yesterday."

"Yeah, no problem. I'm fine. And this time I'm not lying."

"And I heard you joined the Dark Daughters."

Shaunee and Erin sucked air together. I was careful not to look at them.

"Yep."

"That's cool. That group needs some new blood."

"You say 'that group' like you don't belong to it. Aren't you a Dark Son?"

"Yeah, but it's not the same as being a Dark Daughter. We're just ornamental. Kinda the opposite of how it is in the human world. All the guys know that we're just there to look good and keep Aphrodite amused."

I looked up at him, reading something else in his eyes. "And is that what you're still doing, amusing Aphrodite?"

"As I said last night, not anymore, which is one reason I don't really consider myself a member of the group. I'm sure they'd officially kick me out if it wasn't for that little acting thing I do."

"You mean 'little' as in Broadway and LA already being interested in you."

"That's what I mean." He grinned at me. "It's not real, you know. Acting is all pretend. It's not what I really am." He bent down to whisper in my ear. "Really, I'm a dork."

"Oh, please. Does that line work for you?"

He exaggerated a look of being offended. "Line? No, Z. That's no line, and I can prove it."

"Sure you can."

"I can. Come to the movies with me tonight. We'll watch my favorite DVDs of all time."

"How does that prove anything?"

"It's *Star Wars*, the original ones. I know all the lines for all the parts." He leaned closer and whispered again. "I can even do Chewbacca's parts."

I laughed. "You're right. You are a dork."

"Told you."

We'd come to the end of the salad bar and he walked with me over to the table where Damien, Stevie Rae, and the Twins were already seated. And, no, they weren't making any attempt to hide the fact that they were all totally gawking at the two of us.

"So, will you go . . . with me . . . tonight?"

I could hear the four of them holding their breaths. Literally.

"I'd like to, but I can't tonight. I—uh—I already have plans."

"Oh. Okay. Well . . . next time. See ya." He nodded at the table and walked away.

I sat down. They were all staring at me. "What?" I said.

"You have lost every last bit of your mind," Shaunee said.

"My exact thoughts, Twin," Erin said.

"I hope you have a really good reason for blowing him off," Stevie Rae said. "It was obvious you hurt his feelings."

"Think he'd let me comfort him?" Damien asked, still gazing dreamily after Erik.

"Give it up," Erin said.

"He doesn't play for your team," Shaunee said.

"Shush!" Stevie Rae said. She turned to look me straight in the eyes. "Why did you tell him no? What could be more important than a date with him?"

"Getting rid of Aphrodite," I said simply.

—

CHAPTER TWENTY-TWO

"She has a point," Damien said.

"She joined the Dark Daughters," Shaunee said.

"What!" Damien squeaked, his voice going up about twenty octaves.

"Leave her alone," Stevie Rae said, instantly coming to my defense. "She's reconnoitering."

"Reconnoitering, hell! If she joined the Dark Daughters she's engaging the enemy full on," Damien said.

"Well, she joined," Shaunee said.

"We heard her," Erin said.

"Hello! I'm still right here," I said.

"So what are you going to do?" Damien asked me.

"I don't really know," I said.

"You better get a plan and get one quick or those hags are gonna have you for lunch," Erin said.

"Yep," Shaunee said, biting viciously into her salad for effect.

"Hey! She doesn't have to figure this out on her own. She has us." Stevie Rae crossed her arms over her chest and glared at the Twins.

I smiled my thanks to Stevie Rae. "Well, I kinda have an idea."

"Good. Tell us and we'll brainstorm," said Stevie Rae.

Everyone looked expectantly at me. I sighed. "Well. Um . . . ,"

I started hesitantly, afraid I was sounding like a moron, and then I decided I might as well tell them what had been on my mind since I talked to Grandma, so I finished in a rush. "I thought I'd perform an ancient purification prayer based on Cherokee ritual and ask Nyx to help me come up with a plan."

The silence at the table seemed to last forever. Then Damien finally said, "Asking for Nyx's help isn't a bad idea."

"Are you Cherokee?" Shaunee asked.

"You look Cherokee," Erin said.

"Hello! Her last name is Redbird. She's Cherokee," Stevie Rae said with finality.

"Well, that's good," Shaunee said, but she looked doubtful.

"I just think that Nyx might actually hear me and—maybe— give me some kind of clue as to what I should do about horrid Aphrodite." I looked at each of my friends. "Something inside me says it's just wrong to let her get away with all the crap she's getting away with."

"Let me tell them!" Stevie Rae suddenly said. "They won't tell anyone. Really. And it'd help if they knew."

"What the F?" Erin said.

"Okay, now you have no choice," Shaunee said, pointing at Stevie Rae with her fork. "She knew if she said that we would pester the crap outta you till you told us whatever it is she's talking about."

I frowned at Stevie Rae, who shrugged her shoulders sheepishly and said, "Sorry."

Reluctantly, I lowered my voice and leaned forward. "Promise you won't tell anyone."

"Promise," they said.

"I think I can feel the five elements when a circle is cast."

Silence. They just stared. Three of them shocked, Stevie Rae smug.

"So, you still think she can't take down Aphrodite?" Stevie Rae said.

"I *knew* there was more to your Mark than falling down and hitting your head!" Shaunee said.

"Wow," Erin said. "Talk about good gossip."

"No one can know!" I said quickly.

"Please," Shaunee said. "We're just sayin' that someday this is gonna be great gossip."

"We know how to wait for great gossip," Erin said.

Damien ignored both of them. "I don't think there's a record of any High Priestess who has had an affinity with all five elements." Damien's voice got more excited as he spoke. "Do you know what that means?" He didn't give me a chance to respond. "It means you could potentially be the most puissant High Priestess the vampyres have ever known."

"Huh?" I said. *Puissant?*

"Strong—powerful," he said impatiently. "You might actually be able to take out Aphrodite!"

"Now, that's some seriously good news," Erin said, as Shaunee nodded in enthusiastic agreement.

"So when and where are we doing the purification thingie?" Stevie Rae said.

"We?" I said.

"You're not in this alone, Zoey," she said.

I opened my mouth to protest—I mean, I wasn't even sure what I was going to do. I didn't want to get my friends mixed up in something that might be—actually, would probably be—a total mess. But Damien didn't give me time to tell them no.

"You need us," he said simply. "Even the most puissant High Priestess needs her circle."

"Well, I hadn't really thought about casting a circle. I was just gonna do a kind of purification prayer thing."

"Can't you cast a circle and then pray the prayer and ask for Nyx's help?" Stevie Rae asked.

"Seems logical," Shaunee said.

"Plus, if you really do have an affinity for the five elements, I'll bet we'll be able to sense it when you cast your own circle. Right, Damien?" Stevie Rae said. Everyone looked at the gay scholar of our group.

"Sounds like good logic to me," he said.

I was still going to argue, even though everything inside of me felt relieved and happy and grateful that my friends would be there with me, that they wouldn't let me face all of this uncertainty alone.

Value them; they are pearls of great price.

The familiar voice floated through my mind, and I realized that I shouldn't question the new instinct within me that seemed to have been born when Nyx kissed my forehead and permanently changed my Mark and my life.

"Okay, I'm going to need a smudge stick." They looked at me blankly, and I went on to explain. "It's for the purification part of the ritual because I don't have any running water handy. Or do I?"

"You mean like a stream or a river or something like that?" Stevie Rae asked.

"Yeah."

"Well, there's a little stream that runs through the courtyard outside the dining hall and disappears somewhere under the school," Damien said.

"That's no good; it's too public. We'll need to use the smudge stick. What works best is dried lavender and sage mixed together, but if I have to I can use pine."

"I can get the sage and lavender," Damien said. "They have that kind of stuff in the school supplies store for the fifth and sixth former's Spells and Rituals class. I'll just say I'm helping out an upperclassman by picking some up for him. What else do you need?"

"Well, in the purification ritual Grandma always thanked the seven sacred directions the Cherokee people honor: north, south, east, west, sun, earth, and self. But I think I want to make the prayer more specific to Nyx." I chewed my lip, thinking.

"I think that's smart," Shaunee said.

"Yeah," Erin added. "I mean, Nyx isn't allied with the sun. She's Night."

"I think you should follow your gut," Stevie Rae said.

"Trusting herself is one of the first things a High Priestess learns to do," Damien said.

"Okay, then I'll also need a candle for each of the five elements," I decided.

"Easy-peasy," Shaunee said.

"Yeah, the temple is never locked and there are zillions of circle candles in there."

"Is it okay to take them?" Stealing from Nyx's Temple definitely did not feel like a good idea.

"It's fine as long as we bring them back," Damien said. "What else?"

"That's it." I think. Hell, I wasn't sure. It's not like I actually knew what I was doing.

"When and where?" Damien asked.

"After dinner. Let's say five o'clock. And we can't go together. The last thing we need is for Aphrodite or any of the other Dark Daughters to think we're having some kind of meeting and get curious about us. So let's meet at a huge oak tree by the eastern wall." I smiled crookedly at them. "It's easy to find if you pretend that you've just run out of one of the Dark Daughter's rituals in the rec hall, and you want to get the hell away from the hags."

"That doesn't take much pretending," Shaunee said.

Erin snorted.

"Okay, we'll bring the stuff," Damien said.

"Yeah, we'll bring the stuff; you bring the puissantness," Shaunee said, giving Damien a smartass look.

"That is not the correct form of that word. You know, you really should do more reading. Maybe your vocabulary would improve," Damien said.

"Your *mom* needs to read more," Shaunee said, and then she and Erin dissolved in giggles at the really bad "your mom" joke.

I, for one, was glad that they shifted the subject away from me and I could eat my salad and think in relative privacy while they bickered back and forth. I was chewing and trying to remember all the words to the purification prayer when Nala hopped up on the bench beside me. She looked at me with her big eyes and then leaned into me and started to purr like a jet engine. I don't know why, but she made me feel better. And when the bell rang and we all hurried off to class, each of my four friends smiled at me, gave me a secret wink, and said, "Later, Z." They made me feel better, too, even though their easy adoption of Erik's nickname for me gave my heart a twinge.

Spanish class zoomed by: a whole lesson on learning how to say that we like things or don't like things. Profe Garmy was cracking me up. She said it would change our lives. *Me gusta gatos.* (I like cats.) *Me gusta ir de compras.* (I like shopping.) *No me gusta cocinar.* (I don't like to cook.) *No me gusta lavantar el gato.* (I don't like to wash the cat.) Those were Profe Garmy's favorites, and we spent the hour coming up with our own favorites.

I tried not to scribble things like *me gusta Erik* . . . and *no me gusta el hag-o Aphrodite.* Okay, so I'm sure *el hag-o* is not how you say "hag" in Spanish, but still. Anyway, class was fun and I actually understood what we were saying. Equestrian class didn't quite zoom by. Mucking stalls was good for thinking—I went over and over the purification prayer—but the hour definitely seemed to take an hour. This time Stevie Rae didn't have to come get me. I was way too anxious to lose track of time. As the bell rang I was quickly putting up the curry combs, happy that Lenobia had let me groom Persephone again, and preoccupied because she had also told me that starting next week she thought I might actually begin riding her. I hurried out of the stables, wishing that the hour wasn't so late back in the "real" world. I'd have loved to call Grandma and tell her how well I was doing with the horses.

"I know what's going on."

I swear I almost choked. "God, Aphrodite! Could you make a sound or something! What are you, part spider? You scared the hell outta me."

"What's wrong?" she purred. "Guilty conscience?"

"Uh, when you sneak up behind people, you scare them. Guilt has nothing to do with it."

"So you're not guilty?"

"Aphrodite, I don't know what you're talking about."

"I know what you're planning for tonight."

"And yet I still don't know what you're talking about." *Ah, crap! How could she have found out?*

"Everyone thinks you're so damn cute and so damn innocent and they're so damn impressed by that freakish Mark of yours. Everyone but me." She turned to face me, and we stopped in the middle of the sidewalk. Her blue eyes narrowed and her face twisted until it was scarily haggish. Huh. I wondered (briefly) if the Twins realized how accurate their nickname for her was. "No matter what bullshit you've heard he's still mine. He'll always be mine."

My eyes widened and I felt a wash of relief so intense it made me laugh. She was talking about Erik, not about the purification prayer! "Wow, you sound like Erik's mom. Does he know you're checking up on him?"

"Did I look like Erik's mom when you watched me suck his dick in the hall?"

So she did know. Whatever. I suppose it was inevitable that we would have this conversation. "No, you didn't look like Erik's mom. You looked like what you are—desperate—while you pathetically tried to throw yourself at a guy who was clearly telling you he didn't want you anymore."

"Fucking bitch! Nobody talks to me like that!"

She raised her hand and, clawlike, moved to slash at my face. Then it seemed that the world stopped, leaving the two of us in a little bubble of slow-motion. I caught her wrist, stopping her easily—too easily. It was like she was a small, sick child who had struck out in anger, but was really too weak to do any harm. I held her there for a moment, meeting her hateful eyes.

"Don't ever try to hit me again. I'm not one of the kids you can bully. Get this, and get this now. I am not scared of you." Then I flung her wrist away from me, and was totally shocked to see her stagger back several feet.

Rubbing her wrist, she glared at me. "Don't bother showing up tomorrow. Consider yourself uninvited and no longer a Dark Daughter."

"Really?" I felt unbelievably calm. I knew I held the trump card on this and I pulled it. "So you want to explain to my mentor, High Priestess Neferet, the vamp whose idea it was for me to join the Dark Daughters in the first place, that you kicked me out because you're jealous that your ex-boyfriend likes me?"

Her face paled.

"Oh, and you may be very sure that I'll be totally, completely upset when Neferet asks me about it." I sniffed and sobbed a little like I was fake crying.

"Do you know what it's like to be a part of something and have *no one* else in the group want you there?" she snarled between her clenched teeth.

I felt my stomach clench and had to force myself not to let her see she'd struck a nerve. Yes, I knew exactly what it was like to be a part of something—a supposed family—and have it feel like *no one* else wanted me there, but Aphrodite wasn't going to know it. Instead I smiled, and in my sweetest voice I said, "Why, whatever do you mean, Aphrodite? Erik is part of the Dark Sons and just today at lunch he told me how happy he was that I'd joined the Dark Daughters."

"Come to the ritual. Pretend you're part of the Dark Daughters. But you'd better remember something. They're *my* Dark Daughters. You're the outsider; the one who is not wanted. And remember this, too. Erik Night and I have a bond that you'll never understand. He's not my *ex* anything. You didn't stay to see the end of our little game in the hall. He was then and he is now exactly what I want him to be. Mine." Then she tossed her very big, very blond hair and stalked away.

About two breaths later Stevie Rae stuck her head out from behind an old oak that was not far from the sidewalk and said, "Is she gone?"

"Thankfully." I shook my head at Stevie Rae. "What are you doing back there?"

"Are you kidding? I'm hiding. She scares the bejezzus outta me. I was coming to meet you and saw the two of you arguing. Man, she actually tried to hit you!"

"Aphrodite has some serious anger-management issues."

Stevie Rae laughed.

"Uh, Stevie Rae, you can come out from behind there now."

Still laughing, Stevie Rae practically skipped over to me and linked her arm with mine. "You really stood up to her!"

"I really did."

"She really, *really* hates your guts."

"She really, *really* does."

"You know what that means?" Stevie Rae said.

"Yep. I don't have any choice now. I'm going to have to take her down."

"Yep."

But I knew that I'd had no choice even before Aphrodite tried to scratch my eyes out. I hadn't had any choice since Nyx had placed her Mark on me. As Stevie Rae and I walked together in the gaslight-illuminated richness of the night, the Goddess's words repeated over and over through my mind: *You are old beyond your years, Zoeybird. Believe in yourself and you will find a way. But remember, darkness does not always equate to evil, just as light does not always bring good.*

CHAPTER TWENTY-THREE

—

"I hope the rest of them can find it," I said, glancing around me while Stevie Rae and I waited by the big oak tree. "It didn't seem this dark last night."

"It wasn't. It's really cloudy tonight, so the moon's having trouble shining through. But don't worry, the Change is doing really cool things for our night vision. Heck, I think I can see as good as Nala." Stevie Rae scratched the cat affectionately on her head and Nala closed her eyes and purred. "They'll find us."

I leaned against the tree and worried. Dinner had been good—seriously yummy broiled chicken, seasoned rice, and baby snow peas (one thing I could say for this place, they could really cook)—yeah, everything had been great. Until Erik had come by our table and said hi. Okay, it wasn't really a "hi, Z, I still like you" hi. It was a "hi, Zoey." Period. Yep. That was it. He'd gotten his food and was walking with a couple other guys the Twins called hotties. I will admit that I didn't even notice them. I was too busy noticing Erik. They came to our table. I looked up and smiled. He met my eyes for a millisecond, said, "Hi, Zoey," and walked on. And all of a sudden the chicken didn't taste nearly as good.

"You just hurt his ego. Be nice to him and he'll ask you out again," Stevie Rae said, bringing me and my thoughts back to the present under the tree.

"How'd you know I was thinking about Erik?" I asked. Stevie Rae had quit petting Nala, so I reached down to scratch the cat on top of her head before she started complaining at me.

" 'Cause that's what I'd be thinking about."

"Well, I should be thinking about the circle I have to cast but have never cast before in my entire life, and the purification ritual I have to perform, and not some boy."

"He's not 'some boy.' He's some *fiiine* boy," Stevie Rae drawled, making me laugh.

"You must be talking about Erik," Damien said, stepping out of the shadow of the wall. "Don't worry. I saw the way he was looking at you at lunch today. He'll ask you out again."

"Yeah, take it from him," Shaunee said.

"He is our group expert on All Things Penile," Erin said as they joined them under the tree.

"Quite true," Damien said.

Before they could make my head hurt I changed the subject. "Did you get the stuff we need?"

"I had to mix the dried sage and lavender together myself. I hope it's okay that I tied them like this." Damien pulled the smudge stick of dried herbs out of his jacket sleeve and handed it to me. It was thick and almost a foot long, and right away I smelled the familiar sweetness of lavender. He'd wrapped the bundle tightly together on one end with what looked like extra-thick thread.

"It's perfect." I smiled at him.

He looked relieved, and then said, a little shyly, "I used my cross-stitch thread."

"Hey, I told you before you shouldn't be ashamed that you like to cross-stitch. I think it's a cute hobby. Plus, you're really good at it," Stevie Rae said.

"I wish my dad thought so," Damien said.

I hated hearing the sadness in his voice. "I wish you'd teach me sometime. I've always wanted to learn how to cross-stitch," I lied, and was glad to see Damien's face brighten.

"Anytime, Z," he said.

"How about the candles?" I asked the Twins.

"Hey, we told you. Easy . . ." Shaunee opened her purse and pulled out green, yellow, and blue votives in correspondingly colored thick glass cups.

"Peasy." From her purse Erin took a red and purple votive in the same kind of colored containers.

"Good. Okay, let's see. Let's move over here, a little way from the trunk, but close enough that we're still standing under the branches." They followed me as I walked a few paces from the tree. I looked at the candles. What should I do? Maybe I should . . . And as I thought about it, I knew. Without stopping to wonder how or why or question the intuitive knowledge that had suddenly come to me, I simply acted on it. "I'm going to give each of you a candle. Then, just like the vamps in Neferet's Full Moon Ritual, you're going to represent that element. I'll be spirit." Erin handed me the purple votive. "I'm the center of the circle. The rest of you take your places around me." Without hesitation I took the red candle from Erin and handed it to Shaunee. "You'll be fire."

"Sounds good to me. I mean, everyone knows how hot I am." She grinned and shimmied to the southern edge of the circle.

The green candle was next. I turned to Stevie Rae. "You're earth."

"And green's my favorite color!" she said, happily moving to stand across from Shaunee.

"Erin, you're water."

"Good. I used to like to lay out, which involves swimming when I needed to cool off." Erin moved to the western position.

"So I must be air," Damien said, taking the yellow candle.

"You are. Your element opens the circle."

"Kinda like I wish I could open people's minds," he said, moving to the eastern position.

I smiled warmly at him. "Yep. Kinda like that."

"Okay. What's next?" Stevie Rae asked.

"Well, let's use the smoke from the smudge stick to purify ourselves." I set the purple candle at my feet so I could concentrate on the smudge stick. Then I rolled my eyes. "Well, hell. Did anyone remember matches or a lighter or whatever?"

"Naturally," Damien said, pulling a lighter from his pocket.

"Thanks, air," I said.

"Don't mention it, High Priestess," he said.

I didn't say anything, but when he called me that a shiver of excitement tingled through my body.

"Here's how you use the smudge stick," I said, glad that my voice sounded way calmer than I felt. I stood in front of Damien, deciding that I should begin where the circle would be started. Realizing that I was eerily echoing my Grandma and the lessons of my childhood, I began explaining the process to my friends. "Smudging is a ritual way to cleanse a person, place, or an object of negative energies, spirits, or influences. The smudging ceremony involves the burning of special, sacred plants and herbal resins, then, either passing an object through the smoke, or fanning the smoke around a person or place. The spirit of the plant purifies whatever is being smudged." I smiled at Damien. "Ready?"

"Affirmative," he said in typical Damien fashion.

I lit the smudge stick and let the fire burn the dry herbs for a little while, and then I blew them out so that all that was left was a nicely smoking ember. Then, starting at Damien's feet, I wafted smoke up his body while I continued my explanation of the ancient ceremony.

"It's really important to remember that we're asking the spirits of the sacred plants we're using to help us, and we should show them proper respect by acknowledging their powers."

"What do lavender and sage do?" Stevie Rae asked from across the circle.

While I smudged my way up Damien's body I answered Stevie Rae. "White sage is used a lot in traditional ceremonies. It drives out negative energies, spirits, and influences. Actually, desert sage does the same thing, but I like white sage better because it smells sweeter." I'd made it to Damien's head and I grinned at him. "Good choice, Damien."

"Sometimes I think I might be a little psychic," Damien said.

Erin and Shaunee snorted, but we ignored them.

"Okay, now turn clockwise and I'll finish up with your back," I told him. He turned and I continued. "My grandma always uses lavender in all of her smudge sticks. I'm sure part of the reason is that she owns a lavender farm."

"Cool!" Stevie Rae said.

"Yeah, it's an awesome place." I smiled over my shoulder at her, but I kept smudging Damien. "The other part of the reason she uses lavender is because it is able to restore balance and create a peaceful atmosphere. It also draws loving energy and positive spirits." I tapped Damien's shoulder so he'd turn around. "You're done." Then I moved around the circle to Shaunee, who was representing the element fire, and I began smudging her.

"Positive spirits?" Stevie Rae said, sounding young and scared. "I didn't know we'd be calling anything more than the elements to the circle."

"Please. Just please, Stevie Rae," Shaunee said, frowning through the smoke to Stevie Rae. "You can not be a vampyre and be afraid of ghosts."

"Nope. It doesn't even sound right," Erin said.

I glanced across the circle at Stevie Rae and our eyes met

briefly. We were both thinking about my encounter with what might have been Elizabeth's ghost, but neither of us seemed willing to talk about it.

"I'm *not* a vampyre. Yet. I'm just a fledgling. So it's okay for me to be scared of ghosts."

"Wait, isn't Zoey talking about Cherokee spirits? They probably won't pay much attention to a ceremony done by a bunch of vampyre fledglings whose non–Native American-ness outweighs our High Priestess's Cherokee-ness four to one," Damien said.

I finished with Shaunee and moved on to Erin. "I don't think it matters that much what we are on the outside," I said, instantly feeling the rightness of what I was saying. "I think what matters is our intent. It's kinda like this: Aphrodite and her group are some of the best looking, most talented kids at this school, and the Dark Daughters should be an awesome club. But instead we call them the hags and they're basically a bunch of bullies and spoiled brats." Wonder how Erik fit into all of that? Was he really just 'whatever' about the group, like he told me, or was he into it more deeply than that, as Aphrodite implied?

"Or kids who have been bullied into joining and who are just along for the ride," Erin said.

"Exactly." I mentally shook myself. Now was not the time to daydream about Erik. I finished smudging Erin and walked over to stand in front of Stevie Rae. "What I mean is that I do think the spirits of my ancestors can hear us, just like I think the spirits of the sage and the lavender are working for us. But I don't think you have anything to be afraid of, Stevie Rae. Our intention is not to call them here so that we can use them to kick Aphrodite's ass." I paused in my smudging and added, "Even though the girl definitely needs a good ass-kicking. And I don't think there will be any scary ghosts hanging around tonight," I said firmly, then handed Stevie Rae the smudge stick and said, "Okay, now you do me." She began mimicking my actions and I relaxed into the familiar sweet smoke as it drifted around me.

"We're not going to ask them to help us kick her ass?" Shaunee definitely sounded disappointed.

"Nope. We're purifying ourselves so that we can ask for Nyx's guidance. I don't want to beat Aphrodite up." I remembered how good it'd felt to toss her away from me and tell her off. "Well, okay, I might enjoy it, but the truth is that doesn't solve the problem of the Dark Daughters."

Stevie Rae was done smudging me and I took the stick from her and carefully rubbed it out on the ground. Then I returned to the center of the circle where Nala was curled contentedly in a little orange ball beside the spirit candle. I looked around at my friends. "It's true that we don't like Aphrodite, but I think it's important not to focus on negatives like kicking her ass or pushing her out of the Dark Daughters. That's what she would do in our place. What we want is what's right. More like justice than revenge. We're different than her, and if we somehow manage to take her place in the Dark Daughters, that group will be different, too."

"See, that's why you'll be the High Priestess and Erin and I will just be your very attractive sidekicks. Because we are shallow and we just want to knock her bobble-head off her shoulders," Shaunee said while Erin nodded.

"Positive thoughts only, please," Damien said sharply. "We are in the middle of a purification ritual."

Before Shaunee could do anything more than glare at Damien, Stevie Rae chirped, " 'Kay! I'm thinkin' only positive things, like how great it would be if Zoey was leader of the Dark Daughters."

"Good idea, Stevie Rae," Damien said. "I'm thinking the same."

"Hey! That's my happy thought, too," Erin said. "Peter Pan with me, Twin," she called to Shaunee, who stopped scowling at Damien and said, "You know I'm always up for some happy thoughts. And it would be damn nice if Zoey was in charge of the Dark Daughters and on her way to being High Priestess for real."

High Priestess for real . . . I wondered briefly whether it was a good or bad thing that those words made me feel as if I might need to puke. Again. Sighing, I lit the purple candle. "Ready?" I asked the four of them.

"Ready!" they said together.

"Okay, pick up your candles."

Without hesitating (which meant I also wasn't giving myself time to chicken out), I carried the candle over to Damien. I wasn't experienced and brilliant like Neferet, or seductive and confident like Aphrodite. I was just me. Just Zoey—that familiar stranger who had gone from being an almost normal high school kid to a truly unusual vampyre fledgling. I took a deep breath. As my grandma would say, all I could do was try my best.

"Air is everywhere, so it only makes sense that it is the first element to be called into the circle. I ask that you hear me, air, and I summon you to this circle." I lit Damien's yellow candle with my purple one and instantly the flame began to flicker crazily. I watched Damien's eyes get big and round and startled-looking as wind suddenly whipped in a mini-whirlwind around our bodies, lifting our hair and brushing softly against our skin.

"It's true," he whispered, staring at me. "You can actually manifest the elements."

"Well," I whispered back, feeling lightheaded, "one of them at least. Let's try for two."

I walked over to Shaunee. She raised her candle eagerly and made me smile when she said, "I'm ready for fire—bring it on!"

"Fire reminds me of cold winter nights and the warmth and safety of the fireplace that heats my grandma's cabin. I ask that you hear me, fire, and I summon you to this circle." I lit the red candle and the flame blazed, much brighter than should have been possible for an ordinary votive. The air around Shaunee and me was suddenly filled with the rich, woody scent and homey warmth of a roaring fireplace.

"Wow!" Shaunee exclaimed, her dark eyes dancing with the reflection of the candle's shimmering flame. "Now, that's cool!"

"That's two," I heard Damien say.

Erin was grinning when I took my place in front of her. "I'm ready for water," she said quickly.

"Water is relief on a hot Oklahoma summer day. It's the amazing ocean that I really would like to see someday, and it's the rain that makes the lavender grow. I ask that you hear me, water, and I summon you to this circle."

I lit the blue candle and felt instant coolness against my skin, as well as smelled a clean, salty scent that could only be the ocean I'd never seen.

"Awesome. Really, really awesome," Erin said, drawing in a deep breath of ocean air.

"That's three," Damien said.

"I'm not scared anymore," Stevie Rae said when I stood in front of her.

"Good," I said. Then I focused my mind on the fourth element, earth. "Earth supports and surrounds us. We wouldn't be anything without her. I ask that you hear me, earth, and I summon you to this circle." The green candle lit easily, and suddenly Stevie Rae and I were overwhelmed with the sweet scent of freshly cut grass. I heard the rustle of the oak's leaves and we looked up to see the great oak literally bowing its branches over us as though it would shield us from all harm.

"Totally amazing," Stevie Rae breathed.

"Four," Damien said, his voice filled with excitement.

I walked quickly to the center of the circle and lifted my purple candle.

"The last element is one that fills everything and everyone. It makes us unique and it breathes life into all things. I ask that you hear me, spirit, and I summon you to this circle."

Incredibly, it seemed that I was suddenly surrounded by the four elements, that I was in the middle of a whirlpool made up of air and fire, water and earth. But it wasn't scary, not at all. It filled me with peace, and at the same time I felt a surge of white-hot power and had to press my lips tightly together to keep from laughing with pure joy.

"Look! Look at the circle!" Damien shouted.

I blinked my vision clear and instantly felt the elements settle down, as if they were playful kittens who were sitting around me, waiting happily for me to call them to bat at string and whatnot. I was smiling at the comparison when I saw the glowing light that wrapped around the circumference of the circle, joining Damien, Shaunee, Erin, and Stevie Rae. It was bright and clear, and the luminous silver of a full moon.

"And that makes five," Damien said.

"Holy crap!" I blurted, very un–High Priestess-like, and the four of them laughed, filling the night with the sounds of happiness. And I understood, for the first time, why Neferet and Aphrodite had danced during the rituals. I wanted to dance and laugh and shout with happiness. *Another time,* I told myself. Tonight there was more serious work to be done.

"Okay, I'm going to speak the purification prayer," I told my four friends. "And while I say the prayer I'm going to face each of the elements, one at a time."

"What do you want us to do?" Stevie Rae asked.

"Focus on the prayer. Concentrate. Believe that the elements will carry it to Nyx, and that the Goddess will answer it by helping me to know what I should do," I said with way more certainty than I felt.

Once again I faced east. Damien smiled encouragement to me. And I began to recite the ancient purification prayer I'd said so many times with my grandma—with just a few changes I'd decided on earlier.

Great Goddess of Night, whose voice I hear in the wind, who breathes the breath of life to Her children. Hear me; I need your strength and wisdom.

I paused briefly as I turned to the south.

Let me walk in beauty, and make my eyes ever behold the red and purple sunset that comes before the beauty of your night. Make my hands respect the things you have made and my ears sharp to hear your voice. Make me wise so that I may understand the things you have taught your people.

I turned again to the right, and my voice felt stronger as I fell into the rhythm of the prayer.

Help me to remain calm and strong in the face of all that comes toward me. Let me learn the lessons you have hidden in every leaf and rock. Help me seek pure thoughts and act with the intention of helping others. Help me find compassion without empathy overwhelming me.

I faced Stevie Rae, whose eyes were squeezed shut as though she was concentrating with all of her might.

I seek strength, not to be greater than others, but to fight my greatest enemy, the doubts within myself.

I walked back to the center of the circle and finished the prayer, and for the first time in my life, I felt a flush of sensation as the power of the ancient words rushed from me to what I hoped with all my heart and soul was my listening Goddess.

Make me always ready to come to you with clean hands and straight eyes. So when life fades, as the fading sunset, my spirit may come to you without shame.

Technically, that was the conclusion of the Cherokee prayer my grandma had taught me, but I felt the need to add: "And Nyx, I don't understand why you Marked me and why you have given me the gift of an affinity for the elements. I don't even have to know. What I want to ask is that you help me know the right thing to do, and then give me the courage to do it." And I finished the prayer the way I remembered Neferet completed her ritual: "Blessed be!"

CHAPTER TWENTY-FOUR

—

"That was truly the most prodigious circle-casting I've ever experienced!" Damien gushed after the circle had been closed and we were gathering up the candles and smudge stick.

"I thought 'prodigious' meant 'big,'" Shaunee said.

"It also can show exciting wonder and can refer to something stupendous and monumental," Damien said.

"For once I'm not going to argue with you," Shaunee said, surprising everyone except Erin.

"Yeah, the circle was *prodigious*," Erin said.

"Do you know I actually could feel earth when Zoey called it?" Stevie Rae said. "It was like I was suddenly surrounded by a growing wheat field. No, it was more than being surrounded by it. It was like I was suddenly a part of it."

"I know exactly what you mean. When she called flame it was like the fire exploded through me," Shaunee said.

I tried to understand what I was feeling while the four of them talked happily together. I was definitely happy, but overwhelmed and more than a little confused. So it was true, I did have some kind of affinity with all five of the elements.

Why?

Just to bring down Aphrodite? (Which, by the by, I still didn't have a clue how to do.) No, I didn't think so. Why would Nyx touch me with such unusual power just so that I could kick a spoiled bully out of the leadership of a club?

Okay, the Dark Daughters were more than a student council or whatever, but still.

"Zoey, are you all right?"

The concern in Damien's voice made me look up from Nala, and I realized that I was sitting in the middle of what used to be the circle, with my cat on my lap, completely engrossed in my own thoughts as I scratched her head.

"Oh, yeah. Sorry. I'm fine, just a little distracted."

"We should get back. It's getting late," Stevie Rae said.

"Okay. You're right," I said, and got up, still holding Nala. But I couldn't make my feet follow them as they started to head back to the dorms.

"Zoey?"

Damien, the first to notice my hesitation, stopped and called back to me, and then my other friends stopped, looking at me with expressions that ranged from worried to confused.

"Uh, why don't you guys go ahead? I'm going to stay out here for just a little while longer."

"We could stay with you and—" Damien began, but Stevie Rae (bless her little bumpkin heart) interrupted him.

"Zoey needs to do some thinkin' on her own. Wouldn't you if you just found out you were the only fledgling in known history to have an affinity for all five elements?"

"I suppose," Damien said reluctantly.

"But don't forget that it'll be getting light soon," Erin said.

I smiled reassuringly at them. "I won't. I'll be back at the dorm soon."

"I'll make a sandwich for you and try to scare up some chips to go with your brown non-diet pop. It's important that a High

Priestess eats after she performs a ritual," Stevie Rae said with a smile and a wave as she pulled the rest of the four along with her.

I called thanks to Stevie Rae as they disappeared into the darkness. Then I walked over to the tree and sat down, resting my back against its thick trunk. I closed my eyes and petted Nala. Her purr was normal and familiar and incredibly soothing, and it seemed to help ground me.

"I'm still me," I whispered to my cat. "Just like Grandma said. All the other stuff can change, but what's really Zoey—what's been Zoey for sixteen years—is still Zoey."

Maybe if I repeated it over and over enough to myself, I'd actually believe it. I rested my face in one hand and scratched my cat with the other, and told myself that I was still me . . . still me . . . still me . . .

"See how she leans her cheek upon her hand! O, that I were a glove upon that hand, that I might touch that cheek!"

Nala "me-eeh-uf-owed" in complaint as I jumped in surprise.

"Seems like I keep finding you by this tree," Erik said, smiling down at me and looking like a god.

He made me feel all fluttery in my stomach, but tonight he also made me feel something else. Just exactly why did he keep "finding" me? And just exactly how long had he been watching this time?

"What are you doing out here, Erik?"

"Hi, it's nice to see you, too. And, yes, I would like to have a seat, thank you," he said and started to sit beside me.

I stood up, making Nala mutter at me again.

"Actually, I was just going to go back to the dorm."

"Hey, I didn't mean to intrude or whatever. I just couldn't concentrate on my homework so I went for a walk. I guess my feet carried me this way without me telling them to, 'cause next thing

I knew here I was and here you are. I'm really not stalking you. Promise."

He stuck his hands in his pockets and looked totally embarrassed. Well, totally cute and embarrassed, and I remembered how much I had wanted to say yes to him earlier when he asked me to watch dorky movies with him. And now here I was, rejecting him and making him uncomfortable again. It's a wonder the kid ever talked to me. Clearly, I was taking this High Priestess thing way too seriously.

"So how about walking me back to my dorm? Again," I asked.

"Sounds good."

This time Nala complained when I tried to carry her. Instead she trotted along after us while Erik and I fell into step together as easily as we had before. We didn't say anything for a while. I wanted to ask him about Aphrodite, or at the very least tell him what she'd said to me about him, but I couldn't come up with a good way of saying something that I probably didn't have any business questioning him about.

"So what were you doing out here this time?" he asked.

"Thinking," I said, which technically wasn't a lie. I had been thinking. A lot. Before, during, and after the circle-casting I was conveniently not going to mention.

"Oh. Are you worried about that Heath kid?"

Actually, I hadn't thought about Heath or Kayla since I'd talked to Neferet, but I shrugged, not wanting to get specific about what I'd been thinking.

"I mean, I guess it's probably hard to break up with someone just because you got Marked," he said.

"I didn't break up with him because I got Marked. He and I were pretty much finished before that. The Mark just made it more final." I looked at Erik and took a deep breath. "What about you and Aphrodite?"

He blinked in surprise. "What do you mean?"

"I mean today she told me that you'll never be her ex because you'll always be hers."

His eyes narrowed and he looked truly pissed. "Aphrodite has a serious problem with telling the truth."

"Well, not that it's any of my business, but—"

"It *is* your business," he said quickly. And then, totally and utterly shocking me, he took my hand. "At least I'd like it to be your business."

"Oh," I said. "Okay, well, okay." Once again, I was sure I was astounding him with my witty conversation skills.

"So you weren't just avoiding me tonight; you really had some thinking to do?" he asked slowly.

"I wasn't avoiding you. There's just . . . ," I hesitated, not sure how the hell to explain something I was pretty sure I shouldn't explain to him. "There's a lot of stuff going on with me right now. This whole Change thing is pretty confusing sometimes."

"It gets better," he said, squeezing my hand.

"Somehow, for me, I doubt it," I muttered.

He laughed and tapped my Mark with his finger. "You're just ahead of some of the rest of us. That's hard at first, but, believe me, it'll get easier—even for you."

I sighed. "I hope so." But I doubted it.

We stopped in front of the dorm, and he turned to me, his voice suddenly low and serious. "Z, don't believe the crap Aphrodite says. She and I haven't been together in months."

"But you used to be," I said.

He nodded and his face looked strained.

"She's not a very nice person, Erik."

"I know that."

And then I realized what had really been bothering me and decided, oh, well, what the hell, I'd just say it.

"I don't like it that you'd be with someone who's so mean. It makes me feel funny about wanting to be with you." He opened up his mouth to say something and I kept talking, not wanting to hear excuses I wasn't sure that I should or could believe. "Thanks for walking me home. I am glad you found me again."

"I'm glad I found you, too," he said. "I'd like to see you again, Z, and not just by accident."

I hesitated. And wondered why I was hesitating. I did want to see him again. I needed to forget Aphrodite. Seriously, she *is* really pretty and he *is* a guy. He probably fell into her haggish (and hot) clutches before he knew what was happening. I mean, she did kinda remind me of a spider. I should be glad that she hadn't bitten his head off, and give the guy a chance.

"Okay, how about I watch those dorky DVDs with you Saturday?" I said before I could freakishly talk myself out of going out with the most gorgeous guy at this school.

"It's a date," he said.

Obviously giving me time to pull away if I wanted to, Erik slowly bent down and kissed me. His lips were warm and he smelled really good. The kiss was soft and nice. Honestly, it made me want him to kiss me more. Too soon it was over, but he didn't move away from me. We were standing close, and I realized that I had my hands on his chest. His were resting lightly on my shoulders. I smiled up at him.

"I'm glad you asked me out again," I said.

"I'm glad you finally said yes," he said.

Then he kissed me again, only this time he wasn't hesitant. The kiss deepened, and my arms went up around his shoulders. I felt, more than heard, him moan and as he kissed me long and hard it was like he flipped a switch somewhere deep inside me, and hot, sweet, electric desire flashed through me. It was crazy and amazing, and more than anyone else's kisses had ever made me feel.

I loved the way my body fitted his, hard against soft, and I pressed myself against him, forgetting about Aphrodite and the circle I'd just cast and the entire rest of the world. This time when we broke off the kiss we were both breathing hard, and we stared at each other. As my sense started to return to me I realized that I was totally smushed against him and that I'd been standing there in front of the dorm making out like a slut. I started to pull out of his arms.

"What's wrong? Why do you suddenly look different?" he said, tightening his arms around me.

"Erik, I'm not like Aphrodite." I pulled harder and he let me go.

"I know you're not. I wouldn't like you if you were like her."

"I don't just mean my personality. I mean standing out here making out with you isn't normal behavior for me."

"Okay." He reached one hand toward me as though he wanted to pull me back into his arms, but then he seemed to change his mind and his hand fell to his side. "Zoey, you make me feel different than anyone has ever made me feel before."

I felt my face getting hot and I couldn't tell if it was from anger or embarrassment. "Don't patronize me, Erik. I saw you in the hall with Aphrodite. You've clearly felt this kind of stuff before, and more."

He shook his head and I saw hurt in his eyes. "What Aphrodite made me feel was all physical. What you make me feel is about touching my heart. I know the difference, Zoey, and I thought you did, too."

I stared at him—at those gorgeous blue eyes that had seemed to touch me the first time he looked at me. "I'm sorry," I said softly. "That was mean of me. I do know the difference."

"Promise me that you won't let Aphrodite come between us."

"I promise." It scared me, but I meant it.

"Good."

Nala materialized out of the dark and started winding around my legs and complaining. "I better get her inside and put her to bed."

"Okay." He smiled and gave me a quick kiss. "See you Saturday, Z."

My lips tingled all the way up to my room.

CHAPTER TWENTY-FIVE

—

The next day started with what I looked back on later as suspicious normalcy. Stevie Rae and I ate breakfast, still whispering good gossip about how hot Erik was and trying to figure out what I'd wear on our date Saturday. We didn't even see Aphrodite or the hag triplets, Warlike, Terrible, and Wasp. Vamp Soc class was so interesting—we'd moved from the Amazons to learning about an ancient Greek vampyre festival called Correia—that I'd stopped thinking about the Dark Daughters ritual planned for that evening, and for a little while I'd actually quit worrying about what I was going to do about Aphrodite. Drama class was good, too. I decided to do one of Kate's soliloquies from *The Taming of the Shrew* (I've loved that play ever since I saw the old movie starring Elizabeth Taylor and Richard Burton). Then as I was leaving class Neferet snagged me in the hall and asked how far I'd read in the upper level Vamp Soc book. I'd had to tell her that I really hadn't read much (translation: I hadn't read any) yet, and I was totally distracted by her obvious disappointment in me when I hurried into English class. I'd just taken my seat between Damien and Stevie Rae when all hell broke loose, and everything vaguely resembling anything normal about the day ended.

Penthesilea was reading "You Go and I'll Stay a While," Chapter Four of *A Night to Remember*. It's a really good book, and we were all listening, as usual, then that stupid Elliott kid started coughing. Jeesh, the kid was totally and completely annoying.

Somewhere in the middle of the chapter and the obnoxious coughing I started to smell something. It was rich and sweet, delicious, and elusive. Automatically, I inhaled deeply, still trying to concentrate on the book.

Elliott's coughing got worse, and with the rest of the class, I turned to give him a dirty look. I mean, please. Could he not get a cough drop or a drink or whatever?

And then I saw the blood.

Elliott wasn't in his usual slouched and sleeping position. He was sitting straight up, staring at his hand, which was covered with fresh blood. As I watched him, he coughed again, making a nasty, wet sound that reminded me of the day I'd been Marked. Only when Elliott coughed, bright scarlet blood spewed from his mouth.

"Wh—?" he gurgled.

"Get Neferet!" Penthesilea snapped the command as she jerked open one of her desk drawers, yanked out a neatly folded towel, and moved quickly down the aisle to Elliott. The kid who was sitting closest to the door took off.

In utter silence we watched Penthesilea make it to Elliott just in time for his next bloody cough, which she caught in the towel. He clutched the towel to his face, hacking and spitting and gagging. When he finally looked up, bloody tears were running down his pale, round face, and blood was running from his nose like it was a faucet someone had left on. When he turned his head to look up at Penthesilea, I could see that there was a red stream coming from his ear, too.

"No!" Elliott said with more emotion than I'd ever heard him show. "No! I don't want to die!"

"Soon," Penthesilea soothed, smoothing his orange hair back from his sweaty face. "Your pain will end soon."

"But—but, no I—" He started to protest again, in a whiny voice that sounded more like his own, then he was interrupted by another round of hacking coughs. He gagged again, this time puking blood into the already soaked towel.

Neferet entered the room with two tall, powerful-looking vampyre men close behind her. They carried a flat stretcher and a blanket; Neferet was carrying only a vial filled with milky-colored liquid. Not two breaths behind them, Dragon Lankford burst into the room.

"That's his mentor," Stevie Rae whispered almost soundlessly. I nodded, remembering when Penthesilea had chastised Elliott for letting Dragon down.

Neferet handed Dragon the vial she'd been holding. Then she stood behind Elliott. She put her hands on his shoulders. Instantly, his gagging and coughing subsided.

"Drink this quickly, Elliott," Dragon told him. When he started to weakly shake his head no, he added gently, "It will make your pain end."

"Will—will you stay with me?" Elliott gasped.

"Of course," Dragon said. "I won't let you be alone for even a moment."

"Will you call my mom?" Elliott whispered.

"I will."

Elliott closed his eyes for a second, and then, with shaking hands he held the vial to his lips and drank. Neferet nodded to the two men, and they picked him up and lay him on the stretcher as if he was a doll and not a dying kid. With Dragon by his side, they hurried from the room. Before Neferet followed them she turned to face the shocked classroom of third formers.

"I could tell you that Elliott will be fine—that he will recover, but that would be a lie." Her voice was serene, but filled with commanding strength. "The truth is his body has rejected the

Change. In minutes he will die the permanent death and will not mature into a vampyre. I could tell you not to worry, that it won't happen to you. But this would be a lie, too. On average, one out of every ten of you will not make the Change. Some fledglings die early in their third former year, as is Elliott. Some of you will be stronger and last until your sixth former year, and then sicken and die suddenly. I tell you this not so that you will live in fear. I tell you for two reasons. First, I want you to know that as your High Priestess I will not lie to you, but will help ease your passing into the next world if that time comes. And second, I want you to live as you would be remembered if you would die tomorrow, because you might. Then if you do die your spirit can rest peacefully knowing that you leave behind an honorable memory. If you do not die, then you will have set the foundation for a long life rich with integrity." She looked straight into my eyes as she finished, saying, "I ask that Nyx's blessing comfort you today, and that you remember death is a natural part of life, even a vampyre life. For someday we all must return to the bosom of the Goddess." She closed the door behind her with a sound that seemed to echo finality.

Penthesilea worked quickly and efficiently. Matter-of-factly she cleaned up the spatters of blood that stained Elliot's desk. When all evidence of the dying kid was gone, she returned to the front of the class and led us in a moment of silence for Elliott. Then she picked up the book and began reading where she'd left off. I tried to listen. I tried to block out the vision of Elliott bleeding out through his eyes and ears and nose and mouth. And I also tried not to think about the fact that the delicious smell I'd noticed had been, without a doubt, Elliott's lifeblood pouring from his dying body.

* * *

I know things are supposed to go on as usual after a fledgling dies, but apparently it was unusual for two kids to die so close together, and everyone was unnaturally quiet for the rest of the day. Lunch was silent and depressing, and I noticed that most of the food was picked at rather than eaten. The Twins didn't even bicker with Damien, which might have been a nice change if I hadn't known the awful reason behind it. When Stevie Rae made some lame excuse to leave lunch early and go back to the room before fifth hour started, I was more than happy to say I'd go with her.

We walked along the sidewalk in the thick dark of another cloudy night. Tonight the gaslights didn't feel cheerful and warm. Instead they seemed cold and not bright enough.

"No one liked Elliott, and somehow I think that makes it worse," Stevie Rae said. "It was weirdly easier with Elizabeth. At least we could feel honestly sorry she was gone."

"I know what you mean. I feel upset, but I know I'm really upset that I saw what can happen to us and now I can't get it out of my mind, and not upset that the kid's dead."

"At least it happens fast," she said softly.

I shivered. "I wonder if it hurts."

"They give you something—that white stuff Elliott drank. It makes it stop hurting, but it lets you be conscious till the end. And Neferet always helps with the actual dying."

"It's scary, isn't it?" I said.

"Yeah."

We didn't say anything for a while. Then the moon peeped through the clouds, painting the leaves of the tree with an eerie silver watercolor, and reminding me suddenly of Aphrodite and her ritual.

"Any chance Aphrodite will cancel the Samhain ritual tonight?"

"No way. The Dark Daughters' rituals are never cancelled."

"Well, hell," I said. Then I glanced at Stevie Rae. "He was their refrigerator."

She gave me a startled look. "Elliott?"

"Yeah, it was really gross, and he acted all drugged and weird. He must have been starting to reject the Change even then." There was an uncomfortable silence, and then I added, "I didn't want to say anything to you before, especially after you told me about . . . well . . . you know. Are you sure Aphrodite won't cancel tonight? I mean, what with Elizabeth and now Elliott."

"It won't matter. And the Dark Daughters don't care about the kid they use as a refrigerator. They'll just get someone else." She hesitated. "Zoey, I've been thinking. Maybe you shouldn't go tonight. I heard what Aphrodite said to you yesterday. She's going to make sure no one accepts you. She'll be really, really mean."

"I'll be okay, Stevie Rae."

"No, I have a bad feeling about it. You don't have a plan yet, do you?"

"Well, no. I'm still in the reconnoitering stage," I said, trying to lighten up the conversation.

"Reconnoiter later. Today's been too awful. Everyone's upset. I think you should wait."

"I can't just not show up, especially after what Aphrodite said to me yesterday. She'll think she told me and now she can intimidate me."

Stevie Rae took a deep breath. "Well, then I think you should take me with you." I started to shake my head but she kept right on talking. "You're a Dark Daughter now. Technically, you can invite people to the rituals. So invite me. I'll go and watch your back."

I thought about drinking blood and liking it so much that it was obvious, even to Warlike and Terrible. And I tried, and failed, not to think about the scent of blood—Heath's and Erik's and even Elliott's. Stevie Rae would find out someday how blood affected me, but it wouldn't be tonight. Actually, if I could help it, it wouldn't be anytime soon. I didn't want to chance losing her or the Twins or Damien—and I was afraid I would. Yes, they knew I was "special," and they accepted me because that uniqueness meant High Priestess to them, and that was good. My bloodlust was not so good. Would they accept it as easily?

"No way, Stevie Rae."

"But, Zoey, you shouldn't go into that hag pack alone."

"I won't be alone. Erik will be there."

"Yeah, but he used to be Aphrodite's boyfriend. Who knows how good he'll be at standing up to her if she gets real hateful with you."

"Honey, I can stand up for myself."

"I know, but—" She broke off and gave me a funny look. "Z, are you vibrating?"

"Huh? Am I what?" And then I heard it, too, and started laughing. "It's my cell phone. I stuck it in my purse after it charged up last night." I pulled it out of my purse, glancing at the time on the face dial. "It's past midnight, who the heck . . ." Flipping the phone open I was shocked to see that I had fifteen new text messages and five missed calls. "Jeesh, someone's been calling and calling, and I didn't even notice." I checked the text messages first, and felt my stomach start to clench as I read them.

Zo call me
I stl luv u
Zo call me plz
Got 2 see u
U & Me
Will u call?

I wnt 2 tlk 2 u
Zo!
Call me bak

I didn't need to read any more of them. They were all basically the same. "Ah, crap. They're all from Heath."

"Your ex?"

I sighed. "Yeah."

"What does he want?"

"Apparently, me." Reluctantly, I keyed in the code to access my voice messages, and Heath's cute, dopey voice shocked me with how loud and animated he sounded.

"Zo! Call me. Like, I know it's late, but . . . wait. It's not late to you, but it's late to me. But that's okay 'cause I don't care. I just want you to call me. Okay. So. Bye. Call me."

I groaned and deleted it. The next one sounded even more manic.

"Zoey! Okay. You need to call me. Really. And don't be mad. Hey, I don't even like Kayla. She's lame. I still love you, Zo, only you. So call me. I don't care when. I'll just wake up."

"Man oh man," Stevie Rae said, easily overhearing Heath's gushing. "The boy's obsessed. No wonder you dumped him."

"Yeah," I mumbled, quickly deleting the second message. The third was much like the first two, only more desperate. I turned the volume down and tapped my foot impatiently while I went through all five messages, not listening except to see when I could delete and move on to the next one. "I gotta go see Neferet," I said, more to myself than to Stevie Rae.

"How come? You need to block him from calling or something?"

"No. Yeah. Something like that. I just need to talk to her about, well, about what I should do." I avoided Stevie Rae's curious gaze.

"I mean, he's already showed up here once. I don't want him to come by again and cause any trouble."

"Oh, yeah, that's true. It'd be bad if he ran into Erik."

"It'd be awful. Okay, I better hurry and try to catch Neferet before fifth hour. I'll see you after school."

I didn't wait for Stevie Rae's good-bye, but took off in the direction of Neferet's room. Could this day get any worse? Elliott dies and I'm attracted to his blood. I have to go to the Samhain ritual tonight with a bunch of kids who hate me and want to make sure I know it, and I've probably Imprinted my ex-almost-boyfriend.

Yep. Today really, really sucked.

CHAPTER TWENTY-SIX

—

If Skylar's hissing and growling hadn't caught my attention, I would never have seen Aphrodite slumped in the little alcove down the hall from Neferet's room.

"What is it, Skylar?" I held my hand out gingerly, remembering what Neferet had said about her cat being a known biter. I was also sincerely glad that Nala wasn't tagging long after me as usual—Skylar would probably eat my poor little cat for lunch. "Kitty-kitty," the big orange tom gave me a considering look (probably considering whether or not to bite the crap out of my hand). Then he made his decision, un-puffed himself, and trotted over to me. He rubbed around my legs, then he gave the alcove one more good hiss before he took off, disappearing down the hall in the direction of Neferet's room.

"What the hell was his problem?" I looked hesitantly into the alcove, wondering what would make a mean cat like Skylar puff up and hiss, and I felt a jolt of shock. She was sitting right on the floor, hard to see in the shadow under the ledge that held a pretty statue of Nyx. Her head was tilted back, and her eyes were rolled so that only their whites were showing. She scared the total crap out of me. I felt frozen, expecting any second to see blood pouring down her face. Then she moaned and muttered something I couldn't understand while her eyeballs shifted around behind her closed lids as though she was watching a scene. I realized what must be happening. Aphrodite was having a vision. She'd probably felt it coming on and hidden in the alcove so no one would find her and she could keep her info about the death and destruction she could prevent to her hateful self. Cow. Hag.

Well, I was done letting her get away with that crap. I bent down and grabbed her under the arms, pulling her to her feet. (Let me tell you, she's a lot heavier than she looks.)

"Come on," I groaned, half carrying her while she lurched blindly forward with me. "Let's take a little trip down the hall and see what kind of tragedy you want to keep quiet about."

Thankfully, Neferet's room wasn't far away. We staggered in and Neferet jumped up from behind her desk and rushed to us.

"Zoey! Aphrodite! What?" But as soon as she got a good look at Aphrodite, her alarm changed to calm understanding. "Help me bring her over here to my chair. She'll be more comfortable there."

We led Aphrodite to Neferet's big leather chair, and let her sink into it. Then Neferet crouched beside her and took her hand.

"Aphrodite, with the Goddess's voice I beseech you to tell her Priestess what it is you see." Neferet's voice was soft, but compelling, and I could feel the power in her command.

Aphrodite's eyelids instantly began to flicker, and she drew a deep, gasping breath. Then they opened suddenly. Her eyes looked huge and glassy.

"So much blood! There's so much blood coming out of his body!"

"Who, Aphrodite? Center yourself. Focus and clear the vision," Neferet commanded.

Aphrodite drew another gasping breath. "They're dead! No. No. That can't be! Not right. No. Not natural! I don't understand . . . I don't . . ." She blinked her eyes again, and her gaze seemed to clear. She looked around the room, like she didn't recognize anything. Her eyes touched me. "You . . . ," she said faintly. "You know."

"Yeah," I said, thinking that I sure did know that she was trying to hide her vision, but all I said was, "I found you in the hall and—" Neferet's raised hand stopped me.

"No, she's not finished. She shouldn't be coming to so soon. The vision is still too abstract," Neferet told me quickly, and then she lowered her voice again and assumed the compelling, commanding tone. "Aphrodite, go back. See what it is you were meant to witness, and what you were meant to change."

Ha! Got you now. I couldn't help being a little smug. After all, she had tried to scratch my eyes out yesterday.

"The dead . . ." Getting more and more difficult to understand, Aphrodite murmured something that sounded like "Tunnels . . . they kill . . . someone there . . . I don't . . . I can't . . ." She was frantic, and I almost felt sorry for her. Clearly, whatever she was seeing was freaking her out. Then her searching eyes found Neferet, and I saw recognition flash through them and I started to relax. She was coming around and this whole weirdness would be cleared up. And just as I thought that, Aphrodite's eyes, which seemed to be locked on Neferet, widened unbelievably. A look of pure terror blanked her face and she screamed.

Neferet clamped her hands on Aphrodite's trembling shoulders. "Awaken!" She spared hardly a glance over her shoulder at me to say, "Go now, Zoey. Her vision is confused. Elliott's death has upset her. I need to be certain she is herself once more."

I didn't need to be told twice. Heath's obsession forgotten, I got the hell outta there and headed to Spanish class.

I couldn't concentrate on school. I kept replaying the weird scene with Neferet and Aphrodite over and over in my head. She'd obviously been having a vision about people dying, but from Neferet's reaction it hadn't behaved like a normal vision (if there was such a thing). Stevie Rae had said that Aphrodite's visions were so clear that she could direct people to the right airport and even the specific plane she'd seen crashing. Yet today, all of a sudden, nothing was clear. Well, nothing but seeing me and saying weird stuff, and then screaming her brains out at Neferet. It so didn't make sense. I was almost looking forward to seeing how she'd act tonight. Almost.

I put away Persephone's curry brushes and picked up Nala, who'd been perched on top of the horse's feeder watching and making her weird me-eeh-uf-ows at me, and started slowly back to the dorm. This time Aphrodite didn't hassle me, but when I rounded the corner by the old oak Stevie Rae, Damien, and the Twins were huddled together doing a lot of talking—that suddenly shut up when I came into view. They all looked guiltily at me. It was pretty easy to guess who they'd been talking about.

"What?" I said.

"We were just waiting for you," Stevie Rae said. Her usual perkiness was missing.

"What's wrong with you?" I asked.

"She's worried about you," Shaunee said.

"We're worried about you," Erin said.

"What's going on with your ex?" Damien asked.

"He's buggin', that's all. If he didn't bug, he wouldn't be my ex." I tried to speak nonchalantly, without looking any of the four of them in the eye too long. (I've never been a particularly good liar.)

"We think I should go with you tonight," Stevie Rae said.

"Actually, we think *we* should go with you tonight," Damien corrected.

I frowned at them. No possible way I wanted all four of them to watch me drink whatever loser kid's blood they managed to mix into the wine tonight.

"No."

"Zoey, it's been a really bad day. Everyone's stressed. Plus, Aphrodite is out to get you. It makes sense that we should stick together tonight," Damien said logically.

Yeah, it was logical, but they didn't know the whole story. I didn't want them to know the whole story. Yet. The truth was, I cared too much about them. They made me feel accepted and safe—they made me feel like I fit in here. I couldn't risk losing that right now, not when all of this was still so new and so scary. So I did what I had learned to do too well at home when I was scared and upset and didn't know what else to do—I got pissed and defensive.

"You guys say that I have powers that will someday make me your High Priestess?" They all nodded eagerly and smiled at me, which squeezed my heart. I gritted my teeth and made my voice real cold. "Then you need to listen to me when I say no. I don't want you there tonight. This is something I have to deal with. Alone. And I don't want to talk about it anymore."

And then I stomped away from them.

Naturally, within half an hour I was sorry I'd been so awful. I paced back and forth under the big oak that had somehow become my sanctuary, annoying Nala and wishing that Stevie Rae would show up so I could apologize. My friends didn't know why I didn't want them there. They were just looking out for me. Maybe . . . maybe they would understand about the blood thing. Erik seemed to understand. Okay, sure, he was a fifth former, but still. We were all supposed to go through it. We were all supposed to start craving blood—or we died. I brightened a little and scratched Nala's head.

"When the alternative is death, blood drinking doesn't seem so bad. Right?"

She purred, so I took that as a yes. I checked the time on my watch. Crap. I had to go back to the dorm, change my clothes, and go meet the Dark Daughters. Listlessly, I started following the wall back. It was a cloudy night again, but I didn't mind the darkness. Actually, I was starting to like the night. I should. It was going to be my element for a very long time. If I lived. As though she could read my morbid thoughts, Nala "me-eeh-uf-owed" grumpily at me as she trotted along beside me.

"Yeah, I know. I shouldn't be so negative. I'll work on that right after I—"

Nala's low growl surprised me. She'd stopped. Her back was arched and her hair was standing on end, making her look like a fat little puffball, but her slitted eyes were no joke, and neither was the ferocious hiss that snaked from her mouth. "Nala, what . . ."

A terrible chill fingered its way down my spine even before I turned to look in the direction my cat was staring. Later, I couldn't figure out why I didn't scream. I remember my mouth opening so I could gulp air, but I was absolutely silent. It seemed I'd gone numb, but that was impossible. If I'd been numb there's no way I could have been so thoroughly petrified.

Elliott was standing not ten feet from me in the darkness that shadowed the space next to the wall. He must have been heading in the same direction Nala and I were walking. Then he'd heard Nala, and half turned back toward us. She hissed again at him and, with a frighteningly quick movement he whirled around to fully face us.

I swear I couldn't breathe. He was a ghost—he had to be, but he looked so solid, so real. If I hadn't watched his body rejecting the Change, I would have thought he was just looking especially pale and . . . and . . . *weird.* He was abnormally white, but there was more wrong about him than that. His eyes had changed. They reflected what little light there was and they glowed a terrible rust red, like dried blood.

Exactly as the ghost of Elizabeth's eyes had glowed.

There was something else different about him, too. His body looked strange—thinner. How was that possible? The smell came to me then. Old and dry and out of place, like a closet that hadn't been opened in years or a creepy basement. It was the same smell I'd noticed just before I'd seen Elizabeth.

Nala growled and Elliott dropped into an odd, half crouch and hissed back at her. Then he bared his teeth, and I could see that *he had fangs!* He took a step toward Nala as if he was going to attack her. I didn't think, I just reacted.

"Leave her alone and get the hell out of here!" It amazed me that I sounded like I wasn't doing anything more exciting than yelling at a bad dog, because I was definitely scared totally shitless.

His head swiveled in my direction and the glow of his eyes touched me for the first time. *Wrong!* The intuitive voice inside me that had become familiar was screaming. *This is an abomination!*

"You . . ." His voice was horrible. It was raspy and guttural, as if something had damaged his throat. "I will have you!" And he began to come toward me.

Raw fear engulfed me like a bitter wind.

Nala's battle yowl rent the night as she hurled herself at Elliott's ghost. In complete shock I watched, expecting the cat to go spitting and clawing through empty air. Instead she landed on his thigh, claws extended, scratching and howling like an animal three times her size. He screamed, grabbed her by the scruff of her neck, and threw her away from him. Then, with impossible speed and strength he literally leaped to the top of the wall, and disappeared into the night that surrounded the school.

I was shaking so hard that I stumbled. "Nala!" I sobbed. "Where are you, little girl?"

Puffed up and growling, she padded over to me, but her slitted eyes were still focused on the wall. I crouched beside her, and with shaking hands checked to make sure she felt all in one piece. She felt unbroken, so I scooped her up and began jogging away from the wall as fast as I could.

"It's okay. We're okay. He's gone. What a brave girl you were." I kept talking to her. She perched halfway over my shoulder so that she could see behind us, and she continued to growl.

When I got to the first gaslight, not far from the rec hall, I stopped and shifted Nala's position so that I could look more closely to see that she was really okay. What I found made my stomach clench so hard I thought I was going to throw up. On her paws was blood. Only it wasn't Nala's. And it didn't smell delicious like other blood had smelled. Instead it carried the scent of musty dryness, old basements. I forced myself not to retch as I wiped her paws on the winter grass. Then I picked her up again and hurried down the sidewalk that led to the dorm. Nala never stopped looking behind us and growling.

Stevie Rae, the Twins, and Damien were all conspicuously absent from the dorm. They weren't watching TV—they weren't in the computer room or the library, and they weren't in the kitchen, either. I climbed quickly up the stairs, hoping desperately that at least Stevie Rae would be in our room. No such luck.

I sat on my bed, petting the still distraught Nala. Should I try to find my friends? Or should I just stay here? Stevie Rae would eventually come back to our room. I looked at her gyrating Elvis clock. I had about ten minutes to get changed and to the rec hall. But how could I go on to the ritual after what had just happened?

What *had* just happened?

A ghost had tried to attack me. No. That wasn't right. How

could ghosts bleed? But had it been blood? It didn't smell like blood. I had no idea what was going on.

I should go directly to Neferet and tell her what had happened. I should get up right now and take myself and my freaked-out cat to Neferet and tell her about Elizabeth last night and now Elliott tonight. I should . . . I should . . .

No. This time it wasn't a scream within me. It was the strength of certainty. I could not tell Neferet, at least not at that moment.

"I have to go to the ritual." I said aloud the words that were echoing through my mind. "I have to be at this ritual."

As I pulled on the black dress and searched around the closet for my ballet flats I felt myself becoming very calm. Things here didn't play by the same rules as they did in my old world—in my old life—and it was time I accepted that and started getting used to it.

I had an affinity for the five elements, which meant that I had been gifted with incredible powers by an ancient goddess. As Grandma had reminded me, with great power comes great responsibility. Maybe I was being allowed to see things—like ghosts that didn't act or look or smell like ghosts should—for a reason. I didn't know what that meant yet. Actually, I didn't know much besides the two thoughts that were clearest in my mind: I couldn't tell Neferet, and I had to go to the ritual.

Hurrying to the rec hall I tried to at least think positively. Maybe Aphrodite would not show up tonight, or be there but forget to harass me.

It turned out, as my luck would have it, neither was the case.

CHAPTER TWENTY-SEVEN

—

"Nice dress, Zoey. It looks just like mine. Oh, wait! It used to be mine." Aphrodite laughed a throaty, I'm-so-grown-up-and-you're-just-a-kid laugh. I really hate it when girls do that. I mean, yes, she's older, but I have boobs, too.

I smiled, purposefully putting an extra dose of cluelessness into my voice and launched into a gihugic lie, which I think I pulled off pretty well considering I'm a bad liar, I had just been attacked by a ghost, and everybody was staring at us and listening in.

"Hi, Aphrodite! Gosh, I was just reading the chapter in the Soc 415 book Neferet gave me about how important it is for the leader of the Dark Daughters to make every new member of the group feel welcome and accepted. You must be proud that you're doing your job so well." Then I stepped a little closer to her and lowered my voice so she alone could hear me. "And I must say you look better than you did the last time I saw you." I watched her pale and was sure fear flickered through her eyes. Surprisingly, it didn't make me feel victorious and smug. It just made me feel mean and shallow and tired. I sighed. "Sorry. I shouldn't have said that."

Her face hardened. "Fuck off, freak," she hissed. Then she laughed as though she'd just made a huge joke (at my expense), turned her back on me, and with a hateful flip of her hair walked to the middle of the rec hall.

Okay, I didn't feel bad anymore. Hateful cow. She raised one slim arm, and everyone who had been gawking at me now turned their attention (thankfully) to her. Tonight she had on an antique-looking red silk dress that fit her as if it had been painted on. I'd like to know just exactly where she got her clothes. Goth ho store?

"A fledgling died yesterday, and then another one died today."

Her voice was strong and clear, and sounded almost compassionate, which surprised me. For a second she really did remind me of Neferet, and I wondered whether she was going to say something profound and leader-like.

"We all knew both of them. Elizabeth had been nice and quiet. Elliott had been our refrigerator for the past several rituals." She smiled suddenly; it was feral and mean, and any resemblance she might have had to Neferet ended. "But they were weak, and vampyres do not need weakness in their coven." She shrugged her scarlet-covered shoulders. "If we were humans we'd call it survival of the fittest. Thank the Goddess we're not humans, so let's just call it Fate, and be happy tonight that it didn't kick any of our asses."

I was totally grossed out to hear sounds of general agreement. I hadn't really known Elizabeth, but she'd been nice to me. Okay, I admit that I hadn't liked Elliott—no one had. The kid was annoying and unattractive (and his ghost or whatever seemed to be carrying on those traits), but I was not glad he died. *If I'm ever leader of the Dark Daughters I won't make fun of the death of a fledgling, no matter how insignificant.* I made the promise to myself, but I was also conscious of sending it out like a prayer. I hoped Nyx heard me, and I hoped she approved.

"But enough gloom and doom," Aphrodite was saying. "It's Samhain! The night when we celebrate the end of the harvest season and, even better, it is the time when we remember our ancestors—all the great vampyres who have lived and died before us." The tone of her voice was creepy, like she was getting into the show she was putting on way too much, and I rolled my eyes as she continued. "It's the night when the veil between life and death is thinnest and when spirits are most likely to walk the earth." She paused and looked around the audience, being careful to ignore me (like everyone else was). I had a moment to wonder about what she'd just said. Could what have happened with Elliott have something to do with the veil between life and death being thinnest, and the fact that he had died on Samhain? I didn't have time to wonder any more about it because Aphrodite raised her voice and shouted, "So what are we going to do?"

"Go out!" the Dark Daughters and Sons yelled back.

Aphrodite's laugh was way too sexual to be appropriate, and I swear she touched herself. Right there in front of everyone. Jeesh, she was nasty.

"That's right. I've chosen an awesome place for us tonight, and we even have a new little refrigerator waiting for us there with the girls."

Ugh. By "the girls" did she mean Warlike, Terrible, and Wasp? I glanced quickly around the room. Didn't see them anywhere. Great. I could only imagine what those three plus Aphrodite would consider "awesome." And I didn't even want to think about the poor kid who had somehow been talked into being their new refrigerator.

And, yes, I was going to be in total denial about the fact that my mouth watered when Aphrodite mentioned that there was a refrigerator waiting for us, which meant I was going to get to drink blood again.

"So let's get out of here. And remember, be silent. Focus your minds on being invisible, and any human who happens to still be awake will simply not see us." Then she looked right at me. "And may Nyx have mercy on anyone who gives us away, because we certainly won't." She smiled silkily back at the group. "Follow me, Dark Daughters and Sons!"

In silent pairs and small groups, everyone followed Aphrodite out the back door of the rec hall. Naturally, they ignored me. I almost didn't follow them. I really didn't want to. I mean, I'd had enough excitement for one night. I should go back to the dorm and apologize to Stevie Rae. Then we could find the Twins and Damien, and I could tell them about Elliott (I paused to consider whether my gut feeling was warning me against telling my friends, but it stayed silent). Okay. So. I could tell them. That sounded like a better idea than following bitchy Aphrodite and a group of kids who couldn't stand me. But my intuition, which had been quiet when I'd thought about talking to my friends, suddenly reared up again. I had to go to the ritual. I sighed.

"Come on, Z. You don't want to miss the show, do you?"

Erik was standing by the back door, looking like Superman with his blue eyes smiling at me.

Well, hell.

"Are you kidding? Hateful girls, totally cliquish drama-trauma, and the possibility for embarrassment and bloodletting. What's not to love? I wouldn't miss a minute of it." Together Erik and I followed the group out the door.

Everyone was walking quietly to the wall behind the rec hall, which was too close to where I'd seen Elizabeth and Elliott for me to feel comfortable. And then, weirdly, the kids seemed to disappear into the wall.

"What the—?" I whispered.

"It's just a trick. You'll see."

I did. It was actually a trap door. Like the kind you see in those old murder movies, only instead of a door in a library wall or inside a fireplace (as in one of the Indiana Jones movies—yes, I'm a dork), this trap door was a small section of the thick, otherwise solid-looking school wall. Part of it swung out, leaving an open space just big enough for one person (or fledgling or vamp or possibly even a freakishly solid ghost or two) to slip through. Erik and I were the last ones through. I heard a soft *whoosh,* and looked back in time to see the wall closing seamlessly.

"It's on an automatic keypad, like a car door," Erik whispered.

"Huh. Who all knows about this?"

"Anyone who's ever been a Dark Daughter or Son."

"Huh." I suspected that was probably most of the adult vamps. I glanced around. I didn't see anyone watching us, or following us.

Erik noticed my look. "They don't care. It's school tradition that we sneak out for some of the rituals. As long as we don't do anything too stupid, they pretend like they don't know we're going." He shrugged. "It works out okay, I guess."

"As long as we don't do anything too stupid," I said.

"Shush!" Someone in front of us hissed. I closed my mouth and decided to concentrate on where we were going.

It was about four thirty A.M. Uh, no one was awake. Big surprise. It was weird to be walking through this really cool part of Tulsa—a neighborhood filled with mansions built by old oil money—and have nobody notice us. We were cutting through amazingly landscaped yards and no dogs were even barking at us. It was as if we were shadows . . . or ghosts. . . . The thought gave me a creepy chill. The moon that earlier had been mostly obscured by clouds was now shining silver-white in an unexpectedly clear sky. I swear that even before I was Marked I could have read by its light. It was cold, but that didn't bother me like it would have just a week ago. I tried not to think about what that meant about the Change that was going on inside my body.

We crossed a street, then slid soundlessly between two yards. I heard running water before I saw the little footbridge. The moonlight lit up the stream as though someone had spilled mercury across the top of it. I felt captured by its beauty, and I automatically slowed down, reminding myself that night was my new day. I hoped that I would never get used to the dark majesty of it.

"Come on, Z," whispered Erik from the other side of the bridge.

I looked up at him. He was silhouetted against an incredible mansion that stretched up the hill behind him with its huge, terraced lawn and pond and gazebo and fountains and waterfalls (these people clearly had entirely too much money), and he reminded me of one of those romantic heroes out of history, like . . . like . . . Well, the only two heroes I could think of were Superman and Zorro, and neither of them were truly historical. But he did look very knight-like and romantic. And then it registered on me exactly which amazing mansion we were trespassing on, and I hurried across the bridge to him.

"Erik," I whispered frantically, "this is the Philbrook Museum! We're really going to get in trouble if they catch us messing around here."

"They won't catch us."

I had to scramble to keep up with him. He was walking fast, much more eager than me to catch up with the silent, ghostlike group.

"Okay, this isn't just some rich guy's house. This is a *museum*. There are twenty-four-hour security guards here."

"Aphrodite will have drugged them."

"What!"

"Ssssh. It doesn't hurt them. They'll be groggy for a while and then go home and not remember anything. No big deal."

I didn't reply, but I really didn't like that he was so 'whatever' about drugging security guards. It just didn't seem right, even though I could understand the need for it. We were trespassing. We didn't want to get caught. So the guards needed to be drugged. I got it. I just didn't like it, and it sounded like yet another thing that was begging to be changed about the Dark Daughters and their holier-than-thou attitudes. They reminded me more and more of the People of Faith, which was not a flattering comparison. Aphrodite wasn't God (or Goddess, for that matter), despite what she called herself.

Erik had stopped walking. We stepped up to join the group where it had formed a loose circle around the domed gazebo situated at the bottom of the gentle slope that led up to the museum. It was close to the ornamental fishpond that ended right before the terraces leading up to the museum began. It really was an incredibly beautiful place. I'd been there two or three times on field trips, and once, with my Art class, I'd even been inspired to sketch the gardens, even though I definitely can not draw. Now the night had changed it from a place with pretty, well-tended gardens and marble water features into a magical fairy kingdom all washed in the light of the moon and shaded by layers of grays and silvers and midnight blues.

The gazebo itself was amazing. It sat on the top of huge round stairs, throne-like, so that you had to climb up to it. It was made of carved white columns, and the dome was lit from beneath, so that it looked like something that could have been found in ancient Greece, and then restored to its original glory and lit for the night to see.

Aphrodite climbed the stairs to take her place in the middle of the gazebo, which immediately sucked some of the magic and beauty from it. Naturally, Warlike, Terrible, and Wasp were there, too. Another girl was with them, who I didn't recognize. Of course I could have seen her a zillion times and wouldn't have remembered—she was just another Barbie-like blond (although her name probably meant something like Wicked or Hateful). They'd set up a little table in the middle of the gazebo and draped it with black cloth. I could see that there were a bunch of candles on it, and some other stuff, including a goblet and a knife. Some poor kid was slumped with his head down on the table. A cloak had been pulled around him, so that it covered his body, and he looked a lot like Elliott on the night he'd been the refrigerator.

It must really take a lot out of a kid to have his blood drained for Aphrodite's rituals, and I wondered whether that had anything to do with bringing on Elliott's death. I blocked from my mind the fact that my mouth started watering when I thought about the kid's blood being mixed with the wine in the goblet. Weird how something could totally gross me out and make me want it really bad at the same time.

"I will cast the circle and call the spirits of our ancestors to dance within it with us," Aphrodite said. She spoke softly, but her voice traveled around us like a poisonous mist. It was spooky to think about ghosts being drawn to Aphrodite's circle, especially after my own recent experiences with ghosts, but I have to admit that it intrigued me almost as much as it scared me. Maybe I was so certain I had to be here because I was meant to get some clue about Elizabeth and Elliott tonight. Plus, this ritual was obviously something the Dark Daughters had been doing for a while. It couldn't be that scary or dangerous. Aphrodite played all big and cool, but I had a feeling that it was an act. Underneath she was what all bullies are—insecure and immature. Also, bullies tended to avoid anyone tougher than them, so it was only logical that if Aphrodite was going to call spirits into a circle it meant that they were harmless, probably even nice. Aphrodite was definitely not going to face down a big, bad, boogie monster.

Or anything as truly freaky as what Elliott had become.

I started to relax into welcoming what was already becoming a familiar hum of power as the four Dark Daughters took candles that corresponded to the element they were representing, and then moved to the correct area of the mini-circle in the gazebo. Aphrodite summoned wind, and my hair lifted gently in a breeze that only I could feel. I closed my eyes, loving the electricity that tingled across my skin. Actually, in spite of Aphrodite and the stuck-up Dark Daughters, I was already enjoying the beginning of the ritual. And Erik was standing beside me, which helped me not to care that no one else there would talk to me.

I relaxed more, certain suddenly that the future wasn't going to be that bad. I'd make up with my friends, we'd figure out together what the hell was going on with the weird ghosts, and maybe I'd even get a totally hot boyfriend. Everything would be okay. I opened my eyes and watched Aphrodite move around the circle. Each element sizzled through me, and I wondered how Erik could stand so close to me and not notice it. I even snuck a peek at him, half expecting him to be staring at me as the elements played over my skin, but, like everyone else, he was looking at Aphrodite. (Which was actually annoying—wasn't he supposed to be sneaking looks at me, too?) Then Aphrodite began the ritual of summoning of the ancestral spirits, and even I couldn't keep my attention from her. She stood at the table, holding a long braid of dried grass over the purple spirit flame, so that it lit quickly. She allowed it to burn for a little while, and then blew it out. She waved it gently around her as she began to speak, filling the area with tendrils of smoke. I sniffed, recognizing the scent of sweet grass, one of the most sacred of ceremonial herbs because it attracted spiritual energy. Grandma used it often in her prayers. Then I frowned and felt a tendril of worry. Sweet grass should be used only after sage has been burned to cleanse and purify the area; if not, it might attract any energy—and "any" didn't always mean good. But it was too late to say anything, even if I could have stopped the ceremony. She had already begun calling to the spirits, and her voice had taken on an eerie, singsong quality that was somehow intensified by the smoke that curled thickly around her.

On this Samhain night, hear my ancient call all you spirits of our ancestors. On this Samhain night, let my voice carry with this smoke to the Otherworld where bright spirits play in the sweet grass mists of memory. On this Samhain night I do not call the spirits of our human ancestors. No, I let them sleep; I have no need for them in life or in death. On this Samhain night I call magical ancestors— mystical ancestors—those who were once more than human, and who, in death, are more than human.

Completely entranced, I watched with everyone else as the smoke swirled and changed and began to take on forms. At first I thought I was seeing things, and I tried to blink my vision clear, but soon I understood what I was seeing had nothing to do with blurry vision. There *were* people forming within the smoke. They were indistinct, more like the outlines of bodies than actual bodies themselves, but as Aphrodite continued to wave the sweet grass they grew more substantial, and then suddenly the circle was filled with spectral figures that had dark, cavernous eyes and open mouths.

They didn't look anything like Elizabeth or Elliott. Actually, they looked exactly as I imagined ghosts would—smoky and transparent and creepy. I sniffed the air. Nope, I definitely didn't smell any old basement yuckiness.

Aphrodite put down the still-smoking grass and picked up the goblet. Even from where I was watching, it seemed that she looked unusually pale, as though she had taken on some of the physical characteristics of the ghosts. Her red dress was almost painfully bright within the circle of smoke and gray and mist.

"I greet you, ancestral spirits, and ask that you accept our offering of wine and blood so that you may remember what it is to taste life." She lifted the goblet, and the smoky shapes churned and roiled with obvious excitement. "I greet you, ancestral spirits, and within the protection of my circle I—"

"Zo! I knew I'd find you if I tried hard enough!"

Heath's voice sliced through the night, cutting off Aphrodite's words.

CHAPTER TWENTY-EIGHT

—

"Heath! What in the hell are you doing here!"

"Well, you didn't call me back." Oblivious to everyone else, he hugged me. I didn't need the bright light of the moon for me to see his bloodshot eyes. "I missed you, Zo!" he blurted, wafting beer breath all over me.

"Heath. You need to go—"

"No. Let him stay," Aphrodite interrupted me.

Heath's gaze swiveled up to her, and I imagined what she must look like through his eyes. She stood in the pool of light made by the gazebo's spotlights shining through the sweet grass smoke, illuminating her almost as though she was underwater. Her red silk dress clung to her body. Her blond hair was thick and heavy down her back. Her lips were tilted up in a mean-looking smile, which I'm sure Heath would misunderstand and think she was being nice. Actually, he probably wouldn't even notice the smoky ghosts that had stopped hovering around the goblet and had now turned their blank eyes toward him. He also wouldn't notice that Aphrodite's voice had a weird, hollow sound to it and that her eyes were glassy and staring. Hell, knowing Heath he wouldn't notice anything except her big boobies.

"Cool, a vampyre chick," Heath said, totally proving me right.

"Get him out of here." Erik's voice was tight with worry.

Heath tore his eyes from Aphrodite's boobs to glare at Erik. "Who're you?"

Ah, crap. I recognized that tone. It was the one Heath used when he was getting ready to have a jealous fit. (Another reason he was my ex.)

"Heath, you need to get out of here," I said.

"No." He stepped closer to me and put his arm possessively around my shoulders, but he didn't look at me. He kept staring down Erik. "I came to see my girlfriend, and I'm gonna see my girlfriend."

I ignored the fact that I could feel Heath's pulse where his arm rested against my shoulders. Instead of doing something utterly gross and disturbing, like biting into his wrist, I shrugged off his arm and then yanked at it so he had to face me and not Erik.

"I am *not* your girlfriend."

"Aw, Zo, you're just sayin' that."

I gritted my teeth. God, he was dumb. (Yet *another* reason he was my ex.)

"Are you stupid?" Erik said.

"Look, you bloodsucking fuck, I'm—" Heath began to say, but Aphrodite's strangely echoing voice drowned him out.

"Come up here, human."

Like our eyes were magnets to her freaky attraction, Heath, Erik, and I (and, for that matter, the rest of the Dark Daughters and Sons) stared up at her. Her body looked weird. Was it pulsing? How could it? She flipped back her hair and ran one hand down her body like a nasty stripper, cupping her breast and then moving down to rub between her legs. Her other hand lifted and she curled her finger, beckoning Heath.

"Come to me, human. Let me taste you."

This was bad; this was wrong. Something terrible was going to happen to Heath if he went up there and stepped within that circle.

Totally entranced by her, Heath lurched forward without any hesitation (or common sense). I grabbed one of his arms, and was pleased to see Erik grab his other.

"Stop it, Heath! I want you to go. Now. You don't belong here."

With an effort, Heath pulled his eyes from Aphrodite. He jerked his arm from Erik's grip and practically growled at him. Then he turned on me.

"You're cheating on me!"

"Can you not listen? It's impossible for me to cheat on you. We are not together! Now get out of—"

"If he refuses our summons, then we shall go to him."

My head jerked up to see Aphrodite's body convulse as gray wisps seeped out of her. She let out a gasp that was a cross between a sob and a scream. The spirits, including the ones that had obviously been possessing her, rushed to the edge of the circle, pressing against it in an effort to break free and get to Heath.

"Stop them, Aphrodite. If you don't they'll kill him!" Damien shouted as he stepped out from behind an ornamental hedge that framed the pond.

"Damien, what—" I began, but he shook his head.

"No time to explain," he told me quickly before turning his attention back to Aphrodite. "You know what they are," he called up to her. "You have to contain them in the circle or he'll die."

Aphrodite was so pale she looked like a ghost herself. She moved away from the smoky shapes that were still trying to push against the invisible boundary of the circle, until she was pressed against one edge of the table.

"I won't stop them. If they want him, they can have him. Better him than me—or any of the rest of us," Aphrodite said.

"Yeah, we don't want any part of this kind of shit!" said Terrible before dropping her candle, which sputtered and went out. Without another word, she ran out of the circle and down the gazebo stairs. The other three girls who were supposed to be personifying the elements followed her lead, disappearing quickly into the night and leaving their candles overturned and unlit.

Horrified, I watched one of the gray shapes begin to melt through the circle. The smoke that was his spectral body began seeping down the stairs, reminding me of a snake as it slithered in our direction. I felt the Dark Daughters and Sons stir and glanced around me. They were nervously backing away, looks of fear twisting their faces.

"It's up to you, Zoey."

"Stevie Rae!"

She was standing unsteadily in the middle of the circle. She'd thrown off the cape that had covered her, and I could see the white linen bandages on her wrists.

"I told you we needed to stick together." She smiled weakly at me.

"Better hurry," Shaunee said.

"Those ghosts are scaring the shit right outta your ex," Erin said.

I looked over my shoulder to see the Twins standing beside the white-faced, open-mouthed Heath, and I felt a jolt of pure happiness. They hadn't abandoned me! I wasn't alone!

"Let's get this done," I said. "Keep him here," I told Erik, who was staring at me with obvious shock.

Without needing to look back to be sure my friends were following me, I hurried up the steep stairs to the ghost-filled gazebo. When I reached the boundary of the circle I hesitated for a second. The spirits were slowly dissolving through it, their attention completely focused on Heath. I took a deep breath and stepped inside the invisible barrier, feeling an awful chill as the dead brushed restlessly against my skin.

"You have no right to be here. This is *my* circle," Aphrodite said, pulling herself together enough to wrinkle her lip at me and block my way to the table and the spirit candle, which was the only one still lit.

"*Was* your circle. Now you need to shut up and move," I told her.

Aphrodite narrowed her eyes at me.

Ah, crap. I really didn't have time for this.

"Bobble-head, you need to do what Zoey says. I have been dying to kick the shit outta you for two years," Shaunee said, moving up to stand beside me.

"Me, too, you nasty ho bag," Erin said, stepping up to my other side.

Before the Twins could pounce on her, Heath's scream shattered the night. I whirled around. Mist was crawling up Heath's legs, leaving long, thin tears in his jeans that instantly began to weep blood. Panicked, he was kicking and shrieking. Erik hadn't run away, but was hitting at the mist, too, even though whenever some of it stuck on him it ripped his clothes and tore open his skin.

"Fast! Take your places," I yelled before the seductive smell of their blood could mess with my concentration.

My friends ran to the deserted candles. Hastily they picked them up and waited in the proper positions.

I moved around Aphrodite, who was staring at Heath and Erik, with her hand pressed against her mouth as if to hold back her screams. I grabbed the purple candle and rushed over to Damien.

"Wind! I summon you to this circle," I yelled, touching the purple candle to the yellow one. I wanted to cry with relief when the familiar whirlwind suddenly sprang up, swirling around my body and lifting my hair crazily.

Shielding the purple candle with my hand I ran to Shaunee.

"Fire! I summon you to this circle!" Heat flared with the whirling air as I lit the red candle. I didn't pause, but kept moving clockwise around the circle. "Water! I summon you to this circle!" The sea was there, salty and sweet at the same time. "Earth! I summon you to this circle!" I touched the flame to Stevie Rae's candle, trying not to flinch at the bandages that covered her wrists. She was abnormally pale, but she grinned when the air filled with the scent of freshly cut hay.

Heath screamed again, and I rushed back to the center of the circle and lifted the purple candle. "Spirit! I summon you to this circle!" Energy sizzled into me. I glanced around at the boundary of my circle and, sure enough, I could see the ribbon of power marking its circumference. I closed my eyes for an instant. *Oh, thank you, Nyx!*

Then I put the candle down on the table and grabbed the goblet of bloody wine. I turned to face Heath and Erik and the ghostly horde.

"Here is your sacrifice!" I yelled, sloshing the liquid in the goblet in a messy arc around me, so that it made a blood-colored circle on the gazebo floor. "You weren't called here to kill. You were called here because it's Samhain and we wanted to honor you." I spilled more wine, trying hard to ignore the seductive scent of fresh blood mixed with wine.

The ghosts paused in their attack. I focused on them, not wanting to distract myself with the terror in Heath's eyes and the pain in Erik's.

"*We prefer this warm young blood, Priestess.*" The eerie voice echoed up to me, sending chills over my skin. I swear I could smell his rotting flesh-scented breath.

I swallowed hard. "I understand that, but those lives aren't yours to take. Tonight is a night for celebration, not for death."

"*And yet we choose death—it is dearest to us.*" Ghostly laughter floated through the air with the tainted smoke of sweet grass, and the spirits began to converge again on Heath.

I threw down the goblet and raised my hands. "Then I'm not asking anymore; I'm telling you. Wind, fire, water, earth, and spirit! I command in Nyx's name that you close this circle, pulling back to it the dead who have been allowed to escape. Now!"

Heat surged through my body and shot from my outstretched hands. In a rush of salt-scented wind that was burning hot, a shining green mist whooshed from me down the stairs to whip around Heath and Erik, making their clothes and hair flap like mad. The magical wind caught the smoky shapes and tore them from their victims, and with a deafening roar, it sucked them back into the boundary of my circle. Suddenly I was surrounded by ghostly shapes, from which I could feel danger and hunger pulsing, as clearly as I had felt Heath's blood earlier. Aphrodite was curled up on the chair, cowering from the specters. One of them brushed against her and she let out a little shriek, which seemed to stir them up even more, and they pressed violently around me.

"Zoey!" Stevie Rae cried my name, her voice shrill with fear. I saw her take a hesitant step toward me.

"No!" Damien snapped. "Don't break the circle. They can't hurt Zoey—they can't hurt any of us, the circle is too strong. But only if we don't break it."

"We're not going anywhere," Shaunee called.

"Nope. I like it right here," Erin said, sounding only a little breathless.

I felt their loyalty and trust and acceptance like a sixth element. It filled me with confidence. I straightened my spine and looked at the swirling, angry ghosts.

"So—we're not leaving. Which means you guys have got to go."

I pointed down at the spilled blood and wine. "Take your sacrifice and get out of here. It's all the blood that is owed to you tonight." The smoky horde paused in their seething. I knew I had them. I drew a deep breath and finished it.

"With the power of the elements I command you: Go!"

Suddenly, as though an invisible giant slapped them down, they dissolved into the wine-soaked floor of the gazebo, somehow absorbing the blood-tinged liquid and making it disappear with them.

I breathed a long, ragged sigh of relief. Automatically, I turned to Damien.

"Thank you, wind. You may depart." He started to blow out his candle, but didn't need to, a little puff of wind, which felt surprisingly playful, did it for him. Damien grinned at me. And then his eyes got huge and round.

"Zoey! Your Mark!"

"What?" I lifted my hand to my forehead. It tingled, as did my shoulders and my neck (which figured, I always get shoulder/neckaches when I'm over-stressed), plus my whole body was still humming with the aftereffects of elemental power, so I hadn't even noticed it.

His shocked look changed to happiness. "Finish closing the circle. Then you can use one of Erin's many mirrors to see what's happened."

I turned to Shaunee to say good-bye to fire.

"Wow . . . amazing," Shaunee said, staring at me.

"Hey, how did you know I have more than one mirror in my purse?" Erin was complaining from across the circle at Damien when I turned to her and sent water away. Her eyes got big when she caught a good look at me, too. "Holy shit!" she said.

"Erin, you really shouldn't curse in a sacred circle. Y'all know it's not—" Stevie Rae was saying in her sweet Okie twang when I turned to say good-bye to earth, and her words were suddenly cut off as she gasped, "Oh, my *goodness!*"

I sighed. *Hell, what now?* I went back to the table and lifted the spirit candle.

"Thank you, spirit. You may depart," I said.

"Why?" Aphrodite stood up so abruptly that she knocked over the chair. Like everyone else, she was staring at me with a ridiculously shocked expression. "Why you? Why not me?"

"Aphrodite, what are you talking about now?"

"She's talking about this." Erin handed me a compact she pulled out of the chic leather purse she always had slung over her shoulder.

I opened it and looked. At first I didn't understand what I was seeing—it was too foreign, too surprising. Then, from my side, Stevie Rae whispered, "It's beautiful . . ."

And I realized she was right. It was beautiful. My Mark had been added to. A delicate swirl of lace-like sapphire tattooing framed my eyes. Not as intricate and large as an adult vamp, but unheard of in a fledgling. I let my fingers trace the curling design, thinking that it looked like something that should decorate the face of an exotic foreign princess . . . or maybe the High Priestess of a goddess. And I stared hard at the me that wasn't really me— this stranger who was becoming more and more familiar.

"And that's not all Zoey. Look at your shoulder," Damien said softly.

I glanced down at the deep, off-the-shoulder neckline of my cool dress and felt a jolt of shock surge through my body. My shoulder was tattooed, too. Stretching from my neck, down my shoulder and back, were sapphire tattoos in a swirling pattern much like that on my face, only the blue marks on my body looked even more ancient, even more mysterious, because they were interspersed with letterlike symbols.

My mouth opened, but words wouldn't come out.

"Z, he needs help." Erik broke through my shock and I looked up from my shoulder to see him stumbling into the gazebo, half carrying an unconscious Heath.

"Whatever. Leave him here," Aphrodite said. "Someone will find him in the morning. We need to get out of here before the guards wake up."

I whirled on her. "And you ask why me and not you? Maybe because Nyx is sick and tired of you being selfish, spoiled, indulged, hateful . . ." I paused, so pissed I couldn't think of any more adjectives.

"Nasty!" Erin and Shaunee added together.

"Yeah, and a nasty bully." I took a step closer to her and got all in her face. "This whole Change is hard enough without someone like you. Unless we want to be your"—I glanced up at Damien and smiled—"your sycophants, you make us feel like we don't belong—like we're nothing. That's over, Aphrodite. What you did tonight was totally, completely wrong. You almost caused Heath to die. And maybe even Erik and who knows who else, and it was all because of your selfishness."

"It wasn't my fault your boyfriend tracked you here," she yelled.

"No, Heath wasn't your fault, but that's the only thing that wasn't your fault tonight. It was your fault that your so-called friends wouldn't stand by you and keep the circle strong. And it was your fault that negative spirits found the circle to begin with." She looked confused, which pissed me off even more. "Sage, you hateful hag! You're supposed to use sage to clear out negative energy before you use sweet grass. And it's not surprising that you drew such horrid spirits."

"Yeah, 'cause you're horrid," Stevie Rae said.

"You don't have shit to say about it, refrigerator," Aphrodite sneered.

"No!" I put my finger in her face. "This refrigerator crap is the first thing that's ending."

"Oh, so now you're going to pretend that you don't crave the taste of blood more than any of us?"

I glanced up at my friends. They met my eyes without flinching. Damien smiled encouragement. Stevie Rae nodded at me. The Twins winked. And I realized that I'd been a fool. They weren't going to shun me. They were my friends; I should have trusted them more, even if I hadn't learned to trust myself yet.

"We'll all eventually crave blood," I said simply. "Or we'll die. But that doesn't make us monsters, and it's time the Dark Daughters stopped acting the part. You're finished, Aphrodite. You're no longer leader of the Dark Daughters."

"And I suppose you think that now you're the leader?"

I nodded. "I am. I didn't come to the House of Night asking for these powers. All I wanted was a place to fit in. Well, I guess this is Nyx's way of answering my prayer." I smiled at my friends and they grinned back at me. "Clearly, the Goddess has a sense of humor."

"You stupid bitch, you can't just take over the Dark Daughters. Only a High Priestess can change their leadership."

"Convenient, then, that I am here, isn't it?" Neferet said.

CHAPTER TWENTY-NINE

—

Neferet stepped from the shadows and into the gazebo, moving quickly to Heath and Erik. First, she touched Erik's face and checked the bloody slash marks on his arms from where he'd struggled futilely to try to pull the ghosts off Heath. As she passed her hands over his wounds I could actually see the blood drying. Erik breathed a sigh of relief, like his pain had disappeared.

"These will heal. Come to the infirmary when we get back to school and I'll give you some salve that will lessen the sting from your wounds." She patted his cheek and he blushed bright red. "You showed the bravery of a vampyre warrior when you stayed to protect the boy. I am proud of you, Erik Night, as is the Goddess."

I felt a rush of pleasure at her approval; I was proud of him, too. Then I heard murmured agreement all around me and realized that the Dark Daughters and Sons had returned and were crowding the stairs of the gazebo. How long had they been watching? Neferet turned her attention to Heath, and I forgot about everyone else. She lifted the torn legs of his jeans and examined the bloody marks there and on his arms. Then she cupped his pale, rigid face in her hands and closed her eyes. I watched his body stiffen even more and convulse, and then he sighed and, like Erik, he relaxed. After a moment, he looked like he was sleeping peacefully instead of fighting silently against

death. Still on her knees beside him, Neferet said, "He will recover, and he will remember nothing of this night except that he
got drunk and then lost trying to find his ex-almost-girlfriend."
She looked up at me as she said the last of it, her eyes kind and
filled with understanding.

"Thank you," I whispered.

Neferet nodded slightly to me, before she stood to confront
Aphrodite.

"I am as responsible for what happened here tonight as you are.
I have known for years of your selfishness, but I chose to overlook
it, hoping that age and the touch of the Goddess would mature
you. I was wrong." Neferet's voice took on the clear, powerful
quality of a command. "Aphrodite, I officially release you from
your position as leader of the Dark Daughters and Sons. You are
no longer in training for High Priestess. You are now no different
than any other fledgling." With one swift movement, Neferet
reached out, grasped the silver and garnet necklace of rank that
dangled between Aphrodite's breasts, and tore it from her neck.

Aphrodite didn't make a sound but her face was chalky and
she stared unblinkingly at Neferet.

The High Priestess turned her back on Aphrodite and approached me. "Zoey Redbird, I knew you were special from the
day Nyx let me foresee that you would be Marked." She smiled at
me and put a finger under my chin, lifting my head so that she
could get a better look at the new addition to my Mark. Then she
brushed my hair aside so that the tattoos that had appeared on my
neck, shoulders, and back could also be seen. I heard the Dark
Daughters and Sons gasp as they, too, got their first look at my unusual Marks. "Extraordinary, truly extraordinary," she breathed,
letting her hand fall back to her side as she continued. "Tonight
you showed the wisdom of the Goddess's choice in gifting you
with special powers. You have earned the position of Leader of the

Dark Daughters and Sons and High Priestess in training, through your Goddess-given gifts as well as through your compassion and wisdom." She handed me Aphrodite's necklace. It felt heavy and warm in my hands. "Wear this more wisely than did your predecessor." Then she made a truly amazing gesture. Neferet, High Priestess of Nyx, saluted me, fist crossed over her heart, head bowed formally, with the vampyre sign of respect. Everyone around us except Aphrodite mimicked her. Tears blurred my vision as my four friends grinned at me and bowed with the other Dark Daughters and Sons.

But even in the midst of such perfect happiness I felt the shadow of confusion. How could I have ever doubted that I could tell Neferet anything?

"Go back to the school. I'll take care of what needs to be done here," Neferet told me. She hugged me quickly and whispered into my ear, "I am so very proud of you, Zoeybird." Then she gave me a little push in the direction of my friends. "Welcome the new Leader of the Dark Daughters and Sons!" she said.

Damien, Stevie Rae, Shaunee, and Erin led the cheering. And then everyone surrounded me and it seemed that I was washed from the gazebo in an exuberant wave of laughter and congratulations. I nodded and smiled at my new "friends," but I wasn't a fool. Silently I reminded myself that only moments before they had been agreeing with everything Aphrodite had said.

It would definitely take a while to change things.

We got to the bridge and I reminded my new charges that we'd have to be quiet as we made our way back through the neighborhood to the school, and I motioned for them to go on ahead of me. When Stevie Rae, Damien, and the Twins started to cross the bridge I whispered, "No, you guys walk with me."

Grinning so broadly they looked goofy, the four of them stood around me. I met Stevie Rae's bright gaze. "You shouldn't have

volunteered to be the refrigerator. I know how scared you were."
Stevie Rae's grin faded at the reprimand in my voice.

"But if I hadn't, we wouldn't have known where the ritual was
going to be, Zoey. I did it so I could text-message Damien, and he
and the Twins could meet me here. We knew you'd need us."

I held up my hands and she stopped talking, but she looked
like she was going to cry. I smiled gently at her. "You didn't let me
finish. I was going to say that you shouldn't have done it, but I'm
so glad you did!" I hugged her, and smiled through tears at the
other three of them. "Thank you—I'm glad you were all there."

"Hey, Z, that's what friends do," Damien said.

"Yep," said Shaunee.

"Exactly," said Erin.

And they closed around me in a giant, smothering group
hug—which I totally loved.

"Hey, can I get in on this?"

I looked up to see Erik standing nearby.

"Well, yes, you absolutely may," Damien said brightly.

Stevie Rae dissolved into giggles, and Shaunee sighed and said,
"Give it up, Damien. Wrong team, remember?" Then Erin pushed
me out of the center of the group and toward Erik. "Give the guy
a hug. He did try to save your boyfriend tonight," she said.

"My *ex*-boyfriend," I said quickly, stepping into Erik's arms,
more than a little overwhelmed by the mixture of the scent of the
fresh blood still clinging to him and the fact that he was, well,
hugging me. Then, to add to everything else, Erik kissed me so
hard that I swear I thought the top of my head would spin off.

"Please, just please," I heard Shaunee say.

"Get a room!" Erin said.

Damien giggled as I stepped self-consciously out of Erik's arms.

"I'm starving," Stevie Rae said. "This refrigerator stuff makes
you hungry."

"Well, let's go get you something to eat," I said.

My friends started over the bridge and I could hear Shaunee bickering with Damien about whether we should have pizza or sandwiches.

"Mind if I walk with you?" Erik asked.

"Nah, I'm getting used to it," I said, smiling up at him.

He laughed and walked onto the bridge. Then from the darkness behind me I heard a very distinct, very annoyed, "me-eeh-uf-ow!"

"Go on, I'll catch up with you guys in a minute," I told Erik and then I walked back into the shadows at the edge of the Philbrook's lawn. "Nala? Kitty, kitty, kitty . . . ," I called. And, sure enough, a disgruntled ball of fur trotted out of the bushes, complaining the entire time. I bent down and picked her up and she instantly started to purr. "Well, silly girl, why did you follow me all the way out here if you don't like walking that far? Like you haven't been through enough tonight already," I murmured, but before I could head back to the bridge, Aphrodite stepped out of the shadows and blocked my way.

"You might have won tonight, but this isn't over," she told me.

She made me feel really tired. "I wasn't trying to 'win' anything. I was just trying to make things right."

"And that's what you think you did?" Her eyes darted nervously back and forth from me to the path that led to the gazebo, as if someone had followed her. "You don't really know what happened here tonight. You were just being used—we were all just being used. We're puppets, that's all we are." She angrily wiped at her face and I realized she was crying.

"Aphrodite, it doesn't have to be like this between us," I said softly.

"Yes it does!" she snapped. "It's the parts we're supposed to play. You'll see . . . you'll see. . . ." Aphrodite started to walk away.

A thought drifted unexpectedly from my memory. It was of Aphrodite, during her vision. As if it was happening again, I could hear her say, *They're dead! No. No. That can't be! Not right. No. Not natural! I don't understand . . . I don't . . . You . . . you know.* Her scream of terror echoed eerily through my mind. I thought of Elizabeth . . . of Elliott . . . the fact that they had appeared to *me.* Too much of what she said made sense.

"Aphrodite, wait!" She looked over her shoulder at me. "The vision you had today in Neferet's office, what was it really about?"

Slowly, she shook her head. "It's only beginning. It's going to get much worse." She turned and suddenly hesitated. Her way was blocked by five kids—my friends.

"It's okay," I told them. "Let her go."

Shaunee and Erin parted. Aphrodite lifted her head, shook back her hair, and marched past them as if she owned the world. I watched her walk over the bridge, my stomach clenching. Aphrodite knew something about Elizabeth and Elliott, and eventually I was going to have to find out what it was.

"Hey," Stevie Rae said.

I looked at my roommate and new best friend.

"Whatever happens, we're in it together."

I felt the knot in my stomach release. "Let's go," I said.

Surrounded by my friends, we all went home.